Paths Not Yet Taken

by

Philip Rennett

First published in Great Britain in 2024
by Pea Arr Books

ISBN: 978-1-7385747-0-4

Cover design by
Daniel Greenhalgh
cargocollective.com/danielgreenhalgh

To Clare, Molly, Pepo and Charlie

1

"There's something very wrong with our man today. I'm almost worried about him."

Martin Barnwell paid no immediate attention to the remark thrown at him from the persistent fog. Instead, Downing Street's chief of staff took a slow, deliberate drag from the cigarette held awkwardly in his yellowing, arthritic fingers. Exhaling slowly, he watched as a slight breeze snatched the smoke away and wafted it unceremoniously towards his assistant as she emerged from the mist.

Amanda Abbott, her bright red coat a vivid contrast to the gloom around her, focused on walking across the uneven ground and barely noticed the smell of tobacco.

In the steel and glass colossus that loomed sixty yards away, a muffled horn announced the end of the early morning shift. Almost instantly, workers rushed out of the exits in the recently opened Grange Brothers food distribution centre. They scurried and scattered like matchstick figures in a Lowry painting across the unfinished parking lot.

At the same time, the nation's media spilled out through the building's main entrance, setting up cameras and jostling for position behind a rope barrier.

The prime minister's hastily arranged visit was ending. In the damp, unrelenting mist, it was time for the fireworks to ignite.

A fleeting scowl briefly marred Barnwell's weathered face, famously compared by an anonymous 'Downing Street insider' in a recently-launched book to that of *a bulldog licking piss off a nettle while dragging its balls over barbed wire*. The assembled reporters, photographers, and TV crews - necessary parasites to be tolerated in his estimation - may have been the scowl's target. Or perhaps his assistant, but after many years in her role, she remained unfazed by her boss's expressions of disdain, displeasure, or disapproval.

In fact, she was completely oblivious, her attention consumed by maintaining her balance. Heels, even modest ones adorning expensive boots, were ill-advised on impromptu visits to industrial sites. Car parks can be treacherous terrains, and this one was about to prove it.

The Grange Brothers operation was the second largest warehouse in the Midlands, the fourth largest in the country and a brand-new building to boot. So new, in fact, that the car park was not yet finished. Today, the warehouse hosted the launch of a new government food quality initiative. The PM's special adviser had created this 'ground-breaking event' just 48 hours earlier, to distract the public from the PM's most recent error of judgement.

How anybody could mistakenly send images of their genitalia to the German Chancellor rather than their mistress was one thing.

Seeking to draw a line under the whole sorry episode on the steps of a building that had replaced a much-loved local hospital was quite another.

That the hospital closure had been approved by the then Health Secretary who now, for God's sake, was the prime minister, was something else entirely. Heads would roll.

If Barnwell had a hand in it, the PM's special adviser would be the first in a line of one.

"The PM's not been at his best for weeks," he responded eventually. "What makes today so special?"

Amanda "Mindy" Abbott came to a halt next to her boss. She took out her smartphone and checked the twenty-six messages she had received in the past five minutes.

"He hasn't put a foot wrong. No embarrassing comments. Hasn't even knocked anything over. Asked all the right questions…"

She stopped to delete the message from her publisher, providing the latest sales figures for her book and requesting an extra chapter based on 'recent events'.

"Miracles happen then. Did the press behave themselves?"

"As quiet as lambs. They're coming to the end of the tour. The PM will have a brief meeting with the directors over tea and biscuits. He'll come out, talk about the initiative, then head to the car. Someone - probably the Mail - will throw him a question about Todgergate. He'll stop, say whatever he's agreed with Michaels, then we're away."

Barnwell nodded grimly. "And he's not put a foot wrong?"

"Not a thing. He's been quiet since we set off this morning."

A sixth sense, honed by thirty years of political experience, was screaming at him, but Barnwell couldn't make out what it was saying.

It didn't matter.

He knew he was in the calm before the inevitable storm.

He threw the rest of his cigarette to the ground and stamped it out.

"We'll wait in the car and watch from there. I don't want to be anywhere near this shambles. Michaels can handle it. Let's see what's so special about the special adviser."

With that, he made for the warmth and shelter of the third

SUV, parked in a convoy waiting to rescue the country's leading politician from too much humiliation.

Anonymous best-selling author Mindy Abbott followed behind, memorising her boss's words for the new chapter, while avoiding workers keen to get home.

Barnwell's sixth sense realised it wasn't being heard, so stopped screaming. It waited, head in hands, for the inevitable.

2

Warehouse operative Simon Pope opened his car door, slumped into the driver's seat and almost swore.

Still wearing his thick warehouse hi-vis jacket, he struggled out from behind the steering wheel and slammed the door shut behind him. He jogged to the warehouse, avoiding emerging stragglers who were as eager to escape the workplace as he was to get back inside.

Inside the staff changing room, he heaved a sigh of relief. The food he'd bought in the on-site shop was where he'd left it, still resting inside the two carrier bags by his locker. He'd been lucky. Anything left unattended typically vanished within a few seconds. If those bags had disappeared, his life would not have been worth living. Picking them up, he hurried back to the car, tossing them onto the front passenger seat.

He barely noticed the bright television lights and the crowd outside the main entrance. He had glimpsed the prime minister at the far end of the warehouse half an hour earlier. The country's leader looked smaller in real life.

Pope had thought about shouting something witty, sarcastic, or insulting, but changed his mind. No need to draw unnecessary attention to himself.

Besides, he couldn't think of anything to shout. He'd craft something clever later and post it on @TheTrth.

Ah, @TheTrth. The dark web platform where he let his imagination run wild, transforming his dull, tragic life into something more exciting. An exclusive realm, full of fiery and dangerous ideas, where fiction flirted with fact and revolution danced with evolution. A simmering forum where like-minded individuals discussed world altering, era-defining deeds, which never progressed any further.

Later that day, after a couple of strong beers, he would join his online comrades-in-words. They would set the world straight in a deluge of righteous fury, deliberate on actions aimed at causing mass disruption and debate the shape of the new society that would evolve.

Then tomorrow, after walking the dogs, he would have a round of golf.

Gunning the engine into life, Pope guided his ageing blue saloon out of the car park, waved to the security guard at the factory exit and set off for home. Neither he nor the guard noticed the peculiar lump concealed beneath the soiled dog hammock that covered his back seat.

And that is how Simon Pope, known as Simmo to his workmates and friends and as Esteban Canafanta to his online brethren and to the intelligence services who monitored them, changed his life forever.

3

The chief of staff strolled towards his car, halting the quiet conversation by the driver's window. Barnwell recognised the couple outside the car, conversing with his driver. All had served as advanced driving instructors in the Metropolitan Police. Now, they were effectively taxi drivers - highly adept in combat and ambush extraction, but still glorified taxi drivers. Both stood tall as he approached.

Unlike many in politics, Barnwell directed his contempt primarily towards politicians and the leeches who thrived off their influence. Beneath his stern exterior, he held sincere but well-concealed respect for his fellow man and woman. He acknowledged them with a nod.

"Best get set, people. He'll be out in three minutes. We leave sixty seconds after that."

They nodded back and moved off to their vehicles.

Barnwell climbed into the back of the car and settled into his seat. A chill swept through the warm air as the opposite door opened and his assistant clambered in.

Affectionately known as Mart and Mindy within Downing Street, they were an unusual couple. The differences in age and personality should have blocked their genuine, if complex, attraction, but had failed miserably.

Keen political instincts, combined with a willingness to shaft anybody who stood in their way, made them a formidable political duo.

Their entrances into politics were very different.

The cut and thrust of politics had fascinated Mindy ever since her father gave her a copy of Hansard - the daily report of proceedings in the Houses of Parliament - for her sixteenth birthday.

Looking back, it was a bittersweet moment. She had been hoping for the keys to a car in which she and her friends could cavort around the county, getting drunk and meeting boys. Mindy's mother had been expecting her daughter to receive the same, except for the drunkenness and sexual liaisons. Neither knew that dad had lost the vehicle deposit on bets at the bookmakers.

Her father bought the Hansard at the time of her birth, but had forgotten about it. He discovered it in an ancient Woolworths carrier bag in the garage, while searching for some rope with which to hang himself.

Suicide, he had decided, was preferable to facing the wrath of his dear lady once she learned of his gambling transgressions.

Fortunately, the discovery of the Hansard had brought him to his senses. Confession and genuine contrition were good for the soul. His wife's wrath had not been as bad as death. Time healed the wounds, especially when the effects of the gift on his teenage daughter's schoolwork, interests, and libido became apparent.

Mindy had decent GCSE results and excellent A-levels. She then achieved a first-class honours degree in politics and economics from the University of Leicester.

During her time in Leicester, Mindy had sought to broaden her knowledge by joining the local branch of each of the main political parties.

Here, she absorbed the discourse at monthly meetings and read everything published by the national party office. She took part in events and demonstrations and canvassed at local and national elections.

She also had an on-and-off love life with several active members.

Moving between parties with this strategy caused issues, especially when lovers were on opposite sides of the police line. Such challenges, she found, were great opportunities to confirm both her ability to think quickly and her powers of persuasion.

Mart and Mindy sat in silence for a short while. Curtis, the driver, reported their return to a small microphone on his lapel and listened to a brief acknowledgment via an equally small earpiece.

Mindy straightened her skirt and leaned forward.

"Everything okay Curtis?"

The driver held her gaze in his rear-view mirror for a couple of seconds, then winked.

"Everything's fine."

He turned away slightly, scanning across the car park towards the factory entrance.

Down the side of the building, a white transit van reversed towards a doorway. The driver jumped out and opened the back doors. Three, maybe four, figures emerged from the building and clambered in. Closing the door, the driver glanced around, climbed into the cab, and drove away past the convoy.

Curtis watched as the van picked up speed and headed toward the security gate. Strange that all the passengers had chosen the discomfort of the back of the van rather than a seat at the front. Perhaps the driver had bad breath. A buzz from the car's back seat interrupted his thought.

Mindy lifted her phone to her ear.

"Yes?"

"We have a slight problem."

Jeremy Michaels, the normally calm and controlled special adviser to the prime minister, sounded anything but calm and controlled now. Mindy moved the phone away from her ear and switched to speaker mode.

"Go on?"

"The PM's missing."

"Say again?"

"We can't find him."

"He must have taken a wrong turn."

"We've checked. Plus, we've put a call out over the PA system. He's just disappeared."

Curtis pressed his earpiece closer to his ear as he received his own message, then started the car. He turned to Barnwell, who was observing the cars in front moving off towards the factory.

"Boss. I'm getting you out of here."

Barnwell knew better than to object. Curtis drove forward, swung around, and made for the exit. The police car behind them followed, then stopped at the security gate. No one else was leaving for now, although some would be arriving.

Police vans and two ambulances approached at speed, then flashed by to join the search and assist with any aftermath. In his wing mirror, he saw the security barrier come down and stay down. At least the area was secure.

Mindy watched as her boss pulled out his secure mobile and hit the prime minister's number. Then she talked to Michaels again.

"What happened, exactly?"

"Tour finished. We went for a cuppa in the executive canteen. He excused himself - wanted a pee - and never came back. Three minutes later, Jackson went to look for him. Couldn't find him."

Listening in, Curtis wondered how many minutes it would be before Freddie Jackson, the PM's close protection officer, was back on the beat.

"Back up's arriving now and the perimeter's secured. We're being shipped out..." Mindy looked enquiringly at Curtis via his rear-view mirror.

"Local police command-and-control centre."

"...shipped out to the local police HQ."

The panic in the special adviser's voice was palpable.

"But what about the press? What about me?"

Barnwell snapped his phone shut. The PM's phone was ringing, but the PM wasn't answering. He leaned forward towards his assistant.

"Just find the PM, then we can all go home."

A thought struck him.

"You've not set this up, have you, Jeremy? This isn't some elaborate hoax to divert attention from Dickgate?"

"Todgergate." Even as she corrected him, Mindy's brain was telling her to stop. Too late. She turned away, feeling her boss's eyes boring into the back of her head.

"Todgergate," Barnwell repeated. "This isn't some inspired scam to..."

"I've got nothing to do with this," the special adviser interrupted. His voice was indignant, tinged with hysteria and a hint of outrage.

"And yet this visit... this media management opportunity... this entire charade was your brilliant idea."

Barnwell felt the shock of realisation at the other end of the line and luxuriated in it for a couple of seconds. "Just find the PM."

Still avoiding looking at her boss, Mindy ended the call, ignoring the deluge of voicemails and text messages waiting for her. She said nothing, as there was nothing to say.

4

Pope reversed into his garage down the short driveway at the bottom of his back garden and pressed the key fob to close the automated garage door.

Despite the early start and the long shift, he didn't feel tired. With three days off, he couldn't wait to get going. He pulled the two shopping bags over and climbed out of the car.

The staff shop was a major bonus of working in a food distribution centre. The workforce could buy foodstuffs from damaged cases and goods that had been returned or were close to their use-by date, all at dirt-cheap prices. Local food banks and pig farmers would pick up anything left over.

The range and quantity of produce varied, depending primarily on how many deranged or drug-addled forklift truck drivers had been on shift and the amount of product damaged as a result.

Pope made the most of the opportunity whenever he could, keeping his dogs happy and his bank balance reasonably healthy.

Walking past the front of the car, he paused for a moment. Whatever had caught his attention had vanished as quickly as it had appeared.

He left the garage through the side door, locked it, and walked down the garden path to his back door. His two dogs, Fred and Ginger, stared through the glass at the bags in his hand.

He navigated his way between his quiet but persistently inquisitive greyhounds into the kitchen. His mobile phone vibrated in his pocket. It could wait. If he left the bags now, they would be empty by the time he returned to unpack them.

A couple of minutes later, the fridge and the food cupboards were nearly full. His phone vibrated again, but Pope's focus had shifted to feeding the dogs, then making himself a toasted cheese sandwich and a cup of tea.

It was only when he finally sat down at the kitchen table with his late lunch that he remembered to dig out his phone to see who had called.

There were two messages, one from Geoff Dobbs, his team leader at the warehouse, and one from a workmate, Pete Strummer. Both conveyed the same message, albeit in different ways. Geoff asked him to call urgently regarding a work incident. Pete was less vague.

"Simmo. The prime minister's disappeared," he said. "Police are searching everywhere for him. All top secret at the mo, but you might get a call to check you've not kidnapped him or taken him out for a pint."

Pope chuckled at the thought. No chance of him having a pint with that pompous prat. More likely he'd have thumped him, or worse. As for kidnapping him? It would boost his online credibility, but he wouldn't have a clue how to do it or what to do if he had miraculously succeeded.

The new distribution centre was massive. They'd probably already found him, freezing his balls off, wandering around the frozen warehouse. Maybe he'd stumbled into a trailer and was now travelling up the M1 towards Glasgow.

Pope chuckled again. He'd have his sandwich and then give Dobbo a call. He hadn't even seen the prime minister, so it'd be a quick one.

5

Central control command at West Cumberton police station was usually a hive of activity. That's assuming a hive of activity could be four people sitting quietly at separate cubicles.

Here, they monitored police radio comms and accessed images from the town council's CCTV cameras via two large, wall-mounted video screens.

The resource was fine for monitoring the town centre and its pubs, but today would be a challenge. The unit manager had closely monitored radio traffic throughout the visit. By the time the chief of staff and his small entourage arrived, the police had taken live control of the council's cameras. Now, each camera was pointing as well as possible towards the roads leading to the Grange Brothers facility.

The team awaited further news from the site. Meanwhile, they monitored the camera feeds for signs of suspicious activity, or a forty-five-year-old man in an ill-fitting suit with a hi-vis vest over the top.

The door opened and the duty sergeant walked in, followed by Barnwell, Mindy and Curtis.

Mindy stopped and took in her surroundings.

"This is it?"

Time froze for a moment. Even the slight crackle of a speaker held its breath.

"This is West Cumberton, Ms. Abbott, not Scotland Yard," said the sergeant evenly. "We make the most of what little budget we have."

Barnwell decided on a change of tack.

"Looks a very tidy operation, sergeant. Now then. What are we looking at?"

While the lead controller explained the monitoring operation, Curtis scanned the eight camera feeds on the wall screens.

He bent down to talk to the controller furthest from the ongoing presentation.

Keeping his voice low, he asked, "How close to the distribution centre is the nearest camera?"

The controller put down his crisp packet and pointed a salty finger at the top right image on the right-hand screen. It showed a crossroads controlled by traffic lights, close to a small supermarket and a row of shops.

"That junction's about half a mile away," he said. "The primary route to Grange Brothers is the road on the right."

Twenty minutes had passed since the PM's disappearance, but he had been missing for the five minutes prior to that.

"Can you go back thirty minutes on the camera and scroll forward?"

The controller pulled the relevant feed onto his own screen, clicked and dragged the timer back, then let the image play. The traffic from the Grange Brothers road grew much busier as shift workers made their escape.

"What am I looking for?"

"The usual." Curtis knew the controller would understand that meant the opposite.

Dragging the timer slowly forward gave the staccato impression of a grainy movie of the early nineteen-hundreds;

a feeling exacerbated by the steady increase in pedestrians. Workers arrived on foot, then vanished from view.

The white van Curtis had noticed earlier flashed straight through the crossroads in a line of other vehicles. A minute later, Curtis himself appeared at the junction and turned left towards his current location.

Suddenly, his earpiece sprang to life. Every controller inadvertently straightened in their seats and both his passengers' mobile phones buzzed. The message to all was the same.

Search of the area completed. PM not found.

Curtis leaned on the controller's desk to get a better view of the screen.

"Let's backtrack," he said. "I want a closer look at that white van."

Martin Barnwell had always been a clever and astute political operator. He had an innate ability to think clearly and strategically, while circumstance overwhelmed others.

He touched his assistant's arm and motioned for her to follow him out of the room.

With everyone else's eyes and ears otherwise occupied, nobody noticed their departure. After finding an empty office, Barnwell closed the door firmly behind them.

"We have a situation," he said - one of the biggest understatements since Tsar Nicholas II acknowledged he might have a problem getting any more eggs from Mr. Faberge, now that Lenin was in St Petersburg. Mindy didn't respond. She knew when her boss needed to talk in order to work things through.

"In fact, we have two. We have a prime minister who is missing. A prime minister who we presume is alive, but who hasn't resigned."

Mindy's face remained deadpan, although her inner panic-stricken, hysterical self was another story altogether.

"We have a third issue," she said. "And they're stood outside a warehouse while all hell breaks loose around them."

"Check social media. I'm willing to bet that bird has already flown."

He waited while Mindy checked her phone. He noticed the slight tremble in her hands. Her look told him all he needed to know.

"Leave that to the press team. Our problem is prime ministers remain in office until their own party or the electorate kicks them out, unless they resign or die in the meantime." Barnwell stared straight ahead at a blank wall. "Like many of our PM's actions in Number 10, this one creates yet another shitstorm."

"The deputy prime minister…"

"That idiot got the title to stop him babbling about the China indiscretion. A Cabinet seat without risking the nation by giving him a government department. He has zero constitutional power, thank God."

Barnwell paused, gazing at the wall.

"Nobody's designated. The Cabinet needs to agree on a nomination and to support them until this situation ends."

Mindy stared at him. "We're screwed then."

"Exactly."

6

Pope listened to Dobbo's phone ring a dozen times before it was finally answered.

"Dobbo. It's Simmo. I hear you've lost a prime minister."

The team leader, respected by his team for his humorous yet calm personality, and his willingness to hit anyone who fooled around, sounded stressed.

His stiff response suggested he wasn't by himself.

"Ah Pope. Thanks for calling back…" Geoff Dobbs was briefly distracted by a muffled voice in the background before returning to the call. "How do you know about the prime minister? What have you heard?"

Pope felt defensive. He didn't want to land Strummer in trouble.

"Just that he's gone AWOL. Have you found him yet?"

"No. We're pretty sure he's not on site. Disappeared into thin air. We're checking with the last shift to see if anybody noticed anything unusual."

"Apart from a bunch of guys in suits or carrying cameras getting in the way and trying to avoid the fork-lifts? No mate. Sorry. Not a thing."

"What about in the car park?"

"Nothing. I saw the group outside the main entrance. Oh,

and I had to come back in because I forgot my shopping…"

"And was it still there?"

"Yeah."

"Damn."

"I know. Unbelievable."

"Okay mate. Let me know if anything comes to mind."

"Will do, Dobbo. See you next week."

The line went dead. Pope smiled grimly to himself. The prime minister had vanished in the exact spot he'd made the local hospital disappear just two years before. How ironic. That'd be his theme on @TheTrth later. He locked the back door, fussed the dogs as they roached on their beds, and went upstairs for a shower.

Back at Grange Brothers, Dobbs listened as Detective Inspector Cauldwell ordered a mobile unit to visit Simon Pope.

"But you heard him, Inspector. He saw nothing."

"I heard, Mr. Dobson." The detective inspector took a sip of his machine-brewed tea… coffee… chocolate… he couldn't tell. "I also heard him dodge your question about how he knew. If Mr. Pope has something to hide, we'll find it."

Geoff Dobson almost protested but decided against it. Simmo had probably picked it up online. #GrangeBrothers was trending worldwide, to the dismay of the brothers themselves, but to the delight of the company's small marketing team.

Two hundred police personnel were already working on the case, with many more to come. If the inspector wanted to waste police time visiting Simon Pope, then that was his call.

7

At the police station, Barnwell and Mindy organised a meeting of Cobra and held a conference call with available Cabinet ministers.

Two controllers continued to monitor the area around Grange Brothers, and two more helped Curtis to track the white van using the patchy CCTV network.

The CCTV coverage was reasonably extensive, but not comprehensive. Budget cuts over the years had left the cameras in varying states of repair, thanks to selective and sporadic equipment upgrades.

The local pubs had excellent coverage, because vandalism resulted in the regular replacement of these cameras with up-to-date models.

The ageing cameras perched high on the road network, however, were mostly the originals.

They were useful for road accidents and serious driving misdemeanours, but not for identifying individuals or registration plates. This posed problems for Curtis and his small team.

The operational focus had changed onto where the PM might be - hence the dedication of resources to help Curtis find the van.

That task was frustrating. It entailed establishing the van's direction of travel, anticipating which camera it may appear on next and checking the relevant images from that location. If the van didn't turn up within a ten-minute window, the team identified other nearby cameras and repeated the process.

The camera issue meant reading the registration plate was difficult, but the controllers finally pieced together the details. To nobody's surprise, the van's plate actually belonged to a red hatchback owned by a vicar in Brighton.

Finally, after painstaking work, video images showed the van in a small public car park in East Cumberton. The controllers scrolled back ten minutes in time and watched four figures emerge from the vehicle, cross the road and enter The Crossroads public house.

"Not the actions of terrorists who've abducted the prime minister," observed Curtis, "But I'm sure there were five people in the van when it left the warehouse."

A controller picked up a radio and called her boss.

8

Simon Pope had been in the shower for two minutes when he heard the front doorbell. He ignored the interruption and carried on washing his hair, luxuriating in the hot water as it soothed away the aches of the day's work. Half a minute later, the bell rang again, followed by an urgent banging that threatened to take the door off its hinges.

Pope cursed silently, turned off the shower, wrapped himself in a towel, and stepped out onto the landing. At the foot of the stairs, the front door letterbox creaked open.

"Mr. Pope?"

"I'm in the middle of a shower. Go away."

"It's the police, sir. I'm Sergeant Morris from West Cumberton. Mind if we have a word?"

Pope tightened the towel around his waist - an action that didn't go unnoticed by the pair of eyes watching him intently from the letterbox.

"I'm soaking wet. What do you want?"

"Just a couple of questions regarding your workplace, sir. Mind if we come in?"

"Mind if I finish my shower first?"

"We'll be quick, Mr. Pope. Then we're gone."

Pope stomped downstairs and opened the door.

In front of him were the smallest and the largest police officers he had ever seen. Not community support officers, either. The real deal. Tooled up and ready for action. Really ready for action. As if they expected something bad to happen but were trying hard to conceal it.

The sight of Pope in a towel seemed to put them at their ease.

Pope led them down the hallway and into the kitchen. Neither dog had moved so much as one inch, despite all the noise.

Both were flat out on their beds, but lifted their heads enquiringly as the visitors entered, then settled down again when no treats appeared.

Pope sat down at the kitchen table and the smaller officer, Sergeant Morris, sat opposite him. The other man - Pope named him Bigfoot - wandered with a slight limp to the back door and looked out at the garden. It was unnerving, wrapped in a damp towel and not in command of his own house. Pope tried to reassert himself.

"Cup of tea?"

Sergeant Morris smiled, creasing the skin near his eyes and ageing immediately. "No thank you, sir. You're aware of the incident at the warehouse today? Around the time you finished your shift?"

"You lost the prime minister."

The smile faltered for a millisecond. "The prime minister has disappeared, sir. He isn't on the warehouse premises. We've searched them. Twice. With dogs." Sergeant Morris gazed at the two greyhounds as one of them let out a gentle fart. "Tracker dogs," he added. "He's gone. The question is where? And how? Of his own volition? Or did somebody abduct him?"

He let the silence settle, just as his police training had taught him.

Lurch - Pope had decided Bigfoot wasn't an appropriate nickname given the limp - turned from the garden and stared at him meaningfully.

Pope stared back but addressed his response to Morris.

"Not sure I can help. I told my team leader all I know, which isn't a lot."

"That's not quite right though, is it sir?"

Pope frowned. He had told Dobbo everything.

"When was the first time you learned of the incident, Mr. Pope?"

"When I called Dobbo… Mr. Dobson… the team leader."

As he answered, Pope was aware of Lurch - yes, a much better name for him - advancing slowly down the kitchen towards him. Sergeant Morris smiled, nodded and produced a standard police notebook with something of a flourish.

"Quote: *Dobbo. It's Simmo. I hear you've lost a prime minister.* Unquote. Isn't that what you said, Mr. Pope?"

Suddenly, sat in his own kitchen, in his own house, and wrapped in his own damp bath towel, Pope didn't feel very assertive at all. He felt the scars on his head burn and knew his face was reddening.

"Mind if I have a quick look round, sir?" Lurch murmured. "While you're chatting with the sergeant? Saves getting a search warrant and a bunch of us ripping the place to pieces." Pope found himself slightly shocked to see that Lurch's smile actually reached his eyes.

"Help yourself," he replied.

Lurch nodded and wandered off past the sergeant and into the hallway.

Pope watched him limp out, then found himself once again staring at Sergeant Morris, who was staring straight back.

"I hear you've lost a prime minister, Mr. Pope. How do you explain that, if the first time you heard of the issue was when you spoke to Mr. Dobson?"

25

Pope tried to think of a believable answer above the clumping of footsteps up the stairs and into his bedroom. He decided the best answer would be the truth.

"A mate of mine had a call from Dobbo before Dobbo called me. He was just giving me a heads up, that's all."

"And you can prove it?"

Pope reached for his phone, which was charging on the nearby cupboard top, found the voicemail message and played it.

Sergeant Morris held his hand out for the phone and checked the recent calls. There were the incoming and outgoing calls. Everything matched correctly.

"Then why didn't you tell Dobson when you called him?"

"He asked me how I knew and what I'd heard. I just answered the second bit first, and the conversation moved on from there."

Lurch's clumping boots signalled his arrival downstairs. He moved from the lounge to the dining room and then to the cloakroom under the stairs.

"All good," he declared at the kitchen door. "I'll just check the garage."

Pope heard a muffled voice in the police officers' earpieces. The expressions on both men's faces changed. In that instant, Pope felt delighted that he wasn't whoever they were going to meet next.

"Actually," said Sergeant Morris, "We'll leave it at that. Many thanks for clarifying the issue, Mr. Pope. We'll be on our way and leave you to your shower."

By the time Morris finished speaking, Lurch was halfway to the police car, parked across the road.

Sergeant Morris turned and smiled apologetically.

"He always gets a bit excited when there's the chance to shoot someone."

With that revelation, he, too, was gone.

Pope closed the door behind them and went back to his shower.

In the police car, Morris acknowledged receipt of the call about the white van and confirmed they were now heading to East Cumberton. Lurch - or Police Constable Dave Westlake, as he preferred to be called - squeezed into the passenger seat.

"Our man looked familiar, but I can't place him," he said. "Looks like he had a missus at some stage, but that's definitely a bachelor's house."

"Pope! Of course!" Morris had a lightbulb moment. "Thought I knew the name from somewhere." And then, seeing the quizzical look on his partner's face. "Hellman's Bridge. Two, maybe three years ago."

He gunned the car into life and set off towards The Crossroads pub.

"Ah, I remember…" Constable Westlake didn't sound as if the revelation completely resolved his puzzlement as he looked across at the house. "Poor sod."

9

In an office at West Cumberton police station, Mindy finished talking to a hysterical special advisor attempting to manage a bloodthirsty press pack, just as Barnwell concluded his call.

"Cabinet's set up for five o'clock," he relayed. "No doubt the phones will be red hot. Cobra meeting will follow in Whitehall. Whoever's nominated as PM will chair. The usual agencies will attend."

The discussion stopped abruptly when Curtis entered the room after knocking on the door.

"Boss. We've located the van. It's parked outside a pub. We've got five police cars *en route*, plus a firearms unit. ETA five minutes at a rendezvous point nearby, then we'll send in a recce unit and take it from there."

Barnwell nodded. "Enough time to grab a tea then."

And there would have been, had it not been for a pool table argument in the pub quickly turning into a street fight.

The control team stared at their screens as vehicles slewed to a halt, narrowly missing each other and, miraculously, the brawlers in the road.

An overturned milk float spilled broken glass and milk.

Two of the fight's original protagonists shifted their focus from each other to a small bus.

It shredded its tyres on the broken glass, then ran out of control and knocked them both over.

As if that wasn't spectacular enough, it finally stopped after careering into the car park and smashing into the side of the white van.

The control unit manager grabbed the nearest headset and issued instructions.

"All units heading for The Crossroads pub. Major incident in progress. There is a riot on the road outside. Vehicles involved. At least two casualties. Ambulance service being informed. Proceed straight to the pub. Contain the incident and secure the area. We have no descriptions of the individuals from the white van."

He watched the video wall as the bloodied driver and his two passengers staggered out of the rear emergency exit of the bus just as the van exploded in a ball of fire.

"Be aware we have no white van. It's just blown up. Fire brigade is being notified."

Martin Barnwell entered the room, having heard an unprofessional, yet accurate "Holy shit" and viewed the carnage on the screens in front of him. The explosion caught everyone in the control room and at the scene off guard. All the fighting stopped. A couple of brave souls tried to reach the van, but the flames drove them back. Others were tending to the bus driver, his passengers and the two brawlers the driver had failed to avoid.

The British public's willingness to come together in difficult times always amazed the chief of staff. The scene unfolding in front of him also helped him to a decision. If the PM was in the van, he was dead. If not, he was still missing. Either way, the country had no leader. He turned to his assistant and driver.

"Come on," he said. "Time to go."

10

Blissfully unaware of the carnage unravelling ten minutes up the road, a clean and refreshed Pope set to work on his household chores. 'Actioning the nasties' now would give him three days of freedom.

There was golf to play, drink to drink, dogs to walk, and sleep to sleep. He would watch televised sport, chat with friends online and put the world to rights. Then it would be back to work.

Pope didn't mind working at the warehouse. His role was straightforward if physically taxing, but it kept him fit, paid the bills and gave him the chance to save some cash. Living by himself hadn't been a choice. He appreciated mixing with other people, but he was happier listening and watching what was going on, rather than getting involved directly.

Since Pippa had gone, work and golf had kept him going - giving him something to do, keeping his mind occupied, providing a focus while he tried to figure out the future. The dogs helped. Greyhounds were low maintenance but still required care, adding a welcome responsibility to his life.

His eyes rested on a photograph of the two of them with the dogs, walking alongside the local canal, emerging out of a mist that wasn't too dissimilar to today's fog.

A local photographer working on a council project had given them a copy in return for their permission to use the shot elsewhere. Three years ago, Pope mused. Where had that time gone?

Two hours later, the washing and ironing were done. He had cleaned the house thoroughly and had made a fresh pot of tea. Grabbing a couple of biscuits, Pope sat down with his tea at the kitchen table and pulled his laptop towards him.

Milliseconds later, Fred and Ginger were by his side. Both dogs were rescues. Both had raced, after a fashion. Fred, a handsome black and white male, had come from a trainer in Ireland, where he had won a couple of races before falling on a tight bend and damaging his leg. Ginger, a fawn greyhound with white paws, ran well in training but tended to stop and sniff interesting objects before peeing on them.

As a result, both dogs were of little value to their original owner. Seeing them as an unnecessary expense, he was on the verge of putting both of them down until a rescue charity intervened and saved them. That had been five years ago.

They had been in the rescue kennels for six months when Simon and Pippa had visited. Fred's leg had healed by then and, after six months in the same kennel, Fred and Ginger were close. For Pippa, it was love at first sight. In her late twenties, she wasn't particularly keen to have children, but she felt a need to care for something and the two dogs wanted a home.

Each dog had its own begging style. Ginger stood quietly, staring at Pope, her nose dribbling onto the kitchen floor. Fred's chin lay on the tabletop, pointing directly at the food, eyes fixed like a sniper staring down a scope at a target. Both would stay put until receiving a morsel or two. Pope normally made them wait, partly because he was trying to wean them off instant gratification; partly because he liked the company.

If he wanted to concentrate on his online activities while he ate, he'd throw a couple of bits onto the dog beds. Fred and Ginger would get the message and would dash off to eat their treats before settling down.

Now that Pope was on his own, checking the Web while eating had become a habit.

Mealtimes were now fuel times, not the fun, special occasions they'd been before. Instead of chatting and laughing with Pip, sharing the key moments of their respective days, Pope ate in silence, staring into space.

Searching the web for world *faux pas* was a poor substitute, but better than nothing. Today's cuppa would be different, however.

Both dogs turned to look at the back garden just as Pope opened his laptop, then ran to the kitchen door.

Strange time for them to decide they need the loo, Pope thought.

He struggled past the two clearly desperate dogs, opened the back door, and stepped to the side.

Ginger and Fred barged past him.

Rather than heading for their favourite toilet spot - a very pale and very dead patch of grass in the lawn - they raced towards the garage at the bottom of the garden. Without a sound, both dogs skidded to a stop by the side door, their gaze locked on the opaque window.

Pope was about to call them back, but a flash of yellow in the garage window changed his mind.

Oh my, he thought. *A burglar.*

He spun back into the kitchen. Weapons. He needed weapons.

The intruder could be dangerous. Doped up to the eyeballs. Positively slavering for a victim. Pope yanked open the nearest drawer and pulled out a roll of paper towel. Useful for stopping bleeding - after all, it was very absorbent - but not much else.

He glanced out of the kitchen window before continuing his search. No sign of anybody. Good. His eyes fell on his cup of tea. The kettle! Pope grabbed the kettle, filled it to the maximum level and put it on to boil. He could launch that from a few feet away if necessary.

On the draining board was the large knife he'd used to cut his cheese toastie. He gave it a quick wash, dried it on the tea towel and shoved it between his belt and his trousers, making sure the handle was in easy reach.

As the kettle boiled and the search for weapons continued, he risked another look outside. The dogs had settled down on the grass, but continued to stare at the garage door.

Pope looked at the garage. The side-on view confirmed the closed overhead door, which was expected since he had the only key fob. So, the burglar hadn't got in that way, and couldn't get out that way either. That meant he must have used the side door, now guarded by the dogs - but Pope had locked that door on his return from work. The burglar was already inside when Pope returned from work or entered when Pope opened the main door and was parking his car.

Either way, he hadn't attacked when Pope was leaving the garage, his hands full of shopping bags and his head elsewhere. And now, he'd been stuck in there for - Pope checked his watch - almost three hours. The stranger would have already made a move or escaped if he could get out. And he must be cold, tired and possibly a little hungry.

The kettle boiled and Pope absent-mindedly made himself another cup of tea while he pondered his next action. He could call the police, but they were obviously busy and may not return quickly. He had reservations about confronting the felon, fearing what he might do to the interloper.

A couple of altercations in local pubs had followed Pope's short dalliance with the military, neither of which he had started, but both of which he had ended.

He sipped his tea and chomped a biscuit. He would talk to the trapped burglar without opening the side door. Depending on the burglar's responses, he would either open the main door and let him go, or he would leave him locked up and call the police.

Pope quietly retrieved the dogs from the garden and returned them to the house. He shut them in the lounge on their beds, with a couple of biscuits each.

Then he dialled 999 from his phone and quickly hung up, ensuring the number was ready for him to redial if necessary.

Deciding weapons weren't required at this stage, he removed the knife and placed it on the worktop, just in case. He put his keys in his pocket, sneaked through the garden, and stopped beside the garage door, hidden from view. Listening carefully, he heard nothing.

Then he watched, amazed, as his fist moved towards the door and rapped on the window. *How the hell did that happen? What had he done that for?* Before he found the answers, he heard himself shouting.

"Hello?" he called. "Anybody there?"

No answer. Pope's alter ego - the idiot who'd knocked on the door and shouted - was about to inform the garage occupant that he had a gun and was not afraid to use it. Fortunately, Pope intervened at the right moment.

"I know you're in there," he said calmly. "I have a phone and I'm not afraid to use it. The police are very good around here. And they hate burglars."

"I'm not a burglar," a voice responded indignantly. Pope recognised the voice but couldn't remember from where.

"Then what are you doing in my garage?"

"Nothing," came the reply. "I'm sorry if I've caused any problems."

"How do I know you're not a burglar?"

"Because I haven't burgled you."

Fair point, thought Pope, whose memory was scanning through all the voices he knew from work and the golf club, plus anybody else he could bring to mind. There was a glimmer of recognition, but he couldn't quite put his finger on it.

"How did you get into my garage?"

"In your car. In the car park. A door was open…"

Instantly, the glimmer of recognition became a blinding light.

Pope inserted the door key into the lock at the third time of asking. He swung the door open. With his hands in the air and wearing a fluorescent warehouse jacket over his shirt and tie, the prime minister of the United Kingdom stepped forward. "Err… I come in peace?" he said.

Pope took a step of his own and thumped the First Lord of the Treasury in the face, slamming him against the car. At least, he did so in his head. In real life, he just stared. Inside, he was quite pleased at his level of self control.

"What are you doing here?" he said instead.

"I don't know. I wish I did."

"There are people looking for you. The police have been here."

The PM looked past Pope, toward the kitchen door, half expecting the county's constabulary to come flying through it at any second. Pope noted the look of concern - possibly even fear - on the face he usually regarded as infuriatingly smug and unquestionably arrogant. A face he despised.

"Are you ill?"

"No. At least… I don't feel very good. I'm sorry. I've had enough. That's all."

The PM retreated into deep thought, his eyes staring into the mid distance without really seeing. Which was just as well, thought Pope, given it had been a couple of days since he'd cleared the dog poop off the lawn.

Time drifted, yawned, stretched its arms, rubbed its eyes, then drifted some more. Pope wondered when and how this surreal madness would end, his eyes fixed on the man he'd always despised. A man disconnected from his surroundings. Lost in his own mind.

"Look," Pope said, innate hospitality coming to the fore. "I'm going to make a cup of tea. Would you like one?"

The PM regarded him curiously, as if seeing him for the first time. Then his eyes regained their focus. He nodded.

"How do you take it?"

The PM stared at him for a couple of seconds.

"It's been so long since I actually made one," he said. "I don't really know."

11

Pope switched on the kettle, placed tea bags in the mugs, and retrieved the milk from the fridge. His hands shook while adding sugar to a mug.

His mind was a seething torrent of emotions and memories - a potent, dangerous mix. He recognised the signs.

He heard the downstairs toilet flush, slipped the knife back into the cutlery drawer, and pulled a packet of biscuits out of a cupboard.

Moments later, a shadow of a PM walked in from the hallway and halted at the kitchen doorway. "I'm very sorry," he said. "I apologise for the shock. Totally my fault. May I sit down?"

Pope gestured towards the small table and continued making the tea. The PM settled into a chair and observed his surroundings and his host properly for the first time.

The end-of-terrace house from the Sixties was an unfamiliar sight for him, unless he was on the campaign trail. It was a long, quite narrow kitchen, meticulously organised, featuring a quaint little table and chairs at the hallway end. Natural light streamed in through the back door and window. It looked to have undergone a fairly recent makeover, boasting modern appliances and sleek units.

The predominantly yellow decor and vibrant red floor tiles added a lively touch to what would have otherwise been a rather dull room.

He was normally quite good at judging character, but current circumstances meant that ability was sadly lacking. Whatever he had sub-consciously expected of the person who first met him after his escape, this man was not it. This man.

"I'm so sorry. With all that's gone on… Unforgivably rude… I haven't asked your name…"

It was an instantaneous decision. The last ten minutes had left Pope startled, shocked and bewildered. So many feelings raged inside.

Each needed processing, evaluating and ordering, so Pope did what he always did. Like he'd done when each of his parents had died. When he'd been told to leave the army and his other job. When they'd told him about Pippa.

Until he calmed down and felt less vulnerable and more in control, he would give nothing away, including his name.

"We should call someone. Let them know you're okay," he said, without looking across at his guest. "Many people are searching for you. They'll be worried about you."

A smile flickered across the PM's face as he slowly shook his head.

"Oh, I very much doubt that," he said. "An embarrassment to the security services? A major but short-term inconvenience to the government? A bonanza for the media and an enormous opportunity for certain individuals in my party? Yes. But worried about me? They'd dance on my grave, the lot of them."

Pope looked at him carefully as he placed the mugs and the biscuits on the table, then sat down and fired up his laptop.

The PM took a sip of his tea. "Apparently I take sugar," he smiled. "It's been so long since I made myself a cuppa."

"You still haven't," Pope reminded him, eyes fixed on the computer, "Oh shit…"

He rotated the laptop so both men could view the screen. The headlines across the news website said it all.

FEARS GROW FOR PM. BODY IN BURNT-OUT VAN.

STREET RIOT HAMPERS INVESTIGATION. TEN IN HOSPITAL.

KIDNAPPER SEARCH CONTINUES. COBRA MEETING AT SIX.

TODGERGATE TERROR.

"Kidnappers? Riots? But I'm here. This is nothing to do with me."

"And yet it is. You must let someone know you're okay."

"I don't have my phone. It was in my jacket pocket. So… it's up to you… but I'd rather you didn't. Not just yet."

"They're looking for you. They'll find out that whoever that man is, he isn't you."

"I don't want to go back."

Pope glanced up from the screen. The PM seemed close to tears. Again.

"I… I really don't want to go back," he stammered, before hesitating a moment - stunned by what he was about to say. "I've had enough."

Pope leaned back and folded his arms, staring at the man.

The PM wiped his eyes and his nose with his shirt sleeves and looked down at his mug.

"You," Pope said, feeling his face flush and failing miserably to keep the contempt out of his voice. "You've had enough."

The PM took a sip of his tea and shrugged his shoulders. "I hate the job. I can't do it."

Pope just looked at the laptop screen.

The PM filled the subsequent silence by taking another sip of tea.

He mulled over what he'd just publicly admitted - albeit to one person who really didn't look that bothered either way. It was so unlike *Question Time*.

"You can't please all the people all the time, a wise politician once said. Actually, it's bloody tough to keep any of them happy for long. Biggest mistake I ever made. Politics. Wanting to improve the world. Believing I knew better."

"You closed hospitals."

The PM looked up, surprised, then nodded. "I did... including a local one I understand, but... look..." He stopped and closed his eyes, exhausted by defending the indefensible once more. "Actually... no..."

He tailed off, focusing on his tea; hunched over the mug; sinking into a silence disturbed only by the gentle tick of the wall clock and the rhythmic snoring of a roaching Ginger.

Pope stared at the laptop screen but saw nothing. Nothing apart from Pippa.

"Go back. For your own sake. Resign. Retire. Whatever. But you have to go back."

The PM sighed. "Not yet," he said. "Please. Give me a couple of hours. I need to make sense of things. I need... I need a bit of humdrum."

"You can't leave the country without a leader. Is there anyone you can call? So they can call off the hunt?"

The PM thought for a second, then smiled a genuine smile.

"How many phone numbers do you actually know? Mine are on my mobile, or I ask someone to call somebody for me."

Pope set to work on his laptop. "Call your Parliament office and get them to put you through. Email Downing Street. You must know your agent's contact details?"

"That's assuming the answerphone or that email account is being monitored, or my agent actually cares enough or is sober enough to answer. Would you be happy for me to use your phone?"

That stopped Pope in his tracks. He didn't want the police, intelligence services or, even worse, the national media looking into his background. He didn't want Pippa dragged into this, or his privacy disturbed. Why should he tolerate that? He could kick his unwanted visitor out, but what would happen then? There were no guarantees.

Besides, wasn't this the opportunity he'd been waiting for? The culprit of his misfortunes sat defenceless before him, relying on him entirely. He could kick him out and announce it to the world. Humiliate him. Destroy him politically. Change both their lives forever. God knows, he'd dreamt of this moment hundreds of times.

"Do you know what you've done to me? How you've ruined my life?" he wanted to scream at him. He wanted him to realise actions had consequences; to be devastated by the guilt. God knows, that's what he'd had to do. Pope wanted him to suffer. To feel distraught. Totally isolated and bereft of help. Suicidal. Dead. *Dead...? Really?* Pope couldn't decide if the notion shocked or excited him.

"Let's leave it for now," he said. "Give you time to get yourself together. Tell me if you think of anything to calm things down."

The PM stared at him for a couple of seconds. As appreciative as he was, it wasn't the response he had been expecting. He nodded.

"Thank you," he said. He leaned back in his chair and stared at the ceiling.

Both men sat. Both engaged with the same question.

What do I do now?

12

With the prime minister missing, possibly abducted, and potentially barbequed, the chief of staff should have flown out by helicopter. After landing, he should have gone to a secure Cobra location to help plan a response to the crisis.

This, however, was a fog-bound England on a busy Friday afternoon. No afternoon on the M1 southbound is anybody's idea of fun, especially when adding miles upon miles of roadworks and patchy fog to the mix. Escort support from police forces en route can only help so much when the traffic lanes are full or blocked by accidents, no matter how minor.

Fortunately, the fog also helped hide the plain vehicle from attack. The lack of marked police cars fussing around it meant it didn't attract attention from surrounding motorists.

"Boss, the traffic's like this for another twenty miles. Fog is all the way to London. Threat level is amber, but they'd have to be very lucky to find us amongst this lot. We could hole up in Northampton until things clear?"

Barnwell looked up from his phone. "No. Just make sure we have an escort as soon as we hit London. Request armed cover on the bridges. If they catch someone with a rocket-propelled grenade, or even a catapult, they have my permission to shoot them."

Curtis nodded, spoke into his mouthpiece, and received an acknowledgment of the plan. The cars and lorries ahead ground to a halt once more. He leaned across to the glove compartment, pulled out a black case and passed it behind him.

"Just in case," he said.

Barnwell flipped open the case to reveal a semi-automatic pistol with three additional magazines.

Mindy looked at him.

"What?" he asked.

"I think you'll find that's for me." The former corporal in the Territorial Army and Olympic pistol-shooting trialist took the gun from him.

She checked the safety catch and inspected the magazine already installed, placed the gun in the door to her left, then returned to the text she was writing. "We're going to miss the Cabinet meeting."

"Pity," he said. "That promises to be something special."

Mindy's phone buzzed for the thousandth time since leaving West Cumberton. Barnwell had insisted people should text or email to create an uncontested digital trail of events and to ensure important calls came through.

She read through the message and stifled a gasp.

"They've recovered the body from the van," she said. "It's unrecognisable but is a physical match and fragments of the jacket suggest close similarities to the PM's. They've also found a badly damaged mobile phone. Still no trace of the others."

The vehicle fell silent as everyone processed the news.

"Shit…"

"There's something else," Mindy interrupted her boss's succinct reaction. "It looks like he was holding a large penis in his hand when he died. Apparently, though, it isn't his."

The chief of staff and his assistant stared at each other.

The car jolted them forward as a distracted Curtis - for the first time in his professional career - almost collided with the lorry in front of them.

"Very sorry folks," he intoned. Then, looking at Mindy in the rear-view mirror, "Did you just say penis?"

13

On the edge of East Cumberton, Sergeant Stuart Morris reversed into a short track marking the entrance to a farmer's field. He switched off the police car's engine and stepped out for a swift toilet break.

Sat in the car, Authorised Firearms Officer Dave Westlake checked his handgun for the fourth time in the last ten minutes. Sadly, there had been no chance to use it at The Crossroads. However, four persons of interest had left the immediate area and a charred corpse in a smouldering van with false number plates.

Car Two-Zero, along with several other patrol cars, was sealing off the boundary of the town. Other units conducted searches spreading out from the riot area. With a touch of luck, the day might not be a total write-off.

"I can't see this fog disappearing soon," Morris observed as he zipped up his flies. "We won't even know if they walk past us on the other side of the road."

"Works for us as well, Sarge." Prior to joining the police, Westlake had completed tours of Iraq and Afghanistan in a British infantry regiment. "If we sit nice and quiet for a bit, they may walk straight into us without realising. Plus, we have a secret weapon."

Westlake stepped out of the car and put his hand deep into his right trouser pocket.

"Check out this beauty," he said, then whipped out his personal thermal monocular. "Courtesy of the US special forces and an amazing poker hand."

Morris grinned at his friend and colleague. He walked around the back of the car, opened the rear door, slung his semi-automatic rifle around his neck, and picked out his rucksack.

"May as well have a coffee while we wait."

Westlake switched on the monocular and navigated to the thermal palette menu.

In Iraq, Afghanistan and now East Cumberton, detecting body heat was the priority. Given the fog's impact, he selected a greyscale palette, which displayed warmer objects as black and cooler objects as white.

Using the monocular, he peered into the misty field. Three hundred yards away, he spotted a small flock of sheep grazing in front of a large oak tree that marked the far boundary of the enclosure.

He used the telephoto zoom to pick out a lamb to the left of the flock, then manually focussed the lens until the lamb was as clear as it would look on his Sunday dinner plate. Zooming out, the thermal image of the flock was much sharper.

"Better," he said to himself.

Morris looked up from pouring his coffee from the flask and followed his partner's line of sight, only to be met by the impenetrable fog.

"Mind if I have a look? Here, I'll do you a swap."

He handed over the cup of coffee and put the monocular to his eye.

"Last time I looked through one of these…" he started. "Where are they off to…?"

The sheep were no longer grazing peacefully in front of the oak. Most looked right, then abruptly turned and trotted the other way. Morris tracked them.

Must be teatime, he thought, but there was no farmer to greet them on the far side. Nothing to suggest why they had moved so quickly. Now they regrouped and turned to look back. Morris scanned slowly to the right, past the oak tree, towards the field's far right corner.

"Well, well, well," he whispered.

There they were. Four distinct dark grey shapes, walking carefully and in a line along the far edge of the field.

"What've you got, Stu?" Westlake responded in similarly hushed tones.

"Who takes a country stroll on a day like this?"

"Nobody."

"Have a look…"

Westlake grabbed the monocular and watched the four men wandering along.

"They're in no rush," he opined. "But they can't see very far in this."

Morris reached for the radio on his chest and called headquarters.

"We have eyes on four men walking along one of the Radlett's Farm fields, the one closest to East Cumberton road," he reported.

"Stand by," came the reply. Seconds felt like minutes. "Two-Zero. Can you see any weapons?"

Westlake took his eye away from the monocular. "They're not carrying anything."

"Negative. No weapons on view."

"Stand by."

Another age passed.

Westlake looked annoyed. "This could've been sorted out by now."

"Two-Zero. Maintain observation. Do not engage. Units on the way."

"Oh, for f…"

"Copy. Maintaining observation."

Westlake maintained observation or would have done had he found something to observe.

"Oh shit. Where've they gone?"

He scanned the far edge again, starting at the sheep, now munching contentedly in the far left corner, and then along the hedgerow. Taking some deliberately deep breaths, he zoomed in on the corner and swung left once more. There. Dark shapes moved behind the light-coloured boundary hedgerow.

"They've gone through the hedge."

"I'm pretty sure there's another field and then the farm buildings beyond."

Morris thought quickly.

"Get after them, but don't approach. Just keep them in view and keep me informed. I'll drive round to the farm."

Westlake strode back to the car and picked up his rifle. Finally. The chance for some action. He climbed over the padlocked gate and set off at a brisk walk, using his scope to guide him and to monitor the figures moving behind the hedgerow at the same time.

Morris watched him disappear into the fog before stowing his own rifle close by in the passenger footwell. He updated headquarters, hesitated a moment, then gunned the engine into life and headed off towards the farm, a mile away by road.

In films, it was always the guy about to retire who never made it to the end. He determined that wasn't happening today.

14

Pope showed his uninvited guest to the second bedroom where he could relax awhile, then went back to the kitchen. From the top of a cupboard, he retrieved a burner phone he'd bought a year earlier and plugged in its charger. Then he fired up his Tor browser and logged on to @TheTrth. It did not surprise him to find he was late for the party.

Under the thread *UK PM missing; probably abducted; possibly dead* were over 40 comments, not one of which voiced an iota of concern over the health, wellbeing or life of the country's Premier.

Some speculated on what had happened.

Others wondered who orchestrated the plot and why.

Fretters fretted over the future direction of the country.

Speculators were already debating the pros and cons of the prospective leadership contenders.

Revolutionaries were mobilising from their bedrooms for the coming revolution.

Those who saw themselves as a threat went offline to avoid arrest.

If you had him, what would you do with him? wrote Pope, then went to make himself another cup of tea. This was not how he'd envisaged his weekend starting.

The initial shock had faded, replaced by numbness he hadn't felt in a while.

Today, however, he didn't have the luxury of time to wallow.

Within the next hour, he was sure his guest would accept the inevitability of his return to the Westminster bubble. Having spent time on that bed, he was probably looking forward to it.

Pope would drop him off somewhere away from prying eyes and CCTV, clean the inside of his car, re-clean the house and get on with his life. The rest was up to the PM.

Pope grabbed three digestive biscuits, threw two towards the dogs, then sat back down in front of the laptop. The responses to his post took him completely by surprise.

There were none.

It was as if the entire community had been shocked into silence, or fear. Canafanta had asked a pressing question that could not wait for the usual pontification and earnest discussion. @TheTrth wasn't a practical advice forum. Had it been for plumbers, the discussions would be about the rights of water and controlling its direction; not about removing blockages or finding leaks.

As Pope pondered the lack of response, one comment appeared from Rebel2Rebel, who rarely posted but commented regularly.

Useful bargaining chip… Chance to make a difference…

The comment opened the floodgates. What was the chip's value? What could the difference be? Now, the @TheTrth community was on much safer ground, able to discuss the amount of power achieved by holding onto such an asset; the ability to keep the asset safely and to utilise him successfully; and the comparative merits of each proposed ransom demand.

The system could barely keep up with the comments.

Pope was quietly pleased to have generated such a volume of response - quickly up to 58 comments, some of which were generating their own fierce debates.

Reading a long paragraph advocating replacing Parliament with a benevolent dictatorship, he received a message from Rebel2Rebel.

Where do you have him?

Pope stared at the screen. He admitted to himself that part of the reason for posting on @TheTrth had been to stir up this kind of speculation and to lift his credibility within the group. But he hadn't expected this. Rebel2Rebel wasn't asking if he held the PM, but where. Why would Rebel2Rebel want to know?

Another message, this time from @Armed–Justice.

Resources across UK at your disposal.

Pope noticed that comments on the @TheTrth page were at 232 and increasing. He closed the laptop, took a beer from the fridge, and headed to the back garden. Perhaps posting was a bad idea. He needed some fresh air.

15

"They seem decent blokes," said Jim Radlett, the fourth generation of his family to run Radlett's Farm. "Wanted somewhere quiet for their caravan in return for a bit of labour around the farm. It's round the back of the barn. Been here about six weeks and they've never been a problem. Quiet. Tidy. Good as gold, really."

Doesn't sound like the behaviour of kidnappers, Morris thought as he sipped his mug of strong tea.

From the farm kitchen window, he peered at the large barn across the yard, approximately fifty yards away. His earpiece told him support units were at the end of the lane, awaiting the imminent arrival of special forces.

Jim Radlett joined him at the window with his own mug of coffee.

"They're usually picked up around half five every morning and arrive back mid-afternoon after a couple of pints down the pub."

Westlake had circled the second field and was using a half-built wall for cover, some fifty yards beyond the barn and caravan.

The farm buildings were breaking up the fog, which wandered around in patches as it cleared.

With his monocular in his pocket, Westlake looked through the scope on his rifle, which now rested on top of an unfinished part of the wall around shoulder height.

He'd reported two suspects in the caravan, with two more stationed outside on camping chairs, drinking what looked like bottled beer.

The occasional snatch of conversation floated across to him. It was clear they weren't speaking English. They also sounded worried.

Suddenly, shouting from inside the caravan silenced the two drinkers, who turned towards the open doorway.

"Heads up. Something's happening," murmured Westlake into his microphone. "Stand by."

He swung his rifle towards the caravan doorway, just in time to see somebody punched in the face and thrown onto the ground outside. A thick-set man followed quickly and started kicking the prone victim, who curled into a ball in a desperate act of self-preservation. "Shit. It's really kicked off. Someone's getting a right pasting."

Morris thumped his tea down on the kitchen table and made for the door. "Can you see the prime minister?"

"Can't tell."

"Shit. With you in fifteen seconds. I'll approach from the left side of the barn. Your right."

"We going in?"

Morris saw his pension and his long, pleasure-filled retirement flash before his eyes. Running in body armour, carrying an assault rifle wasn't easy at the best of times. He'd spent his entire career heading towards trouble as others moved away. Normally, the adrenalin kicked in hard; spurred him on. Not today, though. "Stand by."

Westlake moved quietly from around the wall and walked carefully towards the fight in front of him, watching events through the sight of his rifle.

His earpiece told him that special forces, a police armed response unit, dog handlers and ambulances were making their way up the road towards the farm.

The drinkers at the caravan grabbed hold of their violent friend for a moment, but he broke free and aimed another kick at his victim's head. Westlake still couldn't identify the PM, but...

"Stop! Armed police!" Just for good measure, Westlake fired twice into the air.

The caravan group froze.

Hearing the shout and the shots over their radios, the convoy accelerated towards the incident, switching on sirens as it did so.

Morris stopped for a split second at the end of the barn to catch his laboured breath, then raised the gun to his shoulder and swung around the corner.

His concerns for his partner were immediately put to rest as he saw him walking slowly towards the group at the caravan, gun at the ready. Three were on their knees, hands on their heads. The fourth person remained slumped on the floor.

Morris moved in; rifle still raised. "Armed police lads," he said, as calmly as he could, with his heart racing and his chest tight. Heads flicked left in surprise. "Nice and steady now. You all speak English?"

He saw heads nod but didn't hear any response, just a cacophony of sirens, quickly drowned out by a growing roar. The gun grew impossibly heavy and slipped from his hands, the weight of it swinging round his neck knocking him off balance. He staggered sideways and fell, first to his knees and then hitting his head on the ground.

The vehicles he saw emerging from behind the barn blurred quickly and then disappeared into blackness. The noise stopped. Everything stopped.

16

Pope was in the back garden about to start his third beer. He sat at a small outdoor table, cleaning his golf clubs with warm, soapy water. The PM appeared dishevelled, even more so than before, at the back door.

Both dogs lifted their heads, but then resumed their prone position on the lawn when no treats arrived.

"They're excellent dogs, aren't they?"

"Typical greyhounds, really. Happy to lie around all day. Like the occasional walk. Great pets."

"I thought they'd race around all the time. Chasing anything and everything."

"That's what people believe. It's not the reality."

"Tell me about it."

Pope motioned for him to sit and pushed the untouched beer towards him.

"You look like you need it."

"Thank you."

The PM took a swig, then inspected the label, which featured an illustration of a curly-haired footballer from the Seventies heading a football.

Pope wandered into the house, pulled another beer out of the fridge, and returned to his seat.

"I can't remember the last time I drank beer from a bottle… Perm's a strange name…"

"It's a hairstyle. The Monk sisters took the family microbrewery on when their father died. It was on its knees. Rather than change the beer, they changed the branding. There are four beers and eight labels in this range. Two labels per beer, one aimed at men, the other at women. Each beer is named after a hairstyle - perm, quiff, buzz and bob. Bottles for the male market feature a cartoon of a footballer with the required hairstyle. Women get film or pop stars. The brewery's never looked back."

The PM took another swig.

"Not bad," he observed. "Not bad at all."

Pope used a wire brush to clean the grooves of his seven iron before drying it on an old cloth. He loved seeing the dirt flush out, revealing the hidden sparkling metal. Immediate reward for his effort. If only life could be that way. Result after result after result. Boost after boost after boost. Pope didn't mind hard work. It kept him busy; occupied his mind. But it was a way to stay alive, not truly live.

To do that, you needed goals. A purpose: something to aim for; then something else. Small steps; enormous achievements. Pope used to feel that way. With Pippa, he felt he swam in the middle of an archipelago, each island more interesting and exciting than the last. Now he was just treading water, and that wasn't a long-term option.

He sensed his guest was relishing the peace; the luxury of nowhere to be, nobody to meet, and nothing to say. That was fine by Pope. He was used to the silence. Wrapped himself up in it.

Half an hour later, the clean clubs lay resplendent in Pope's golf bag. Two more bottles stood open on the table. The dogs had moved indoors, possibly miffed at the lack of food and having to share their garden with no tangible reward.

Neither man felt compelled to talk. It probably surprised both how comfortable the silence felt.

Pope used the time to weigh up his guest surreptitiously. He looked shorter than he did on television - probably Pope's height but a few kilogrammes heavier. His face seemed exhausted, pale, and slightly more wrinkled than expected. His hair was a mess, but at least he had some.

In fact, he wasn't that different from the coiffured character illustrated on the beer bottle label.

The PM had been looking down for a while. Pope wondered where in the world his mind was.

Turned out it had been in the garden all the time. He'd been looking at Pope's golf clubs.

"I used to play a bit of golf in a previous life," he said. "Mind if I have a swing?"

Pope shrugged. "Help yourself," he said, and took another swig of beer. He watched the PM take out a six iron and examine the head.

"Blades," the PM observed. "Never got along with them. Not good enough at ball control."

"They've changed in recent years. A bit more forgiving than they used to be."

The PM took a couple of swings that redefined the term 'rusty' forever. The second took a huge divot out of the lawn and flung it towards the garage.

"Oh no. I'm ever so sorry."

Pope picked up the divot and threw it back to the PM. He walked into the garage and emerged with a golf carry bag holding another set of clubs. By the time he returned, the divot was back in the lawn.

"My previous set. Cavity backs," he announced. "Have a go with them." He rescued his six iron and gave it a quick clean before returning it to his bag and the bag to the garage, well out of harm's way.

He went into the house and came back out with two more beers and his laptop.

The PM tried several swings with the newly arrived clubs.

"Much better," he pronounced. "More weight in the head. Easier to swing."

Certainly the swing was looking better. Slower but smoother, although a ball might alter things a bit.

Pope opened his laptop. The browser was still open - a schoolboy error, but no harm done. Comments had grown to over 800. Several arguments between various factions had broken out, which he'd check later.

He also had a further seventeen messages to open, plus several more from Rebel2Rebel and @Armed_Justice. They could wait as well. He deleted history, quit the browser, then opened another to check on the news.

The PM noticed the laptop and realised reality was about to interrupt his enjoyment.

"They've announced the body in the back of the van isn't you, although it appears he was wearing your jacket," Pope said. "There were reports he was holding a penis in his hand when he died. Apparently, it was a sausage. Something is happening at a local farm. Oh, it's the Radlett's place."

Pope knew Jim from the golf club, although he'd rarely played with him.

The PM heard every word but remained focused on bending his knees slightly when trying a flop shot with the lob wedge. Pope continued trawling through the coverage.

"Cobra's meeting, chaired by the Cabinet Secretary. Apparently, the Cabinet's still to decide on who's taking your role. Surely there's a plan for something like this. What if you were sick or in an accident?"

"Like the poor chap in the back of the van?"

Both men felt embarrassed and disturbed, but for different reasons.

Pope felt embarrassed by his original question and disturbed by the crassness of the answer.

The PM was embarrassed because the government certainly was unprepared for this situation. Also, he was disturbed by the lack of an announcement.

Either members of the Cabinet were fighting fiercely for the role, or nobody wanted it. He wasn't sure it was the former. He now understood the role, and these people had watched him struggle and fail from the front row.

Maybe sanity was prevailing over ambition and hubris. Perhaps his colleagues were more human than he had ever imagined. He broke the silence.

"Bratwurst," he said. "The sausage was a bratwurst. One month ago, at a G7 dinner, I chatted with the German chancellor about how various foodstuffs are associated with specific mealtimes. I gave the example of sausage at breakfast - not the best example, but we were on our third bottle of wine by then. He extolled the virtues of German sausage as an accompaniment to beer in the evening. Couple of weeks later, I find some fine-looking bratwurst in a deli, buy half a kilo then send him a picture of one of them along with a message…"

"Guess what's for supper…"

"Exactly! He finds it funny, sends me a LOL and shows it to his team."

"And word gets out…"

"Some Germans dislike me more than the British media."

The PM put the lob wedge in the carry bag and raised his bottle in a mock salute.

"Todgergate was born. A special adviser said we should explain all and knock it on the head. I wasn't sure if pictures of me waving a sausage would be a good career move."

"People believe what they want to believe."

"Even if it isn't the reality."

Both men sat, lost in their own thoughts and nursing their Perms as the dogs - having heard the word sausage - ran out into the garden.

17

Five o'clock had been and gone, unlike the traffic on the M1 southbound and the fog that swirled around it.

Barnwell stared at his assistant, who stared right back at him, and the silence hung heavy in the air.

Curtis thanked the Almighty that he was a simple driver. He had no role except for following instructions, transporting people, and occasionally extricating them and himself from dangerous situations.

His eyes fixed on the registration plate of the stationary coach in front of the car, and they didn't move from that position. He had no desire to throw even a cursory glance at his rear-view mirror to witness this moment. Why should he? He was part of it.

A disembodied female voice cleared her throat. "Hello? Have I lost you?"

"You lost us for a few seconds, Emma," Mindy lied to the civil servant from the Cabinet secretariat, playing for a bit more time. "Can you repeat, please?"

"Oh, sorry. Yes, of course. I was asked to take the minutes at the 5pm Cabinet meeting and I'm in the Cabinet room at Number Ten. It's now ten past five and I'm the only person here. Just confirming the time and place."

"It should have started at five. The Cabinet secretary..."

"... asked me to contact you. We have people trying to contact ministers, but we're not having any luck. Calls are ringing out or going to voicemail. That's why I wondered if the venue's changed..."

"No, you're in the right place. Give me a minute..." Mindy muted the call. "Curtis, can you make sure other ministerial security details..."

Curtis nodded and murmured into his lapel microphone. Thirty seconds later, he had his answer.

"All operational, but currently static. Constituency offices. Department meetings. A couple are just leaving their minister's home."

"And none of them are moving towards Downing Street." Barnwell couldn't believe what he was saying. "The most scheming, ambitious, selfish bunch of clowns I've ever had the displeasure of working with. Now the top job's there for the taking, they've all run a mile..."

"So the country has no leader..."

Barnwell gestured for Mindy to unmute her phone.

"Emma, it's Martin Barnwell here, chief-of-staff."

"Yes, Mr. Barnwell?"

"Please remain in the Cabinet room until 7pm. The Cabinet will be with you by then. It's vital that the media doesn't pick up on this delay. And put me through to the Cabinet secretary, please."

A few seconds later, Cabinet secretary David Slayton was on the line, learning that he was currently the most powerful man in the country. The most powerful person, excluding media moguls, sports stars, celebrities, and social media influencers.

"Call the Cobra meeting straightaway and chair it," Barnwell suggested. "The police and intelligence agencies are probably meeting already. No need for everyone to be in the same room. We need to crack on. The security services have well-rehearsed plans for such scenarios. It's just a matter of getting these implemented while the Cabinet focuses on the leadership."

"Will you be joining us?" Slayton asked, hoping for some moral support. The intelligence agencies always scared him. Their representatives always looked at you as if they knew something about you that you'd rather they didn't.

"I'll call you later. I've some threats to make."

Just before six o'clock, ministers started to arrive at Downing Street, their sombre faces broadcast live to the world. Not one of them acknowledged the cameras or even thought about making a statement. To the viewer, each displayed the heavy responsibility of office at this critical juncture in the country's history.

Privately, each minister knew their reputation, career, wealth, and even their marriage were at stake if they weren't present when the chief of staff arrived.

Half an hour later, Curtis swept the car past armed members of the Metropolitan Police Diplomatic Protection Group into Downing Street. He pulled up immediately outside the black, blast-proof steel front door of Number Ten. Before the media could react, Barnwell was already in the building. Mindy handed the repacked handgun back to Curtis. Their eyes locked.

"Tonight's off then?" he asked.

She smiled at him. "I'll call you tomorrow."

In an instant, she was gone, leaving just a familiar whisper of perfume as a parting gift.

Curtis swung the car around and headed back out of Downing Street, waving at the DPG guys at the gate. He smiled to himself. A great night last night. Today, he'd been at the centre of history in the making, at least for a while.

18

Pope switched off the oven and removed the two Cornish pasties. Carefully observed by the dogs, he put a pasty on each plate and added baked beans from a pan on the stove.

The lingering fog patches had reluctantly disappeared, chilling the approaching evening. The men had retreated into the house for something to eat and more to drink.

"You still haven't told me your name."

Pope hesitated for a second.

"Simmo."

"Well Simmo," the PM picked up his latest beer, "Here's to you. I'm very grateful for your hospitality."

Pope put the plates on the table, then picked up his own beer to clink the proffered bottle. They ate in silence for a while.

"Simmo. May I ask you something?"

"As long as you don't take exception to my answer."

The PM cocked his head to one side as he considered the condition, then nodded.

"Do you live here by yourself? It's only just occurred to me that someone may…"

"I live here by myself."

The PM nodded again, then swallowed a forkful of beans.

"Have you always lived by yourself?"

"No." The answer was final.

The PM liked to think his success in politics was down in part to his ability to judge others; knowing when to push, insist or bully; knowing when to back off.

This was one of the latter moments.

Suspecting his host wasn't eating the crust of his pasty because of the dogs staring at the table, the PM did the same. He took another swig of his beer. His host was comfortable at home, but there was a noticeable melancholy in him and the house.

Pope took a swig of his beer and looked hard at his guest.

"I have some questions for you."

"As long as you don't take exception to my answers."

"Last year's trade summit with the Yanks. Did you really call them gullible and naïve?"

"No. I made the observation to our own team. All trade issues to be decided by American courts?" He took another mouthful of pasty. "Someone took exception and leaked it. But they made it a comment about the US. Difficult to row that one back and explain our own people were the idiots."

"Do you already have offers in place for when you step down?"

A wry smile. "If I did, I suspect they're off the table after today."

"Did you decide to close Cumberton District Hospital when you were Health Secretary?"

"I ratified it just after I joined the department, along with several others. Made me look dynamic apparently. The department conducted investigations and finalised the closures well before then. It just so happened my predecessor keeled over in the arms of his mistress the week before the announcements were due."

"You reviewed nothing?"

"It was the ultimate point of a three-year process."

"People died. The hospital wasn't there for them anymore."

"And I'm very sorry for every single one of them."

Pope fell silent and finished the rest of his tea. The PM did the same. The direction the questions had taken unnerved him. Normally he'd be fielding - or rather ignoring - questions from Joe Public about something mundane, like his love life... Then it hit him.

"I have a number. Do you have a pen and paper?"

Pope grabbed the whiteboard and pen from the side of the fridge and handed it over. The PM wrote quickly.

"Who is it?"

"Mindy. Amanda Abbott. Assistant to my chief-of-staff."

"And hers is the number you remember?"

The PM didn't look up as he finished writing.

"Just came to me. Don't know why."

"That's the first thing you've said today that I don't believe."

The PM sighed and looked up.

"She worked as an intern for me when I first became an MP. Best assistant I ever had. Sharp. Beautiful. Funny. After a year, we had a bit of a fling for eighteen months. Then she dumped me. Poached by a junior minister who now sells eggs to food companies across the Home Counties. She ended up working for Martin Barnwell and they've been a formidable pairing ever since. Formidable."

"In Downing Street..."

The PM shrugged. "We'd both moved on. And I'd rather she was working for me rather than against me."

"So, what do you do now?"

The PM wasn't ready to return yet. He needed time to figure out how to explain his disappearance, and that depended on his future plans, which currently didn't exist.

"I wouldn't mind a game of golf," he said.
Pope laughed.
The PM looked hopefully across the table.
Pope frowned.
"Wow," he said, "You're serious."

19

Sometimes strangers entering a new pub hit a wall of silence and sense a cold, if not outwardly hostile, reception. The Cabinet room in 10 Downing Street was no different, although it wasn't necessary to be a stranger in the room or to the people in it to elicit that reaction.

Barnwell was well used to this experience and was oblivious when the hubbub he could hear inside stopped the instant he and Mindy walked in.

Despite its turbulent history, the Cabinet room is a welcoming and roomy space. Not today, though.

Mindy ran her eyes over the occupants. Only half the usual attendees, looking bored like students waiting for detention. Three skulked in a corner, as if sharing a sneaky fag. Several civil servants, who had either been waiting on their minister or talking between themselves, backed away to the fringes.

There was one conspicuous absence. The chair in front of the marble fireplace, the only chair in the room with arms, was unoccupied.

Barnwell stood at the end of the table.

"Ladies and gentlemen. Glad you could make it at such short notice. Please..." He gestured at the table and the sneaky fag sharers slumped into their seats.

"You will appreciate the seriousness of the situation. You need to decide on the interim leader of Her Majesty's Government and how we move forward. Your focus is important, so please give your mobile devices to your advisers and they will leave the room."

Protest flared for several seconds, but a thump of the table by the chief-of-staff quickly extinguished it.

"We don't have time for this nonsense and prevarication," he said evenly. "Please. Now."

Reluctantly, as if handing over their most treasured possessions, all around the table complied. All civil servants left, except for Emma, who had called the car earlier to report the empty room. She had remained in the room since, as requested, despite desperately needing the toilet. Preparing to take the minutes of one of the most important meetings in recent history did nothing to calm her bladder. Quite the opposite, in fact.

Fortunately, help was at hand.

"Emma," Mindy could recognise a fellow female in distress a mile off, especially when her face was as red as Emma's. "We'll be having an off-the-record chat for a couple of minutes. I'll call you back in when we're ready."

Emma smiled in relief, nodded and left quickly.

To the contained fury of the high and mighty around the table, Barnwell checked his own phone while they were handing theirs over. Yet despite the egos within the room, the superiority complexes, the outrageous arrogance, nobody said a word.

He looked up at the faces staring at him, some malevolent, others blank, a few terrified.

"Thank you, genuinely, for attending. I apologise for the brusqueness of my request to you, but I'm sure you understand why it is important that we have a quorum and show a united front."

Finding courage he hadn't thought was within him, the health secretary spoke up.

"There are notable absences from the table…"

Barnwell's face hardened for a moment. Just long enough for the attendees to be grateful they had made the effort to come.

"The foreign secretary has cut short his Middle East trip and is in the air. Defence, education, transport, and three 'without portfolios' are unavailable or unreachable. That's unfortunate."

For them, thought everybody around the table.

Barnwell took a moment to look at Jean Baptiste-Loo's portrait of Sir Robert Walpole - the only picture in the entire room - which hung above the fireplace. The others followed his gaze and stared into the eyes of Britain's first, longest serving and arguably greatest prime minister.

"We face a situation that is unprecedented in our country's history," said Barnwell. "The prime minister vanished. He wasn't in the van that was destroyed at the pub riot. We suspect that the man who died had the PM's jacket, phone, wallet, and sausage."

"Sausage?" The health secretary couldn't believe what he'd just heard.

"Sausage," repeated Barnwell, as if it was the most obvious item in the world for a prime minister to carry, alongside the nuclear codes. "Four other people who were also in the van are in police custody. The prime minister wasn't among them. They're at the local police station, but Special Branch doesn't think they were involved in the disappearance. Apparently, anything not chained down in that distribution centre disappears quickly. A bit like the PM."

He paused for the information to sink in. Unless the prime minister was abducted, he had removed his jacket and left it behind with his belongings before disappearing.

Why would he do that? To avoid being found?

He waited for the inevitable questions, but none were forthcoming.

"Oh, shit." The chancellor - who lived in the flat at Number 10 and therefore had no excuse for missing this meeting - was famous for her pithy comments. This wasn't one of her best, although it was one of the most apt.

"Quite," said Barnwell, "But while we wait to find out what exactly has happened to our beloved leader, we need to find another one."

The group's focus subtly changed from considering others to prioritising themselves. Barnwell needed to keep the meeting moving.

"Chancellor, if nobody has any objection, may I suggest you chair this meeting in the absence of the prime minister? Our aim is to agree on his temporary replacement and on a way forward. The cabinet secretary will join us shortly once the Cobra meeting has finished."

The chancellor walked to the chair with the enthusiasm of a condemned woman taking her last walk. Mindy opened the door and called Emma back in.

20

Pope grabbed another two beers and transferred a pack of four bottles recently installed in the freezer into the fridge. He hadn't normally drunk so much so quickly and so early in the evening, especially with a golf game planned for the morning. He wasn't sure if it was the alcohol talking, but it may actually be possible to play a round with a disguised First Lord of the Treasury.

The PM looked startled.

"Really? It's a goer?"

"We'll play in the afternoon. The course is much quieter. I've some clothes in the guestroom wardrobe that should fit you."

Then, answering the PM's questioning look, "I used to be bigger than I am now. Stored the stuff in case I put the weight back on."

"People will still recognise me, won't they?"

"You look different in real life. Heavier. Paler. Besides..." He took a long pull at the bottle. "You're going to cut your hair."

"My hair? But it's... Actually..." The PM sat back in his seat and shook his head. "You really think it'll work? What if somebody recognises me?"

"It's a golf club. What happens on the course stays on the course. Actually, that's not quite right, but it won't go any further than the clubhouse."

"But what if someone mentions it when they're home, or in the pub later?"

"And says what? *You know that the prime minister's gone missing? I saw the dead spit of him on the fourth hole this afternoon. Thinner, mind, not as tall and with shorter hair, but the dead spit.*"

The PM stared. "Not as tall?"

"Do you watch yourself on television?"

"Rarely," the PM lied.

"You surround yourself with people shorter than yourself. Now I've seen you, it looks as if you appoint people based on their height, or rather their lack of it."

The PM pictured himself talking to colleagues and meeting members of the public. Invariably, he was looking down at them. It had never occurred to him before. Damn, his media team and his chief-of-staff - or rather his chief-of-staff's assistant - were good.

Cutting his hair would be a big statement. A statement to himself and, once he returned to wherever to become whatever, to everybody else. A physical break. No more hiding. No more artifice. A new start. New horizons.

"I'll do it," he said. "I'll do it now."

"Clippers are in the bathroom cabinet. Water's hot if you want a shower. Towels are in the airing cupboard. Pick what you like from the wardrobe."

"Sod it. I'll do it. I'm going to do it."

With that, the PM swayed to his feet. Still holding onto his bottle, he staggered out of the kitchen, into the hallway and up the stairs.

Pope shouted after him. "I'm taking the dogs for a walk. Back in half an hour."

"I'm going to bloody do it!"

Pope unplugged the burner phone and entered the phone number the PM had supplied, preceded by 141. Grabbing two slip leads from a wall hook and waste bags and treats from a drawer, he pushed his way between his eager hounds and opened the front door. Both dogs shot out into the small front garden, where they waited for the gate to be opened before running down the country lane towards the open fields.

Pope followed into the chilly dusk, wishing he'd slipped on a jacket before leaving the house. He had no concerns for the dogs. They'd be back soon for a treat or two. It felt good to experience some normality after a while.

He broke into a trot. He needed to distance himself from the house, from the madness of the last few hours. Then, for the first time in his life, he tried speaking aloud in a range of different accents.

21

The Cabinet meeting was going as feared.

Cabinet secretary David Slayton's Cobra report was the only bright spot. Government departments were to implement Operation Mongoose, involving security and police services.

This called for a public manhunt for the prime minister, rather than searching for potential kidnappers who probably didn't exist. Not that the latter notion was completely disregarded.

No ultimatum had been received from any known organisation. There were no claims of success from any credible source, just the usual nutters.

People were speculating online, and AI programmes were analysing lots of data for specific search terms.

Specialised police teams were using online identities and web communities to pinpoint potential leads.

All to no avail.

"The plan is to broaden the search area across the Midlands and into surrounding regions," said Slayton, peering over the top of his rimless glasses. "We have agreed to a programme of high profile policing. Starting at first light, twelve police forces will engage with the public."

"Search teams and dog rescue services will cover rivers, lakes, abandoned mines, etcetera. Helicopters with heat-sensitive cameras will check fields and wooded areas. As I speak, our face recognition platform is downloading images from community CCTV systems across the area. The software will automatically apply the PM's features against all digitally recorded data from 2pm today and will flag any matches."

"We have dedicated medical support ready at ten major hospitals with direct helicopter landing access. We'll also be boosting security at all major transport hubs. Every newspaper in the country will have the PM's photograph on tomorrow's front cover; the same with every online news home page. Cobra is sixty-to-seventy per cent confident we'll have him in 24 hours."

He thought, but didn't add, "Dead or alive."

Slayton took a breath, surveying the room.

The majority of Cabinet members looked down or pretended to read notes. Nobody wanted to make eye contact with anybody else.

Everyone hoped for a discussion where they didn't have to contribute.

Over the last year, the prime minister had faced many problems, only some of which were down to his incompetence and relaxed approach.

The honest ones amongst them could see the seeds sown three elections ago and the arrogance that had grown within the party.

Over that time, familiarity had bred contempt within the media and resentment among the electorate.

"Thank you, David. An excellent and comprehensive report," said Emily Helms.

The chancellor was polite to all, including enemies, and was well aware of the meeting's historical significance.

Her body ached from the rigid position she had adopted in the unfamiliar chair in order to avoid contact with its back or its arms.

In her mind, the less physical contact she had with the damn thing, the less chance there was of her being stuck in it. She had leadership ambitions, but now was not the right time, akin to accepting the captaincy of the Titanic with the iceberg approaching. "Are there any questions for the Cabinet secretary?"

Nobody wanted to speak, but Helms was determined they would do so or would be damned by their silence. She focused on her main long-term competition in the room. The greater their contribution, the more likely that peer pressure would build for them to take on the poisoned chalice.

"Home secretary...?"

Damien Crockett, former police officer, erstwhile police commissioner and a handsome cove to boot, looked deep in thought for several seconds. This operation sat firmly in his area of responsibility and was definitely his area of expertise. Exactly what he didn't want.

He cleared his throat. "Thank you, Emily," he lied, "And thank you David. All very comprehensive. I assume Downing Street will handle the media?"

Rookie mistake thought Barnwell at the end of the table. This meeting would end sooner than he'd expected.

The heavy atmosphere enveloping the ministers at the table lifted quicker than the day's fog as they sensed an escape route opening up in front of them.

Helms recognised the shift in mood. It was the perfect moment to strengthen her value to the senior party members, gain their favour, and weaken a potential future rival.

She settled back in the chair, placed her arms on the rests and cocked her head towards Slayton who, never slow to take advantage of a weakness, responded quickly.

"Downing Street will, of course, provide support. However, I believe that the acting prime minister should announce our response. An ideal opportunity to cement their position in the eyes of the public as the country's leader. The leader of the opposition will likely ask an Urgent Question and request Parliament to meet tomorrow. It would be helpful to have the acting prime minister, firmly endorsed by the public, in position for that event."

Helms nodded at this sage advice before looking around the table. "Dominic?"

The secretary of state for work and pensions had served ten years in the unpopular role and despised ambitious young colleagues.

He eagerly accepted the invitation to join the discussion and to push in the knife.

"This is a critical time in our recent history, chancellor. A unique moment," he observed, savouring every word and glancing quickly across at Emma to make sure she was recording his contribution in the minutes. "We must unite as a nation. People rally behind those they trust and believe in during challenging times."

Out of the corner of his eye, he could swear that bastard Crockett was shaking, perhaps even sweating slightly. *Welcome to realpolitik, punk.*

"I realise I am not the person to fulfil this role," he admitted. Most around the table relished his faux self-deprecation and resolved to utilise a similar strategy when their time came to speak.

Damien Crockett resolved not to give them the opportunity. He had two options: take charge or do something incredibly foolish to eliminate himself from consideration.

Not that the latter option had prevented the incumbent from securing the position.

This was a historic moment. The lady from the Cabinet office should record that he volunteered to be the leader, instead of being forced into it.

He looked up and raised his hand slightly.

"If I may, Emily? It is now several hours since the prime minister disappeared. I hope we find him safe soon, but the government shouldn't prevaricate. Leadership and decisive action are needed now."

The group around the table held its collective breath. Sat next to her boss on a row of chairs by the wall close to the door, Mindy felt her personal mobile vibrate in her jacket pocket. If it was anything important, they'd leave a message. A second vibration told her they had.

Crockett decided the dramatic pause had been long enough. "With that in mind and with humility, I offer myself for the role of acting prime minister in this unprecedented situation. I believe that my experience and my expertise, allied to the relevance of my ministerial portfolio, makes me the right choice for this role. I suggest I hold that position until the PM is with us once again or until the 1922 Committee decides on the way forward for the Party and the country."

Helms cocked her head to the other side, as if she hadn't actually considered the home secretary taking on the role.

"Thank you for your offer, Damien. Certainly, I know the role would be safe in your very capable hands." She looked around the table, hiding a triumphant smirk. "Thoughts please. Is there anybody else who would like to throw their hat in the ring?"

22

Stuart Morris was in Heaven. An angelic female face in soft focus wafted into his view and looked at him with a gentle smile. She mouthed some words, but he couldn't tell what she had said. Hopefully, it was "Welcome to Heaven. Happy hour's... well... it's always happy hour."

His eyes grew more accustomed to the bright light. Shapes were becoming better defined. The wail of a tortured banshee gradually replaced the buzz in his ears.

A dark mass shifted slowly behind the angel; drifted alongside her. Perhaps he wasn't in Heaven after all. Maybe agents of both afterworlds were still arguing over his soul; weighing up the balance of his time on earth; determining his eternal fate. Surely being a copper had stood for something worthwhile. The people he'd helped. The populations he'd protected.

"Good God, Stu. You scared the shit out of me."

Sergeant Stuart Morris GC, QPM, felt the tears prick his eyes and slowly venture down his cheek.

The concerned face of Dave Westlake loomed into view and smiled through tears of his own.

"You're in an ambulance, mate. You'll be okay. Just rest easy. And welcome back."

23

The prime minister stared at the mirror, his curly locks now nestling in the bathroom sink. Not knowing how to operate the electric clippers, he had just started mowing, feeling as if he was sweeping away his current trials and tribulations; the pressure on his shoulders lifting with each clump of hair that hit the bowl. As a result, he was now the proud owner of a harsh crew cut.

He looked younger. Thinner. Almost gaunt, in fact. People would think he looked ill. He ran his hand from the nape of his neck, over the back of his head. There were no outcrops of hair hanging on to what they were, fearful of what the future held for them. They'd all gone.

His eyes, no longer partially hidden by an overlong fringe, shocked him initially. They seemed much bigger; greener; a rabbit in headlights. He looked more vulnerable. He was more vulnerable. Dear God.

"What on earth have I done?" he asked himself.

The reflection didn't answer. Didn't need to. The eyes said it all.

He gathered the hair and disposed of it in the toilet, then wiped the sink with damp tissue paper. That went into the toilet as well.

Then he stood, flushed and watched as it all span around the bowl, seemingly reluctant to leave, and then quickly disappeared.

Two minutes later, after a quick shower, he was back in front of the mirror, drying himself off. Second time around, his eyes were getting used to the lack of hair. They didn't look as startled as they had such a short time ago. Didn't look as big.

The PM smiled, picturing familiar faces clocking his new look for the first time.

He watched as the smile creased the skin by the side of each eye. He liked that look. He didn't smile enough. It was rare that a smile reached anything other than his mouth.

He wandered back into the guest room and opened the wardrobe doors.

Four pairs of chinos, half a dozen T-shirts, and a couple of jumpers hung neatly on the left-hand side. Three shirts, four ties, a suit and a dinner jacket on the right. The latter surprised him. A warehouse worker with his own dinner jacket?

He took it out for a closer look. In the inside pocket was a four-page A5 booklet, folded vertically in half. A menu for a regimental dinner, held almost two years earlier.

The PM returned the menu to the jacket and the jacket to the wardrobe.

He caught sight of a stationer's box file on the shelf above the hanging rail. His curiosity piqued by the discovery of the menu, he removed the heavy file and sat down with it on the bed.

He skimmed through the papers, pictures, and press clippings, making sure not to disturb their order and keeping an ear out for his host. Once the box was back in the wardrobe, his eyes were the same size as when he first saw his cropped head.

"What have I done?" he whispered, for the second time in fifteen minutes.

Picking a light blue polo shirt and light grey trousers, he dressed quickly, tidied the bathroom, and made his way downstairs.

Aware of his recent alcohol intake, he made a cup of tea and turned on the television in the lounge. He was just in time to see Damien Crockett stride to the lectern in the lights of the world's media.

The PM smiled wryly. So, Crockett had drawn the short straw and was facing his very own Alamo. Taking a sip of tea, he settled back to enjoy the fun.

24

Martin Barnwell sat in his office and watched the scene outside his window unfurl on his laptop. It was only his general contempt for all politicians that prevented him from feeling sympathy for the home secretary. Contempt, plus decades of experience that told him this moment may well turn into Damien Crockett's finest hour. The man who stepped up. The capable leader who guided the country through tough times.

The uncertainty of Barnwell's own political future didn't bother him. He didn't play their game. There were too many rules; goalposts that could shift; unreliable people you needed to rely on. The goalposts were shifting now. Crockett would bring in his own team and ideas if he stayed. All of which was fine by Barnwell. It was how the world moved. He wasn't short of offers and more would undoubtedly arrive, even over the next few days, if the current situation remained unresolved.

Just as the acting prime minister started speaking, Mindy entered Barnwell's office and closed the door behind her.

"He's alive," she announced, waving her personal mobile phone.

"Really? Where is he?"

"I don't know."

"Is he okay?"

"Not sure."

"Who's…"

"Look," she interrupted, sensing his rising level of exasperation, which was matching her own. "Shall I tell you what I know?"

Barnwell bit his lip and nodded.

"This voicemail came while we were in the Cabinet room."

A male voice, part lilting Irish, part broad Glaswegian, quite breathless and possibly inebriated, filled the room.

"This is a message for Miss Abbott concerning your prime minister," it said. "He is safe. Physically, he is well." There was a break as Pope caught his breath, steadied his nerve, and tried to remember the key message the PM had given him. "He says call off the hunt. Unnecessary. Waste of resource. He'll be with you again soon. He promises this time he won't bring white lilies."

The caller rang off.

Barnwell looked at his assistant.

"White lilies?"

Mindy nodded. "About ten years ago, he gave me lilies. Or rather he tried to. I hate them. Kill cats. Remind me of death. Also, it's my mobile; not the work one. Definitely a message from him, or two incredibly lucky guesses."

Barnwell nodded. If his assistant had more to say, she'd still be talking.

"And the caller?"

"Number withheld. I'll get MI5 onto it, but I'm willing to bet triangulation will put the caller in a field miles away from civilisation."

"And he's definitely not Irish or Scottish."

"The Irish bits weren't bad, but he's definitely not Scottish."

Barnwell's gaze drifted back to his laptop, although his mind remained on the voicemail. Crockett had finished his statement.

Basking in the lights and the attention, he ignored the plan to nod, then march briskly back into Number Ten to get on with the job. He answered one question about how he felt, taking on the role. Now he was admitting how little he knew and explaining why he wasn't up to the job. With each question, he seemed to become smaller and sweatier.

The chief of staff looked at his assistant.

"Thoughts?"

"Slightly tricky. Sounds as if he's relaying a message from the PM, but *your prime minister* suggests not his prime minister. He could have simply told us where the PM is and we could go get him. Calling off the hunt sounds like a request, not a kidnapper's demand. In fact, there were no demands. There's also a suggestion that mentally or emotionally, the PM has a problem. He certainly wasn't himself earlier today." She hesitated for a second. "This guy either doesn't want to let the PM go, thinks he's protecting him or is simply relaying a message he's been given."

Barnwell nodded.

"We can't call off the search," he said. "Triangulating the call may provide the messenger's location, but not the PM. He could be in a barn in Blackburn or flying out to Florida for all we know."

"Who do we inform about the call?"

Barnwell looked at his laptop. An aide who could stand the torment no longer had interrupted the acting PM halfway through an answer.

He whispered something in his ear along the lines of "This is a complete cock up. Pretend I've just told you something important and run back inside. We'll work the crowd and explain we've just received a new lead."

Crockett was almost running back to the front door and into the sanctuary of the building. Could Mart and Mindy trust this man with this kind of information? Could they trust anyone?

"Nobody," he answered. "Kill it."

Mindy looked down at her mobile and pressed Delete.

25

Watching his home secretary beat a hasty retreat from the podium, the PM felt a mixture of emotions. He had experienced similar uncomfortable moments before, but never shied away from a question. Not until today. Crockett's disappearance had been contrived, no matter how they'd tried to disguise it with an aide suddenly appearing at his side with a supposedly urgent message. The PM's own disappearance, however, was a different matter.

He muted the television and watched the confused faces of the anchors, reporters, and correspondents as they tried to make sense of what had happened.

At a past photo call, two individuals at a Samaritans branch had shared with the PM the stories of their failed suicide attempts. Thankfully, each was in a better place. Neither of them could really explain why they had chosen to end it all. It seemed to be all that was left for them.

That's what had happened those few short hours ago. His own political suicide. Leaving everything behind seemed the only choice. Just to find some peace. Calm. A bit of humdrum. It was a question one of the Samaritans volunteers said they asked frequently.

"Do you really want to die, or are you looking for peace?"

Peace. From his armchair across from the television, he examined his present surroundings. A second armchair, twin of the one he sat on, to his left. On his right, the door into the hallway. Against the wall on the far side of the doorway, a two-seater sofa with a coffee table in front. A small clock ticked on the mantelpiece above the boarded-up fireplace. On the main wall, a framed photograph of a couple walking by a misty canal.

No red boxes, issues, events, personalities, speeches, political infighting or legislative problems all vying for attention. A complete lack of beeps, rings, buzzes, polite coughs, urgent knocks, strident voices, shuffling papers, whining shredders, patronising tones or muffled conversations to disturb him. Just peace.

He closed his eyes and listened to the gentle ticking of the clock.

Normally, staff choreographed every waking second of his day. Not now. He was First Lord of His Own Time. His own space. His own life.

It wouldn't last. He had to go back and explain his actions, but only after deciding on the explanation. But he wouldn't apologise. He'd be out of there as soon as possible. A quick farewell trip to Buckingham Palace and then peace would be his. He'd buy a nameplate for a village home. Welcome to Humdrum.

A key fiddling in the front door lock disturbed his reverie, followed by a clunk and the scampering feet of the two dogs on the hallway tiles.

Both bundled into the front room to say hello, then headed to their beds in the kitchen. He heard Pope lock the latch, hang his keys on a hook, and slip his shoes off and into the rack at the bottom of the stairs.

The next moment, he was filling the doorway.

"Nice hair. Nice clothes too," he observed, then left a beat.

"You're still here then."

The PM gestured at the television. "There's no rush. They've found a replacement."

Pope looked at the screen and grunted. The broadcaster was repeating the press conference. The troubled face of the home secretary filled the screen.

"Did you make the call?"

"Left a message." Pope watched as a replay showed the aide approach the podium, speak briefly to the acting prime minister and then escort him away from the lectern. "Looks like they've received it."

He looked again at his guest. The hair change made him look very different. The clothes also played their part. You might recognise him on the street, but not know why or from where. Possibly the pub. Maybe a market stall, or the golf course.

The PM's face looked thinner, drawn.

"You look tired."

"I'm knackered, to be honest."

"Not surprising. Go get some rest. Big day tomorrow."

"Golf?"

Pope laughed.

"If you're still here tomorrow afternoon, then golf. Who knows?" He gestured at the TV screen, showing Number Ten's door. "You might be back in there before then."

"If that's the case, I'll only be packing my stuff."

Both men looked at each other. Pope spoke first.

"Let's see what tomorrow brings. Who'd have thought today would turn out like it did?"

"Who'd have thought." The PM nodded and made his way past Pope. "Thank you for today, Simmo. Whatever this results in, I'm glad it's given me the opportunity to meet you." He held out his hand. Pope shook it.

"See you tomorrow."

26

Dave Westlake sat quietly in a corner of Lofthouse Hospital's accident and emergency department, nursing a tepid coffee in a small plastic cup.

His mind reflected on the day's events, seeking any clues to the sergeant's apparent heart condition that he may have missed. Around him, the people from the pub riot waited for help, feeling annoyed and frustrated by the delay. The presence of four armed police officers tempered their frustration. Westlake's edgy colleagues hovered around the edges of the room, ready to take on anybody who looked at them.

"Constable Westlake?" Westlake looked up and looked into the hazel eyes of the duty doctor who'd taken control of the situation as Stuart Morris had arrived one hour earlier. Her identity badge revealed the smiling face behind the mask.

"Doctor?"

"I'm Meghan Mills. I'm the doctor responsible for Sergeant Morris. He's fully conscious now and is asking to see you."

"Is he okay?"

"As well as possible after a heart problem. He should be fine. Needs a small op to fix an issue with one of his arteries. He's asked to see you. I take it he has no close family?"

Westlake shook his head as he stood up.

"Divorced. His son and family live in Australia."

"Ah. That'll be why he wants you. There's a dog that needs looking after?" She paused and sized him up. "I understand you kept him alive until the paramedics got to him. You did well."

She marched past the wounded and infirm, down a long corridor, and stopped outside a closed door. Westlake trailed behind like a puppy hoping for treats. All he received was a hard stare.

"In there. Don't excite him. You've got ten minutes. We'll be operating on him later tonight. He knows."

Westlake watched her trim figure sashay to the end of the corridor, where she turned round and looked at him, knowing he'd be looking at her.

"Time's ticking Constable."

And with that, she was gone.

Westlake smiled ruefully. All the times and all the places he could have met the woman of his dreams, and it had to be here and now.

He walked into the private room and closed the door behind him.

Stuart Morris lay in bed, taped up to a heart rate monitor and with an intravenous drip feeding into his arm. His drawn, grey face studied the screen of his mobile phone.

"We've still not got him then."

"No. Those lads were fine. Good lads actually, apart from the gang leader, who'd nicked the van. That's why they were beating the shit out of him. Anyway, what's this about your dog needs looking after?"

He saw the confusion on the sergeant's face. "Yeah. I didn't think you had a dog either."

Confusion turned into a frown on Morris's face, then a smile, and finally a laugh.

"They told me I needed an op and asked me if I had any close family nearby. I thought they were telling me I was dying. I wanted nothing to go to Helen. Think I said to make sure the bitch got nothing. Had an oxygen mask on, though." He laughed again, shaking his shoulders as he tried to stop.

Westlake saw the spikes on the monitor display grow in size and frequency.

"Steady mate, watch that heart of yours," he said, before smiling himself. "They must think nothing's a dog food."

Both men started giggling, tried not to giggle, then giggled at each other giggling.

Tears rolled down their cheeks again, but this time in humour and relief, not shock and concern.

Westlake pointed at the monitor spikes again, eased himself into a chair next to his mate, and attempted to control himself. Morris grabbed a handful of bed sheets and stuffed them into his own mouth, which set Westlake off again.

Flashing lights on the monitor and a loud alarm in the corridor calmed both men down very quickly.

There was time for three slow, calm breaths each before the door crashed open and two nurses entered the room. Both men looked up, nonplussed by the interruption. The nurses didn't give a shit.

They shoved Westlake violently to one side as one nurse placed a stethoscope on Morris's chest while feeling for a pulse in his wrist. The other checked the monitor and the chest connections.

"I feel okay, honest..." Morris's voice trailed away, the room filling with an ominous silence as Meghan Mills appeared in the doorway. The two police officers remained silent, as was their right, while the staff completed their checks and reported everything was normal. The doctor stepped backwards to let her staff exit the room before moving forwards into it.

"I'm not sure what happened here, but I'm hoping, gentlemen, that you understand the seriousness of Stuart's situation."

Westlake renewed acquaintances. "We do doctor. We've almost sorted everything out."

"You have five minutes left. Then, Stuart, we'll be preparing you for the angioplasty. The consultant's arrived and is looking at your scans. She'll be down to see you in due course."

"She...?" Westlake couldn't help himself. He tried desperately to rescue the situation before Mills could respond and crush his fleeting dreams of future romance forever. "That's the first time I've heard that gender attribution for a consultant. About time too."

Mills gave him a look from above her surgical mask, a look that could have been appreciation or gratitude, but was probably contempt or malevolence. Masks had a lot to answer for. She made as if to leave.

"Doctor?" Westlake held his breath. She stopped. "Could I pop by for a quick word on my way out?"

She held his gaze for a moment. "Room 19. Turn right at the end of the corridor." And she was gone. Again.

Westlake turned around, smiling triumphantly. Morris grimaced back at him and shook his head slowly.

"Mate. She'll have you for breakfast."

27

After watching the news for ten more minutes, Pope waited for the noise upstairs to stop. Then he went to the kitchen, grabbed another bottle, sat at the table, and opened his laptop.

@TheTrth was on fire as the USA caught up with events across the Pond. Comments on the Canafanta post slowed as contributors started their own.

As he read through the comments, Pope noticed a definite change in tone.

Excitement over the prime minister's disappearance and keen debate over what might have happened to him had faded.

Comments now focused on the lack of contribution from Canafanta himself and the timing of this unusual change in behaviour.

What's happened to Mister C? He's not backward in coming forward normally.

@Canafanta wotz ur take?

@Canafanta. Arrested, keeping low or beating the shit out of that right wing prick?

Where's canafanta?

@Canafanta. You got him or what mate?

First time I've ever seen someone post on here and not engage in the debate. You'd think he was trying to get us to incriminate ourselves or something... #OldBill #MI5 #scum

The direct messages had changed tone as well. Rebel2Rebel and Armed-Justice were still offering their help, asking for confirmation and situation reports. Others demanded proof and painted a very clear picture of how the lack of it would change their attitude towards him.

@Canafanta Tor will only hide you for so long. We're onto you matey and won't have to travel far to say hello.

@Canafanta fancy name is just that. Throwing bait on the lake and waiting for the fish to bite. Who you working for?

@Canafanta canawhupass traitor!!!

Pope's hand shook slightly as he reached for his beer. His online family, the community he loved to be part of, was turning against him. He may have posted the question and left for various reasons. People wanting answers were hitting out indiscriminately, such was the volatility of the situation.

His immediate thought was to get involved, come up with a reason for the delay, and join the debate. Problem was, engaging might not quell the intense vitriol and might even fuel it. A better solution might be to post a picture of his guest. But that wouldn't shut them up. Providing the evidence would draw more attention than he wanted. Not a good idea.

Not taking part in something he had actually started meant he really stood out from the crowd. Strangers he regarded as friends now suspected him of being part of the security services. By attracting the spotlight, he was now a person of interest to those who definitely were. Both sides would still hold suspicions long after this.

It was time to delete the post, delete his account, his browser and his web history. His Esteban Canafanta days were over.

Leaving his laptop on to complete the secure deletion of his Trash items, Pope let his dogs out for a final toilet break of the day, checked the doors and went to bed.

Around the same time, in the headquarters of Greater Manchester Police, two online officers stared at their computer screens.

"His account's gone completely," reported the officer known on the @TheTrth platform as Rebel2Rebel. "No responses, and the last three messages bounced. That's the only non-response and the first account closure we've had on any target platform today."

"Good job we have an archive then," replied @Armed-Justice. "There might be something in there."

28

After a fitful night's sleep, Martin Barnwell's phone ringing at 5.30am came as a blessed relief.

"Downing Street here. The PM's called a Cobra meeting for 7.30. He's asked that Miss Abbott and you attend."

"Acting PM."

"Ah, yes. The PM feels it might be best if we drop the 'Acting' bit. He feels it may impinge on the willingness of others to do as they're instructed - something we can't really afford when we're all meant to be rowing the same way."

Barnwell sighed inwardly. Hadn't taken Crockett long to enter the spirit of the occasion. "We'll be there."

He slipped on his dressing gown and wandered down the hallway towards the kitchen, stopping briefly to knock on the guest bedroom door.

"Cobra meeting at 7.30. We're to attend."

"Okay," responded Mindy's tired voice. Staying with the Barnwells reminded her of staying with her parents when at university. "I'll get Curtis to pick us up at seven."

She waited for the kettle to go on before patting the bottom of the naked man lying with his back to her. Again, it reminded her of those university days.

"Pick us up at seven," she whispered.

29

Despite the beer and challenges of yesterday, Simon Pope slept deeply, surprising himself.

He woke gently around half seven, one hour later than normal for the weekend but, with golf postponed until later, perfectly acceptable.

The low sun streamed in through the curtains. He looked out of the bedroom window and marvelled at the blue sky over the fields on the other side of the lane. So different from yesterday.

He stopped a moment and listened but could hear nothing. The beauty of living so close to the edge of the countryside. He listened again, more carefully this time. Again, nothing. No dog sounds. No prime minister sounds. Nothing.

He walked onto the landing and looked through the doorway into the second bedroom. The bed linen looked immaculate. There were no traces of the PM using the room. Strange. It felt like yesterday never happened, like a bad dream.

He looked out of the back window.

In the middle of the garden, watched intently by Fred and Ginger, the First Lord of the Treasury swung a golf club at an imaginary ball. Time after time after time.

Occasionally, when changing clubs, he would reach to a plate, pick up a couple of pieces of the crust from yesterday's Cornish pasties, and toss them over to the dogs.

Pope watched him closely. Twenty-four hours earlier, he hated this man. Despised him. His decisions in government had hurt people, Pope included. His words had caused upset, confusion, and ridicule. Sometimes, he'd been arrogant or uncaring in his reaction to global, national and local events that required more. Pope had excoriated this man and what he stood for, advocating protest and action in order to deliver a change of leader by whatever means necessary.

One day earlier, he would have screamed into this guy's face, beaten him to a pulp and told him exactly what he thought about him and why.

Not today, though.

He'd seen weakness and frailty. This man wasn't in charge of a ship. He was on an airbed buffeted by rough waves, malevolent currents and strong unfavourable winds. He was helpless. Frightened. Trying hard just to survive and then - when the opportunity arose - finally finding the courage to step off and accept whatever fate had in store for him.

The venomous online attack on Pope showed how easy it was to become a target for strangers' spite.

It illustrated the difficulty in responding when there were other things to consider. Todgergate, for instance, and the 'gullible and naïve' comment made during the US trade talks.

In the garden, the prime minister dropped a golf iron, walked over to the dogs, sat down between them with his back to the house and stroked the back of their necks.

Fred's tail dropped between his legs, which came as no surprise as Fred hated fuss and was tolerating it solely for the treats that could come his way. Ginger's tail was a different matter. She wagged it so hard she was in a state of perpetual imbalance, relying solely on her front legs for stability.

Eventually, Fred quietly disengaged from the attention, leaving the prime minister free to use both hands to give Ginger a big hug. She had a huge, toothy smile on her face; a smile Pope hadn't seen for quite a while. He realised he'd missed that sunny smile. It shocked him for a moment. He'd been so wrapped up in himself, he had neglected the dogs.

He looked after them well in terms of food and exercise, but emotionally there had been a disconnect and that hadn't worked for any of them.

He dragged his eyes from the scene and walked into the bathroom and caught sight of himself in the mirror. He barely recognised himself.

"Mate," he asked himself. "What are you doing?"

Ten minutes later, clean-shaven, washed and dressed, he walked downstairs and into the kitchen. The dogs had settled on their kitchen beds and the golf clubs were back in the bag against the garage wall.

"Morning Simmo," a voice called from the lounge. "I see they've ignored my request yet again."

The television news showed police roadblocks, army foot patrols, helicopter searches, and vox pop after vox pop. Clearly, Pope's message had not been successful.

People in traffic queues, airport lines, and streets across the country voiced a surprisingly broad spectrum of opinion.

"I expected the resentment," mused the PM, watching a postal worker blink back tears and a candlelit vigil praying for his safe return. "But I didn't expect this."

"How do you feel?"

"Slightly hungover. That Perm beer has quite a kick."

"You know what I mean."

"Flattered by the concern. Embarrassed at all the fuss when I'm safe and well. Nervous about the reaction there'll be when I finally return. Wondering if being found dead in a ditch might be the best outcome for all concerned…"

His voice trailed off, though his eyes never left the television.

He looked beaten, Pope thought. His universe was crumbling around him, and it would devastate him; crush his soul. All that he valued, held onto as validation for what he was, would vanish. All sides would vilify him, either in public or - worse - in private. Allies would disappear. Friends would fade away. By all accounts, his family had already gone.

If he wasn't careful, he'd soon see himself as others viewed him. He would hate himself, then beat himself up emotionally and psychologically for being unable to sort it.

Pope had seen that journey; experienced part of it, but had learned to live with it rather than succumb or trying to escape. He thought of his dogs. Together, they were all surviving rather than living. Life shouldn't revolve around that, leaving two options. Three actually. In that moment, Pope chose the third.

"I'm going to make a cup of tea," he announced. "Want one?"

30

The nondescript Cabinet Office Briefing Room A is the most famous room in the Cabinet Office main building. It is the usual venue for the cross-departmental committee that meets in times of national emergency. Cobra.

The prime minister usually leads the meetings, where government officials and leaders from various sectors discuss important matters and have their heads banged together. Metaphorically.

The expected result is fast, effective decision-making and a co-ordinated response to whatever crisis faces the nation.

Martin Barnwell and Mindy Abbott wondered if they were in the right room. They were the only ones in it and, in fact, they weren't.

"Briefing Room A is being redecorated," explained the civil servant who escorted them into another meeting room. "The prime minister wanted it brightened up; to be a more cheerful environment in which to make stressful life or death decisions. He's gone for yellow and pink." The man's face remained impassive, but both Mart and Mindy spotted the slight, involuntary shudder.

"The others will be here shortly,"said the civil servant, then turned abruptly and left.

Mindy paced to the far end of the room, as if she'd expected to find the other participants crouched behind the table.

Barnwell pulled out the chair nearest to him, tossed his notebook onto the table and sat down.

"What's going on?" she asked the room.

"Everyone who needs to respond is already doing what they're supposed to be doing and co-ordinating their efforts effectively. If they weren't, they'd be in here griping about it," Barnwell answered.

"This is our acting prime minister's attempt to exhibit leadership and control. Convening Cobra is a good way of doing that. Although it usually helps to have other attendees arriving as well."

"So, where is he?"

"Probably leaving Number Ten in a three-car convoy instead of using the back door. Makes for better television."

As he spoke, the door opened again. A civil servant stood aside to allow Damien Crockett to march in purposefully, followed by David Slayton and a couple of aides.

"There should have been more whooshing. Would've made it more dramatic," complained the acting PM to his Cabinet secretary. "As it was, I've seen faster funeral hearses."

"Even for those cars, it's hard to gain speed over such a short distance," opined Slayton. "I daresay the determined strides from the car into the building more than made up for it."

He raised his eyebrows at the chief-of-staff before turning on his heels and walking out, followed by his two aides and the door holder.

Slayton wasn't attending the meeting and opted to leave under his own terms, thus avoiding the ignominy of being dismissed from a room in his own building.

Crockett watched the door close.

He made himself a coffee at the refreshment cabinet, then returned to the main table and abruptly looked up at Barnwell.

"What?" he asked. "No congratulations?"

"Good morning, acting prime minister," Barnwell replied, ignoring the question. "Sleep well?"

Britain's acting First Lord of the Treasury shook his head. "You know I didn't."

"Then what are we doing here at this time of day?" Barnwell asked. "And where the hell is everybody else?"

Slightly taken aback by the questions, Crockett quickly gathered his thoughts.

"You know why we're here. The public expects a Cobra meeting every time a royal farts in public or an MP buys an extra cushion. It's a way of calming the nation's nerve."

"Which explains your presence, but not ours."

Another silence.

"Honestly, I don't know what to do next. No point in pretending I do. I got the gig because nobody else wants it - not even the bastard on the other side of the Commons chamber. He must be pissing himself."

Crockett took another sip of tea while wishing he was an opposition MP. "I'm surrounded by rabbits in headlights. That's no disrespect. We're sailing uncharted waters and that frightens many people…"

Mindy took the bullet. "The response has been good up to now. We have the country locked down tighter than a…"

"But we still don't have him!" Crockett slapped the table, stinging his hand in the process and only just managing to hide the pain. "You guys lost him. He could be dead by now… Jesus, we thought he was roasted in that van yesterday…"

Barnwell ignored the accusation.

Mindy decided this meeting was going to feature prominently in the updated version of her current book.

"If he's still here, the services will find him," Barnwell said. "I'm sure of that. In the meantime, it's your job to keep the country on an even keel. He's first among equals, that's all - just as you are now. Keep the country steady. The nation will always remember if you do that."

Mandy couldn't resist.

"Fail, and the nation will never forget."

Crockett's face reddened as he stared at her and tried to think of a suitable response.

She stared back at him blankly and took a sip of her tea. "Prime minister, however this situation pans out, it creates unprecedented opportunities for you."

Crockett's face lost some of its anger. "I am well aware, Miss Abbott. But I don't assume I know how to make the best of this situation. That's why you and Mister Barnwell are here. Your obligation lies with this office, not with an individual. Whether my tenure lasts eight hours or eight weeks or eight years, I need to know that you will be here for me."

For the first time in a good while, Crockett felt in control.

Once again, his two decades as a police officer proved useful.

No matter what the two faces looking at him tried to convey, he could read the eyes.

"Look, I'm just an honest copper. To survive in this jungle, I will rely on your experience, your political nous and your willingness to use the rod when required. In return for your loyalty, you can expect mine. And something else, assuming I'm still here after the short term. A say in policy and direction."

He was pleased to see the slight widening of the eyes looking at him.

"My focus is law and order. How we resolve the issues in that area is open to debate, as long as we resolve them. Everything else is up for grabs. And if I've followed your own careers correctly, I think this situation represents a significant opportunity for all three of us."

He pulled out two business cards - both blank except for a handwritten mobile phone number - and placed them on the table.

"Have a think about it. Talk about it between yourselves, then let me know."

He stood and took his empty cup to the refreshment table for a refill. By the time he returned, both cards had gone. He sat down once more and opened his own writing pad.

"I have to answer an urgent question at midday and want to avoid a repeat of last night's media disaster. Tell me what I need to say."

31

Heat from the rising sun burned off the mist covering the fields surrounding the village of Sidwell, as a growing drone disturbed the autumnal tranquility of the morning.

Cows munching on the damp cud raised their heads as an elongated shadow swept over them, moments before the blue and yellow twin-engine helicopter of the National Police Air Service did the same.

Helicopters from Birmingham and Leicestershire had maintained surveillance of the local countryside throughout the night, to the annoyance of many, including the cows.

High resolution thermal image cameras had pinpointed several objects of interest.

Forces on the ground - both military and civilian - had investigated each one.

Results so far included several homeless people whose sleep had been rudely interrupted and one drunk driver whose car had slipped into a ditch, trapping him inside.

One foreign farmhand, homesick for his beloved fiancée, had found solace with a sheep.

The sheep's surprise had been nothing compared to the farmhand's, when he suddenly found he had three armed members of the SAS for company.

Overnight, extra helicopters had flown from outlying bases to the two in the region. Once there, ground staff serviced and refuelled them while the crews grabbed a few brief hours of rest. They headed out to take over the search, cruising at 138mph at 8,000 feet.

Once in the right area, they dropped to lower orbits to maximise the effectiveness of their cameras.

By now, the area of interest included the land surrounding the villages slightly further afield.

Civilian pilot Barry "Chopper" Johnson set up an orbit pattern which took the helicopter and its cameras over the borders of several fields. Constable Dylan Spence, the police officer on board, used a thermal image camera to inspect the ditches, hedgerows, and trees.

The pilot maintained contact with the flight controller in the NPAS operations centre in West Yorkshire. Spence communicated directly with the control centre at West Cumberton and with the police officers below him, parked in a lay-by on a country lane.

"Okay, we've established orbit over the fields southwest of Sidwell," he reported, his eyes never leaving the video screen in front of him. The camera zoomed in slightly to improve the view of the narrow ditches, but the white blob signifying a heat source was absent from the frame.

"We have some movement in the field, coming out of the woods directly ahead," reported Chopper Johnson.

Spence moved the camera forwards and picked up two white figures emerging from the copse, followed by a couple of dogs. He grabbed the binoculars next to him and pointed them in the same direction.

"Two people - look like dog walkers - heading in your direction from the woods in the south-east corner of the field closest to you," he said to the police car below.

"Copy that," came the reply. "Stand by."

Spence watched as two police officers emerged from the car and walked over to a wooden stile, situated next to a locked gate in the hedgerow.

The walkers didn't notice the reception committee because they were looking up at the helicopter. The two dogs were more interested in sniffing the occasional cow pat.

Johnson hovered the helicopter over the far end of the field as the two groups met at the gate. It made no sense to get closer.

Both men had a clear view of the discussion. The group at the gate could hear each other much easier without them overhead.

After a couple of minutes, the police officers walked back to their car. The walkers climbed over the stile, while their two dogs squeezed through a small gap by the gate. A voice crackled through the helicopter's speaker.

"Couple of local dog walkers. They've been across this field and the two beyond it. Nothing out of the ordinary. The dogs didn't pick up any unusual scent either."

"Roger that," Spence replied.

Johnson flicked the joystick and banked the helicopter over the far hedge to resume the search.

The police car drove past the walkers and turned left to rejoin the hunt.

The two walkers watched it disappear, then called over their dogs and put them back on their leads.

"Well, I never," said the prime minister. "I'm gobsmacked."

"Told you," said Pope, high on a mixture of fear, elation and adrenalin, "Hair, height and context."

"*Come out for a walk*, you said. *The fresh air will do you good!* I thought it was over. Expected to be in the back of that car now."

"Yeah. With me handcuffed. What would have happened to the dogs?!"

The prime minister watched as a smiling Pope crouched by his hounds and gave them a fuss. The first time he'd seen him do that.

Pope was feeling a similar buzz, but for the prime minister, Pope's question threw a bucket of cold water over his euphoria.

If the police had recognised him, what would have happened to his host and his dogs? Not just in the short term, but after that? What right did he have to jeopardise this man's future?

His fall from grace was one thing, but that was his decision. He couldn't drag somebody down with him. That might be outside of his control. This episode tarnished the country, government, intelligence services, and police. All because he walked out of a door. There'd be repercussions. They'd want a scapegoat. A fall guy. And they'd want to make sure the fall guy didn't talk. His blood turned to ice. Dear God, what was he doing? And how could he sort it?

"You were very good then, Simmo. Incredibly believable."

Pope gave Ginger a good scratch behind her ears. She reciprocated by licking his face.

"The secret's basing your story on the truth. In fact. Once they've accepted that part of the story, it's easier for them to accept the rest."

"Sounds like you've done this kind of thing before…"

"Aaah," Pope smiled, "That was a lifetime ago."

32

As the door clicked shut behind the UK's acting prime minister, Mart and Mindy exchanged glances across the table.

The last hour had been intense. A brief talk introducing an unprecedented political opportunity, followed by a debate on the pressing question in the Commons.

"Wow," said Mindy and then, in case her boss hadn't heard her the first time, "Wow, wow, wow."

"Thoughts?"

"Wow. And meh."

Barnwell nodded. "Pretty succinct."

"He's sharper than I thought. The media embarrassment last night after the Cabinet charade was a masterstroke. Limits expectations. Sets a low bar."

"Which he'll soar over with ease in just over three hours."

"And then he's on an upward trajectory. Possibly an unstoppable force for the next couple of terms."

"Apart from one large PM-shaped fly in the ointment."

"Ah, yes."

They fell silent for a while. Silences between them were always comfortable.

Both were confident that one of them would speak when they had something worthwhile to say.

Mindy pacing the room was a good sign to Barnwell. Each step echoed softly, creating a rhythmic pattern that seemed to guide her thinking. He preferred to sit, his still mind focused on the issue. She stopped and turned near the far end of the room, partly silhouetted by the video screen on the wall behind her.

"Do you think he means it?"

"At the moment? Probably. But can he deliver?"

"No. Not yet anyway." She recommenced her pacing, then checked her jacket pocket and pulled out her mobile phone.

Barnwell watched as she studied the handset, willing it to ring. Her face had a glow he hadn't seen in years. He realised he'd missed it; that he'd probably been responsible for its disappearance. He had taught her a great deal, turning her into a formidable political operator, but at what cost?

Where had the fun gone? The real buzz of achievement? Not only in her journey, but also in his own?

There was a grim determination to keep politicians on track and steer the country in the right direction. Sure, they had their wins, but these were no longer celebrated. Maybe, in grinding others down, they'd done the same to themselves?

With genuine shock, he realised how much he cared for his assistant and her future. Maybe she should use the platform he'd helped her to build and launch on her own trajectory. Now was the perfect time to do that, regardless of the crisis outcome.

He cleared his throat.

"We both know it's possible that the PM could be back with us shortly," he began.

"But we don't know what state he's in, whether he's fit to continue in office or even wants to keep going," she joined in.

"In the meantime, the country needs its government, needs direction…"

"From a party nobody wants to lead, or an opposition that doesn't want to touch Downing Street with a barge pole."

"So if the PM returns, we're weakened."

"And if he doesn't, we're in crisis."

"With one hope. And he just left this room."

"And he sees us as his only chance."

Silence descended once more. Mindy sat down at the table.

"Social justice. Environment. Health. Education. He's offering us a chance to deliver on all of it, Mart. Cohesive, comprehensive change, driven by a persuasive champion on a tidal wave of popularity."

"Just as long as he delivers on law and order."

Mindy smiled. "I'm sure we can do that."

Barnwell smiled back and shook his head gently. "Not we. You."

33

The prime minister watched the news while Pope put the kettle on.

His guest had gone quiet on the walk home and Pope didn't disturb his reverie. Certainly, he had much to consider. They both had.

"I have to get back. It's important…"

Pope didn't look up from making the tea.

"The longer I'm missing, the more they'll search for me. They'll go over old ground. Maybe come back here…"

Pope took milk from the fridge and stirred it into the mugs. He heard a chair scrape behind him as the PM sat down at the kitchen table.

"I want to keep you out of this Simmo. There would be repercussions for you if they discovered your involvement, no matter how innocent. And I'm not sure what they'd be."

Pope set down the mugs and sat at the table. The PM picked up his tea and stared at the froth on the surface.

"What'll you tell them?"

"The truth. I'm ill. I know I need help. Couldn't take it anymore. Hid in a vehicle. Left the vehicle once it stopped. Went into hiding…"

"Cut your hair…"

The PM frowned as he considered the questions he'd need to answer, then smiled at the absurdity of it all. "Found some fresh clothes…"

"Had a couple of showers…"

"Found food and drink whenever I needed sustenance…"

"Slept well on a comfortable bed…"

"Avoided the largest manhunt in recent history…"

"Had a round of golf…"

Both men laughed. The PM shook his head with another smile.

"What am I going to do?"

Pope took a drink from his mug.

"I reckon you have three choices. The second of those possibly results in a huge stain on your character. The third involves you dying in a ditch."

The prime minister sensed a hint of relish, or possibly malice, in Pope's voice. Not surprising, given what he'd found in the box file.

"Many people would love options two and three," he said. "What about you?"

Pope gazed at him for an age, deliberating on how much to say. He left the kitchen and brought back the photograph off the lounge wall. The picture was a romantic scene of two people walking hand in hand alongside a misty canal, flanked by leafy trees on both sides.

Looking closely, the prime minister could see two dogs further down the path. He felt the colour drain from his face and his heart rate increased. Whatever was coming next, he would not like it.

Three years earlier, Cedric Pollock, a photographer collecting images for the local council, took the picture on the spur of the moment. In return for the couple agreeing to forego their modelling rights on the picture, he provided them with this print and a digital version for their own use.

"That's me, my fiancée Philippa, and the dogs by the canal, walking back from the pub. We'd just celebrated getting engaged."

"Oh? Congratulations. It's a lovely picture," said the prime minister appreciatively. He suppressed his instinctive desire to exclaim, "Pippa Pope?"

The contents of the box in the cupboard prepared him for what was coming, but he didn't want to share what he had found. Besides, this was a critical moment for Pope. Knowing his indirect role in what was to come, the PM had no desire to speed things up. His guilt wouldn't let him.

Pope said nothing but disappeared upstairs, returning with three more photographs. "This is Pippa, around seven years ago." The first framed photograph showed an attractive woman surrounded by young children. She was flashing a radiant smile that lit up the squalid hospital ward somewhere in the Middle East. Her red hair peaked from under her beret and the red cross armband and sergeant's chevron on her army uniform revealing her role and her career.

"Were you both in the army?" asked the PM, fully aware of that fact. Pope nodded.

"That's where we met."

"What did you do?"

"As I was told. Mostly."

Knowing not to press, the PM took the second framed photograph. This time, Pippa was in the back garden of the house, trying to pose with the two dogs for the camera. She was in a crisp white shirt and blue jeans, her hair falling onto her shoulders. Her smile remained the same, but her eyes seemed more content and relaxed.

"Three years ago," said Pope. "And this one, about three months later."

The last photograph had no frame. He placed it gently on the table. It was a head and shoulders shot.

Pippa lay asleep on a pillow, her face framed by her hair. She looked pale. At peace. Several minor details on the print seemed to clash with the overall serenity of the shot. The pearlescent skin on the left side of her face appeared bruised. Beyond the pillow's edge, a cream cylinder came into view. Above the pillow was a chrome handle that looked familiar to the PM. Eventually, he recognized it. The inside of an ambulance. He looked up at Pope, whose eyes never left the photograph.

"Not long after the photographer took the canal picture, we walked that way again," Pope murmured. "It was hot and humid. A stroll to the pub and a couple of cool drinks sounded ideal. The trees gave us some shade. We'd just reached Hellman's Bridge, next to the pub…" He stopped briefly. "Do you know lightning can strike three miles from the thunderstorm?"

The PM shook his head.

"I came to on the pavement. Head bleeding. All cramped up. Couldn't hear anything. Couldn't see Pippa." He stopped again and took a drink of tea. The PM noticed his hands shake slightly as he did so. "People from the pub rushed to help. The ambulance was ever so quick. They'd just left another job. Got her heart going again. Got us both in the ambulance. Fifteen minutes later, her heart stopped again. They parked up to have another go. Twenty minutes they worked on her. Another crew arrived and took over. It's exhausting trying to save a life."

Pope hesitated. While he was talking, Ginger had walked over from her bed and rested her head on his knee. He stroked her neck. "That's when I took the picture. She looked so peaceful."

The men silently stared at the four photographs on the table. The kitchen clock ticked. On his bed, Fred rolled onto his back and farted gently.

Eventually, Pope picked up the three photographs and took them upstairs.

After he'd gone, the PM picked up the framed picture and replaced it on the wall in the lounge. Pope found him looking at it when he came downstairs.

"Every decision that government has to make changes lives, Simmo, whichever way the decision goes. You must have experienced something similar in your previous line of work, I imagine."

"Similar."

"The difference, I expect, is that world is black and white. There's not much grey."

"It's a balance. Collateral damage. Jeopardising intelligence assets. Politics. All come into play unless someone's pointing a gun at you or is about to trigger a suicide vest."

The prime minister nodded thoughtfully, then turned to look at his host, trying to stop his lips from trembling.

"I am sincerely sorry you lost Pippa, Simmo. And I bitterly regret that a government decision over West Cumberton hospital was potentially a factor in her death. But I have to say…"

"Her death?" Pope laughed while staring at the PM's bewildered face. Laughed out loud, hysterically, releasing emotions he hadn't realised were so close to the surface. He slumped in an armchair, tears falling down his face. Then, seeing the PM's frown remained in place, he wiped his eyes, stood up and put his hands on the PM's shoulders.

"Pippa didn't die, prime minister. Things aren't as bad as that. The senior paramedic in the second crew got her heart going again. They took her to Birmingham. She had a couple of operations and survived."

"But… That's wonderful news! Wonderful. But where is she now?"

"Living in Solihull. Married to the woman who saved her."

The PM's face twitched, unsure of how to respond to the new information. Pope exploded into laughter again, leaned forward and pulled the PM into a big bear hug. The PM hugged him back, laughing and crying with relief at the same time.

"I'm so sorry Simmo," he sobbed. "At least, I think I am. It's difficult to know how I'm feeling at the moment."

"It's okay, mate," Pope smiled, patting him on the back. "You've done me a big favour today, believe me."

34

In the chief-of-staff's office in Number Ten, Barnwell sat at his desk while his assistant paced the room. On the wall, a split TV screen displayed simultaneous coverage from four news networks. Each showed the heavy front door of their building.

Mindy's head was spinning. Everything she thought she'd ever wanted was so close. Genuine power to make actual change. A unique opportunity, supported by her boss, to advance from apprentice to sorcerer and make a positive impact on the country. But was it a genuine opportunity or a mirage? There'd been no more phone calls. They were the only people in Westminster who knew the PM could reappear at any moment.

"There he goes," observed Barnwell as the door displayed on each network broadcast suddenly opened. Special adviser Jeremy Michaels walked out towards the waiting taxi, with a heavy briefcase in one hand and a carrier bag full of papers in the other.

Unwisely, the missing PM's special adviser put the carrier bag on the pavement while opening the taxi door. He didn't remember it until he was in the back seat of the car. The taxi lurched forward, then halted.

When Michaels emerged again, the bag was fully exposed to the world. Overwhelmed by this exposure, it toppled over into the road and spilled its contents towards the photographers and cameramen.

Michaels scrambled to gather everything, trying to maintain his dignity under the bright flashes and camera lights. He ignored reporters' questions, returned to the taxi, and vanished from politics for at least three months.

Both politicos watched impassively.

"Missed opportunity," commented Mindy. "We should've hidden a dildo or something in that bag. Just in case."

Barnwell nodded.

"Nothing like stuffing a man when he's down. Our acting PM doesn't hang around, does he?"

"Nope... I've been thinking about that."

A ping from Barnwell's laptop interrupted the conversation.

"Security update..."

He clicked on the link and entered his details to access the file, which downloaded and opened automatically. Mindy looked over his shoulder at the screen.

Both read through the MI5 briefing, which was a condensed summary of overnight online surveillance by various parties.

"That Manchester one looks interesting."

Barnwell picked up the phone and asked the switchboard to connect him to the Greater Manchester Police.

One minute later, he was talking with Constable Noel Sutcliffe, a.k.a. Armed-Justice.

"We have profiles on several forums and run a couple of ghost forums, including @TheTrth," Sutcliffe explained. "We've monitored them since the disappearance. Activity has been high, but there's been nothing of genuine interest. However, one of our regular, more vocal contributors is conspicuous by their absence. Started a thread asking what people would do if they had the prime minister, then vanished. Most unlike them."

"Maybe they're at school, or out visiting their gran," proffered Barnwell, combining his disdain for all who talked the talk but didn't even try to walk the walk with the requirement to be non-gender specific wherever appropriate, to Mindy's quiet satisfaction.

"Maybe, but they shredded their files before leaving."

"Shredded?"

"Code obfuscation. You delete and reconfigure your files to make rescuing them much more difficult. It's rather extreme for someone just nipping out to see their gran."

Barnwell ignored the mild jibe.

"And we can't get them?"

"There's always some digital dust, but it's doubtful. It's not exactly a strong lead, so GCHQ won't see it as a priority. We have documented most of his posts and comments in our archive, though. He joined a couple of years ago. Focuses on the ineptitude of the UK government and the current prime minister in particular."

"Where's he based?"

"Tricky to pin down. He could be anywhere in the world. The language he uses makes us think he's closer to home. We've sent what we have to a forensic linguist and to a criminal psychologist."

Mindy could bear it no longer. "What makes you think this person's male?"

"He's dropped his guard slightly over the last few months. Got a bit more radical, more threatening. Used a few phrases that resonated with one lad here who used to be in the military. He thinks this person may be serving, or a former member. Possibly special forces."

"Are there no women in those regiments?"

"Operationally? Not sure. There were no such instances up to three years ago - except for the Special Forces Support Group. And then there's his name, or rather, what we assume is a pseudonym."

"Which is…?"

"Esteban Canafanta."

35

Esteban Canafanta fed his dogs and replenished the water in their bowl. He had already stowed both golf bags in the car, along with one trolley.

"I have a spare," he explained to the PM, "But you'll look even less like a senior government minister if you're carrying your own clubs."

The prime minister agreed, despite not having lifted anything heavy in a while.

"I found this," he said, showing the sports holdall in his hand. "I've packed all my stuff. You know. Just in case."

Pope nodded. "You stay here with the dogs. I won't be long."

He loaded the dishwasher and switched it on. Picking up a pack of alcohol wipes, a polish spray, two disposable rags and a duster, he disappeared into the hallway.

The PM sat on the kitchen step, looking out into the garden. It really was a peaceful place. The dogs squeezed by and ran onto the lawn as the noise of the vacuum cleaner filled the house.

Once the noise stopped, they returned to their beds.

"All done," reported Pope, holding an old, full carrier bag and wiping down the kitchen surfaces and door handles.

He caught sight of the PM looking at him. "You know," he said, putting the rag he'd used into the bag, "Just in case."

The golf course was fifteen minutes away, but today's trip would be longer so Pope could avoid main roads and as many CCTV cameras as possible.

He watched the prime minister climb onto the rear seat and pull the dog hammock over himself as he did so.

"I can't believe I didn't see you," he said.

"You weren't looking for me, so why would you?" came the muffled reply. "You said yourself; context."

Pope locked the side garage door, opened the main door, got in the car, and headed out onto the country lane. He paused while the garage door closed once more, then drove the few yards past his house to the junction. He turned right, retracing the steps they'd taken earlier that morning. As he did so, a police car passed in the other direction.

"Police car," he reported. "They're still keen to find you. You're more popular than you think."

The PM said nothing. There was so much to think through; decisions he needed to make; decisions that others would make.

Had he really had enough of politics? The power buzz? What would people think of him? How would he manage without real influence? How would he explain the last 24 hours? Twenty-four! Was that all?

Could he protect his host and the dogs? Had Simmo broken any laws? Was harbouring an unwanted prime minister a crime under some vague centuries-old law? Had he himself mis-led the police?

He thought of Pippa and the events of two years ago. Simmo had said she was happy in her new relationship, partly, he imagined, as she would never be called Pippa Pope. Fate and the Department of Health had conspired to split them up.

Perhaps the hospital closure had simply brought forward the pain waiting for them further down the line if they'd married? Every decision has an impact - sometimes good, sometimes bad and often both.

Pope turned on the car's entertainment system. His passenger jumped when he heard an unexpected voice until he realised it was the start of a country song.

Night-time. Thunder roars and lightning dances in the sky.
On the road, he's chasing dreams, determination in his eyes.
Raindrops hammer on the roof, a rhythm for his fears.
In the storm, he'll find the strength to quell his inner tears.

The prime minister felt a chill as the car slowed at a crossroads.

The lyrics, the haunting quality of the singer's voice, the car's movement and the smell of dogs created a poignant moment he would remember forever.

Thunderstorms and lightning strikes, a truly awesome sight.
There's some will park up in the dark, refuse to face its might.
But he will drive, he will not hide, he'll chase it through the night.
He'll try restart his broken heart, won't stop until it's right.

The PM pondered parking in the dark. Was that was he was doing? He wondered if the song, or Simmo's affection for it, pre-dated the lightning event and all that followed. Maybe he'd discovered and clung onto it since then. As if it hadn't done enough already, the song continued to poke both men.

Raindrops cleanse his weary soul; they wash away the past.
Through the tempest, he emerges stronger and steadfast.
Thunderstorms may howl and rage, but they can't break his stride.
In their chaos, he finds there's a man that he can't hide.

If the media hadn't found that bloody sausage picture, he wouldn't be here now, thought the PM. Even a harmless photograph could cause chaos nowadays. But, like the hospital closure and Pippa, perhaps the Bratwurst would simply speed up his departure from this damn job.

Maybe there were fewer negative consequences to events than he first thought. People move on to fresh adventures. Rebuild. Reinvent. Most people, he corrected himself. For over two years, Simmo had been stuck. Most unusual for a man of action.

The song ended, followed by a familiar guitar intro. Clearly, this was a compilation. Equally clearly, a theme was developing.

"Ah," he said. "*Thunderstruck*. A fellow AC/DC fan."

"Can't be in the army and not be," said Pope, swinging into an empty lay-by at the last moment, tyres crunching on gravel. "Helps focus the mind when leaping from a helicopter or a patrol vehicle. Stay there."

He put on a disposable glove, grabbed the carrier bag on the passenger seat and jumped out. He returned moments later, and the car resumed its journey.

Ten minutes later, Pope turned into a lay-by hidden from the road. The PM emerged from the car, brushed off as many dog hairs as he could and hauled his set of golf clubs from the boot.

Pope pulled out a red golf cap and set it at a jaunty angle on the PM's head.

"A Tory prime minister carrying his own bag and wearing a red cap," he smiled. "Nobody would ever believe me. The course is two minutes away on the left. I'll be in the car park. Walk up. Introduce yourself. We shake hands. Talk for a couple of minutes. I'll wave my arms around as if I'm referring to different parts of the course. You'll ask if you can join me. I'll say yes, and then we'll take it from there."

"Is all that for the members?"

"It's for the CCTV. I want evidence that this was our first encounter, and I didn't know who you were."

"And what if I meet someone else and they ask me questions?"

"Tell them anything. Won't matter what you say. Golfers like to talk about themselves. Asking a question ticks the civility box. Listening to the answer isn't required."

Pope drove off and the prime minister, who would be David Small for the next few hours, watched him go. Then he shouldered the bag and followed on foot, going over his cover story as he did so.

36

Turning into the golf club's tree-lined drive, it surprised Pope to see how few cars were in the car park.

He parked within view of the CCTV camera and entered the pro shop. The small light on the camera above the till showed he was being recorded, which was fine.

"Too many police around Simmo," explained the pro. "Nobody's staying for more than a pint in case they get stopped at a roadblock. Others have cancelled because it's too much hassle getting here. Bloody prime minister's going to cost us a few quid today."

Pope bought himself a chocolate bar and one bottle of water and checked to make sure the tee was clear.

"Go whenever you like, mate," said the pro. "No more bookings in for today, just roll-ups."

Pope went back to his car and opened the boot. He was just putting on his golf shoes when another car crunched to a halt a couple of spaces away.

He looked up and his heart sank.

Every golf club in the country has members everybody wants a game with and a few members everybody wants to avoid.

The newcomer definitely fell into the second category.

David 'Coldfront' Davies. A man so devoid of golfing talent and social awareness, his approach was always likely to create a low depression. The size of the challenge he posed to golf pro and psychologist alike was the matter of fierce, if only occasional, debate in the clubhouse - mostly between the pro and a member who happened to be a psychologist.

Pope heard the pro shop door shut, followed by the click of the lock. When he turned around, the lights were off, and the pro was sneaking into the clubhouse through the back door.

There was only so much golfing inanity any pro could take. This one had already spent too much time on the practice ground with Coldfront. As Mr. Davies was a tight-fisted teetotaller to boot, the bar was the pro's safest point of refuge until the golfer was well on the course.

Keeping his back to the other car, Pope tied his shoelaces, set his golf bag on his trolley and walked off to the putting green. He heard Davies struggle to ease his heavy frame out of his midsize car, open the boot and drag out his bag. He was planning to play then. Bugger.

Pope took out his putter and tossed a ball onto the green, his mind working through options to avoid his two-ball becoming a three-ball. Trying to decide between faking a heart attack or committing murder, he overheard a conversation in the car park.

Turning slightly, he glimpsed the PM shaking Coldfront's hand.

"Clever," he murmured to himself, having recovered from his initial surprise. In front of the CCTV cameras, too.

Pope relaxed a little as the PM created incontrovertible video evidence that neither had known the other until being introduced by a third party.

This would not be the most enjoyable round of golf he'd ever played, but it certainly promised to be one of the most memorable.

Based solely on Coldfront's side - the only audible side - of the conversation, it was obvious the PM's disguise was working.

The cover story was holding up, although Coldfront didn't appear to be listening.

Yes, Coldfront would be delighted to have a playing partner who could benefit from his course knowledge and some nuggets of advice on how to play the great game. The pro shop was closed - although he could have sworn it was open when he drove into the car park - so Coldfront would be happy to deem the visitor his guest. They'd sort out the green fee at the end of the round, assuming the pro shop would then be open.

Pope resisted the powerful urge to turn around, instead choosing to content himself with a lingering gaze across the course.

As he looked, a sense of tranquility washed over him, permeating his troubled soul. This feeling sometimes lingered even after a four-hour round.

Hidden within the undulating rural expanse of the south Midlands, the course was meticulously maintained.

Lush fairways stretched out before him, bordered by rows of majestic, well-established trees.

The occasional clusters of trees and bushes marked the path to perfectly maintained greens.

Protected by well-placed bunkers, grassy knolls, and the occasional sparkling pond or ditch, each meticulous green was a sight to behold.

As Pope admired the course, his gaze wandered to the views beyond.

Miles upon miles of fields, seamlessly bordered by towering hedgerows, stretched out before him. Interspersed within this picturesque scene were pockets of woodland and the occasional farmstead.

Scattered flocks and herds dotting the landscape made the sight even more breathtaking. The warmth of the glorious sunny afternoon enhanced the beauty of it all, making the scene truly awe-inspiring.

Only the insistent buzz of a helicopter in the distance, combined with the mournful wail of a police siren, broke the idyll.

"How are you, Simmo? It's been a while since I've seen you here this late."

"I'm good, Dave." Pope couldn't bring himself to use Davies's nickname to his face. Few people could. He may be a poor golfer and have a challenging personality, but he was built like a brick shithouse, and had an explosive temper. "Had some stuff to do this morning."

"Story of my life!" Coldfront wafted a hand at the figure alongside him. "My friend here wants a game. His name's Paul. Paul Morgan. Fancy joining us?"

"Sure. Why not?" Pope held out his hand for the PM to shake. "My name's Simon. Simmo on the golf course."

"Alright Simmo? Pleased to meet you."

Pope hesitated for a second, slightly thrown by the change of agreed name and the Welsh accent the PM had appropriated for the occasion, then shook his hand.

"Welcome to the club."

37

In the Barnwell residence, the chief-of-staff and his assistant sat in the Music Room - the empty third bedroom. A small speaker played white noise at a reasonable volume. Mindy paced, while Barnwell sat on a dining chair, nursing a coffee and dying for a cigarette.

For the forty-second time today, she checked her private phone to make sure the volume was up, vibration was on, and she hadn't missed a call.

In the lounge, Mavis Barnwell settled into an armchair with a mug of fresh coffee, selected a rock music channel on the television and turned up the volume. As a former Second Secretary in the Foreign & Commonwealth Office, she knew the implications of her husband's position.

Despite regular security checks, various organisations and nations could still monitor her home. She was also adept at making any monitoring as difficult as possible.

The sixty-year-old was also a Metalhead.

Mindy waited until the muffled yet unmistakable intro to *Highway to Hell* battered its way through the wall before she spoke.

"Thoughts?"

"Let's hear yours."

"We have no choice at the moment. Short term, we support Crockett and see how this pans out. Longer term… He'll want us both, you know…"

Barnwell took a sip of his coffee.

"All in due course. Meantime, it would help if we knew what our previous boss was up to."

Both lapsed into silence once more.

Mavis put in her earplugs and started the vacuum cleaner on the other side of the wall.

A little more noise wouldn't hurt.

38

The first hole at the golf club was a straight par four. The left edge of the course was out-of-bounds, with trees on the right dividing the first and eighteenth fairways.

Having established his guest didn't have a handicap and offering a miserly shot per hole, Coldfront then took the honour himself. He placed a ball on a tee and started his warm-up routine. Pope closed his eyes and offered a silent prayer. He'd forgotten about the routine. Please God, make it shorter than last time. Much, much shorter. The PM watched on with interest.

You won't be so interested after a couple of holes, Pope thought, motioning the PM to take a step or two backwards.

Five steps back from the ball, Coldfront swung his driver back and forth with a violence rarely seen outside Hollywood movie battle sequences. He took two paces forward, repeated the swing routine, then took two more, all while focusing on the distant flag.

Eventually, he settled by the ball and slowly, ever-so-slowly, brought his club down behind it.

The PM held his breath; Pope didn't bother. Coldfront raised the clubhead six inches, then dropped it behind the ball again, then repeated the process. Fifteen times.

A police helicopter emerged over a wood, flew overhead, and disappeared. The PM was oblivious to it. His eyes were fixed on the clubhead. His visual expression, a mix of confusion and fascination.

Coldfront looked up, sighed, shook his head and started again.

Just as Pope was about to scream "Hit the damn ball", the man on the tee drew back the club and swung it forward with all the finesse he'd displayed in his pre-shot routine.

The ball rocketed impressively off the tee, but not quite in the right direction. The three men watched as it ballooned to the right, over trees, onto the empty eighteenth fairway.

"Getting better, Dave," Pope said, using years of experience to remove any trace of sarcasm.

"A work in progress, but getting there. Shortening the pre-shot routine has definitely helped."

For the first time since he entered politics, the PM elected to remain silent.

Pope had a couple of practice swings with a long iron and sent his ball straight down the fairway. The PM didn't bother with a pre-shot routine because he hadn't got one. He put his ball on the tee and took a swing at it with his driver. To his surprise, he made a good connection. The ball ended in the right-hand rough, 150 yards away.

"Shot!" exclaimed Coldfront. "Pity you missed the short stuff, but I think I saw where you went wrong. I'll just play mine, then we'll have a chat." With that, he marched off to the neighbouring fairway.

The PM picked up his golf bag and he and Pope walked off the tee.

"That was his short routine?"

"Used to be twice as long. Changed it when members started pulling out of competitions if they were playing behind him. He was adding a good thirty minutes to a round.

Coldfront, we call him. Creates a depression wherever he goes. Coldfront's his nickname, but not to his face. Never to his face."

"Jesus."

"Nah. Just call him Dave."

Seven minutes later, the three golfers reconvened on the first green. Pope and the PM used the traditional method of hitting the ball down the correct fairway until the green got in their way. Coldfront opted for the neighbouring fairway, a small copse and then two shots out of a green-side bunker.

The PM made a putt from the edge of the green. It had been years since he'd last swung a putter and, as the ball sailed gracefully past the hole and rolled to a halt fifteen feet away, it showed.

"There's some crap on the end of your putter," observed Coldfront. Pope silently cringed as the PM lifted the blade of the putter to inspect and remove the offending muck.

"No Paul," smirked Coldfront. "The other end."

The world paused as the prime minister processed the comment, then smiled and shook his head.

"It wasn't the best, was it?"

He walked over to his ball and weighed up the return putt.

"Dead sheep, Paul," Coldfront continued, with relish. "Still ewe."

"Still you," smiled the PM, shaking his head. "Very good."

Moments later, the ball was on its way once more, a firm stroke tracking right to left and stopping only when it toppled into the hole. "That's a five nett four. My hole I think?"

Pope shook his head as he addressed his own putt, his fourth shot. The ball started left of the hole, then caught a subtle ridge and tracked unerringly towards the pin. He caught the eye of the PM and winked as he heard his ball hit the bottom of the cup.

"Hole halved," declared Coldfront, as he picked his own ball up, unable to match his opponents. "That's the only time you'll see Simmo pleased with a move to the right."

No surprise, the PM thought as the golfers headed to the second tee. Not that he cared. Whatever Pope's political beliefs, the man had taken him in when he was at his lowest ebb. He'd looked after him, protected him, shared his home, his food and, most definitely, his drink with him.

Humanity had prevailed over perception, personalities and politics. It was a massive and humbling lesson the PM vowed to learn from and to follow. And now, here he was, playing a round of golf alongside his unsuspecting, unwilling teacher - maybe his saviour.

Meanwhile, the world outside the fairways occupied itself with looking for a man who didn't want to be found. A man who would be quite happy if the biggest question in the rest of his life was how to pace a putt.

* * *

Pope found himself alone with Coldfront on the second tee as the PM relieved himself behind a small bush several yards away.

"Interesting man, our Paul?" Pope asked.

"No idea," replied Coldfront, selecting a rescue club for the long par three hole and swishing it back and forth before placing a ball on the tee.

Moments later, the PM joined them.

"This, Paul, is a 204-yard downhill par three," intoned Coldfront. "The out-of-bounds area is behind the tree line to the left, and at the back, where the police officers are standing."

Pope and the PM had been selecting clubs from their bags. Both turned as casually as they possibly could.

Sure enough, three figures in hi-vis jackets emerged from the copse behind the green and trudged to the right.

"Must be looking for the prime minister," deduced Coldfront. "Either that or they're very lost."

One officer caught sight of the players on the tee, gestured to his companions, then waved. The officers hurried past the green and into the wooded area to the right.

"Cops in the copse," grimaced Pope, to Coldfront's delight.

"Cops in the copse. I like it." He went through his tee-shot routine, then whooped when he hit the ball straight down the fairway and onto the front of the green.

"Shot," said Pope.

"Well played, Dave," said the PM, fervently hoping his own ball would follow a similar line and not follow the police into the wooded area. Coldfront stared at his ball and held his follow-through pose for the imaginary television cameras. Meanwhile, Pope shoved his own five iron into the PM's hands, swapping it with the three wood the PM was holding.

"Trust me," he whispered. "You'll be short, but you'll be straight."

The PM's hand shook as he placed his ball on a tee. He had a couple of practice swings, thinking of the shots he had played in Pope's garden, watched by the two dogs. Then he stood over the ball, offered a quiet prayer to the golf gods, had one last look at the flag and swung.

A couple of minutes later, Pope lofted his bunker shot onto the green, then joined the PM to watch Coldfront prepare for his birdie putt, some fifty feet from the hole.

He looked down at the PM's ball marker, a mere six feet away from the flag, then up to the PM's flushed, smiling face.

"Fluke," he said.

"Now, now Simmo." The PM's eyes didn't move from Coldfront, who was currently lying flat on the ground behind his ball, with one eye closed.

"It's all about course management."

"You hit a sprinkler head."

"So?"

"Fifty yards away."

"You said I'd be short."

"It was a lucky bounce."

The PM gestured to the row of hi-vis jackets to his right. "My police friends would beg to differ. I got a round of applause."

"They didn't see the shot. Just the result."

"Isn't that what counts?"

"But did you really have to bow?"

"You always take the plaudits when you can."

Both men fell silent as Coldfront finally hit his putt.

The ball rolled quickly, then slowed towards the top of the slope before dropping reluctantly into the hole.

The police roared. Coldfront roared back and raced to them, high-fiving and hugging each of them.

Pope removed the ball from the hole.

"Make sure you miss your birdie," he said. "If you get it, they'll be expecting the same from you."

The PM replaced his ball, took aim and hit the putt with slightly less pace and slightly more to the right than needed.

The ball came to a halt above the ground, causing a groan from the tree line. Pope picked up his own ball.

"Can't beat a birdie, Dave. Well played."

The audience offered a small round of applause, shook Coldfront's hand once more, then disappeared back into the woods to continue their search.

The three golfers walked off in the opposite direction, along a short path to the third hole. Actually, two walked. One floated on air.

* * *

The euphoria from the second hole had worn off by the seventh. While delighted to evade the law yet again, the PM was a little disappointed not to be recognised. The presence of the police officers brought his attention back to his situation and Pope's predicament. This lack of focus meant his golf suffered as a result - a problem exacerbated by growing exasperation with their playing partner's antics.

Poor Coldfront's game had fallen to pieces. Aiming to build on his early success, the man was simply trying too hard. As the pressure grew, his shots worsened, and his pre-shot routine lengthened.

"I don't think I can manage all 18 holes after this," he confessed to his playing partners, as his tee shot went left into the silver birch trees.

"Neither do I," said the PM.

"I'm so sorry," he continued, noticing the look of surprise on his partners' faces, "I hadn't meant to say that out loud."

He gestured vaguely towards the sky. An invisible surveillance aircraft made its presence felt by emitting an unremitting drone. "This constant racket is getting on my nerves."

Coldfront grunted and stomped off to find his ball. Keen to make amends, the PM followed to help him look for it. Pope watched them go, then made his way some 100 yards down the fairway to the resting place of his topped drive. As he had predicted, it wasn't the most enjoyable round he'd ever played, despite the fair weather and the empty fairways. However, it would definitely be one of the most memorable, whatever happened.

He hit an eight iron over the trees at the corner of the dogleg onto the fairway beyond, then wandered into the rough on the right side to locate the PM's own ball. Finding a ball in open ground close to a flowering gorse bush, he shouted across to the others.

"Paul! What ball are you playing?"

"Can't remember," the PM shouted back after a couple of moments' thought.

"How do I know if this is yours, then?"

"I've put my initials on it."

Pope bent down and moved the ball gently to check any markings on it. There they were. Paul Morgan. PM. He smiled to himself as he let the ball settle back where he'd found it, then stood up. He saw the PM grinning back at him.

Coldfront, meanwhile, was becoming increasingly agitated the longer the search for his ball went on. His general bonhomie had been eroding as he focused more intensely on his own game.

"Found it." The PM pointed at the ground near the foot of an old tree stump. "I think you'll have some sort of shot from here."

Coldfront walked over and pulled out a six iron. The ball nestled down slightly, but there was a gap of sorts between several trees that led to the second part of the dogleg.

Abruptly and without warning, he took his stance, swung the club back and brought it crashing down into the back of the ball. A huge divot flew ahead of him.

"I didn't see the ball," he said. "Where's it gone?"

"Didn't see it either," said the PM. "I didn't expect you to hit it so soon. It sounded a good strike, though. I reckon it's fine."

"You reckon it's fine?"

Even from the other side of the fairway, Pope could see Coldfront's face redden.

The danger sign.

He marched swiftly towards his playing partners.

"Did you see the ball land?" Coldfront asked the PM evenly.

"No, but…"

"Have you played here before in a previous life? Can you combine your X-ray vision with your built-in radar to see through solid objects and locate the ball? Is a friend on the International Space Station watching our game through an exceptionally large and powerful pair of binoculars? No? Then how do you know my ball is fine?"

The PM did, indeed, have an acquaintance currently on the ISS, but his finely honed political survival instincts, combined with the red face and surly attitude of the big man in front of him, persuaded him to keep that fact to himself.

"I saw it," Pope shouted across as he kept moving towards them. Coldfront turned and looked at him. "I saw it Dave. Flew out of the trees. Cracking shot. Not sure exactly where it's ended up, but I've a reasonable idea. Paul, why don't you go take your second shot, then we'll all search for Dave's ball?"

The PM didn't need a second invitation. All three were soon walking down the centre of the fairway.

"So, we're thinking about the fairway, or the trees to the right of the bush, or in the fairway bunker?" Coldfront asked, working through each scenario and trying to find a solution for each.

The PM cleared his throat. He hadn't said a word since retreating to his own ball, hitting it reasonably well down the fairway, then rejoining the other two.

He needed to break the ice with the big man on the other side of Pope but didn't want to provoke him.

"Wherever it is, Dave, it won't be any problem if you hit another cracker like your last one."

"That's true, Dave," Pope interjected before Coldfront could respond. "You'll deal with it, whatever it is. It's not worth worrying about it until then."

Both men held their breath while Coldfront slowed his pace and was silent for several seconds.

"I have been through some terrible things in my life, some of which actually happened," he said, turning to look at them both. "Mark Twain."

And with that, he walked on while the other two looked at each other for a moment before stumbling forward in his wake.

The ball was in the first cut of rough close to the fairway bunker, but nowhere near the tree line. Coldfront looked behind him to gauge how good his shot had actually been.

"Told you it was a cracking shot," said Pope. "What made you change your routine though?"

"There was no room in all those trees to do it. Besides, I guess I'm getting fed up with using all that energy to hit bad shot after bad shot."

"So. What are you going to do here, then?"

Coldfront looked at the flag, just over 100 yards away, with a pond to its left. He took out his pitching wedge, had two gentle practice swings, fighting against every muscle memory fibre in his body, then hit the ball. All three men watched in silence as it sailed into the blue sky, landed just short of the green and rolled to the centre.

"That," smiled Coldfront. "I'm going to do that."

* * *

The group was much quieter as they played the par-five ninth hole, leading back towards the clubhouse.

One focused on embedding his new pre-shot routine and maintaining it even when a shot went slightly awry, and his memory yelled at him to go back to the old method.

Another hated the heavy bag, but still tried to enjoy this precious time away from an unpredictable future.

The third member had caught sight of yellow and blue flashes of colour in the car park beyond the bushes and trees.

Pope's mind scrambled to work through the implications of police vehicles at the course and how best to deal with the situation. It was still scrambling as the group walked towards the green and the car park appeared on their right.

Four patrol cars lined up alongside an incident support van bristling with antennae, an ambulance and a dog unit van.

"Oh. They're back again then," observed Coldfront. "Must like the food."

A police officer emerged from the clubhouse carrying wrapped foil packages and distributed them to other officers in the parking lot.

"They've been here before?" asked the PM.

Coldfront nodded confirmation. "Yesterday afternoon. Not as many of them then, though. Word gets around."

He walked up to his ball - yet another shot that had found the fairway - and lofted it with his sand wedge onto the green.

"Gents," he announced, picking his putter out of his bag, "I'm leaving you after this hole. I shall go to the range for a while to make sure the last few holes haven't been a fluke, then I'll be on my way."

"I've another hour before my lift arrives," said the PM to Pope. "Happy to play a few more holes if you like? Or we could go in for some refreshment?"

His eyes said something quite different.

"What do we do now?" they screamed.

39

For the tenth time since the angiogram and the subsequent angioplasty, Stuart Morris selected a ceiling tile above his bed and counted the dots. It passed the time; gave him something to focus on. Yesterday had gone well - eventually.

It had taken a while to stop his wrist from bleeding where they'd inserted the catheter. Happily, the tightness in his chest had eased considerably during the procedure. After twelve hours of observations, they had passed him fit for discharge. All he needed now was a short-term carer, transportation home and time to ponder his future.

His police career was over. By the time he recovered fully, he'd be retired. Until retirement, he'd be on full sick pay. Collapsing on duty in the middle of a potential terrorist incident also meant a gratuity payout on top of his police pension.

"You're a lucky bugger, in more ways than one," the Superintendent had said on her visit that morning. She was right. Having senior paramedics as part of the response to the farm incident meant Morris had received the best possible treatment right from the start.

The hospital itself had been on red alert and he'd been a priority case since his arrival.

Otherwise, he would still be in the waiting room, with a vague promise of an appointment in six months and a letter for his doctor.

Halfway through counting his blessings and hoping retirement wouldn't end up being a curse, a tap on the door disturbed his reverie.

"Woah. You're looking better, mate. Check out that colour in your cheeks." Still in uniform, after spending half the day searching woodland, Dave Westlake sat down on the bed and looked carefully at his friend.

Then a broad smile cracked his serious expression. "Talk about landing on your feet. How are you feeling?"

Stuart Morris smiled at the man who had saved his life the previous day. A man who was like a son and meant more to him than anyone else on the planet. Tears pricked his eyes, and he felt the smile waver on his face.

"Relieved. Sore. Happy. Worried. Sad. Scared. You name it."

"Bloody hell mate." Dave Westlake's military career had been full of incidents that had left him with a similar range of emotions after each event. Most had ended with him never again working or living alongside somebody he regarded as a brother. At least this time, he still had his friend.

"Tell you what we'll do," he said. "Let's grab stuff from yours, then get you to my place. Just for a couple of days. Make sure you're properly okay. We can have a good chat."

"Booze is off limits."

"For you it is. Lord knows, I'll need it if I've got to listen to you droning on for a bit."

Morris chuckled.

"Won't I be disturbing your love life? How's it going with the marvellous Doctor Mills?"

Westlake grimaced as he picked up the sports bag from the floor by the bed.

"Turns out she has a partner." His eyes widened. "You'll never guess who it is."

"Probably true," said Morris. "Who is it?"

"Remember that bloke we were visiting when the shit hit the fan yesterday?"

"Simon Pope...? No!"

"Not him. His ex-fiancée."

40

After completing the tenth hole - a steep uphill par three - Pope and the PM turned and looked at the clubhouse.

Coldfront had ambled off and was hitting balls on the range, after being ignored by the police officers who were more focused on their lunch.

"What do you think?"

"It could be the making of him," said Pope. "He's already hit four decent balls in the time…"

"Not that."

Pope had known what the PM meant. He just didn't have an answer for him. He knew from experience that the best type of action was often inaction.

"The next three holes loop around, so we'll see them again in about thirty minutes from over there. I reckon they'll have gone by then. They're not interested in us. We'll stick to the plan."

"They've dogs with them."

Pope took a breath. "Stick to the plan."

The next two holes dragged on. Thick, ominous clouds rolled in, their dark presence shrouding the woods. The temperature dropped, chilling the air and contributing to the eerie stillness.

The once vibrant and welcoming atmosphere now felt foreboding, as if a sinister presence lurked nearby.

Both golfers found it difficult to concentrate on their game, and their lacklustre play reflected their indifference. Unconcerned with their performance, they paused for a moment on a bench at the thirteenth tee, abandoning the idea of taking a shot.

The prime minister took a moment to absorb his surroundings.

The vibrant blue sky and warm sunshine had vanished completely, and the oppressive grey clouds looked determined to crush him, as well as his spirit.

Even the chorus of dwindling birdsong now carried a mournful tone rather than a joyful melody. Sensing the shift in mood, Pope searched for a way to lift it.

"You played well," he commented.

The furrows on his playing partner's brow diminished slightly.

"I wasn't too bad, was I?"

"Occasionally."

"I enjoyed it."

The distant but growing drone of yet another helicopter suppressed any resurgence of positivity. Neither spoke as the noise grew. The PM's eyes anxiously scanned the strip of grey above them.

"You don't need to worry. It's turning away." Pope's eyes were closed as he spoke.

It may have been the change in light, but the PM could have sworn his playing partner's complexion had paled significantly.

"Are you okay?"

Pope unclenched his fists, exhaled, then took in a slow, long breath as the noise changed in tone and faded away.

"Time to move," he said.

Approaching the fourteenth tee, both men held their breath as the clubhouse and car park came into view. The police vehicles and ambulance had gone. Half a dozen cars remained in the car park. Coldfront continued to hit balls on the practice ground.

"Not sure I want to push our luck any further today," said the PM.

"Agreed," replied Pope.

"I think it's time we made another phone call. On the way back."

Pope looked at him, then nodded.

Once they were back in range of the CCTV cameras, Pope checked and found the pro shop remained closed. A drink was offered, followed by a glance at a watch, a shake of the head, and a handshake.

Pope walked back to his car, dumped his bag in the boot, grabbed his shoes, and wandered into the clubhouse to change his footwear. The PM hoisted his bag onto his shoulder and took a shortcut across the ninth fairway towards the club entrance, then disappeared from sight.

Eight minutes later, Pope reappeared holding his golf shoes, and drove off, waving to a returning Coldfront as he did so and receiving a cheery wave back.

41

Mindy finally put the phone down, having walked around a mile and a half during a ninety-minute call with the acting PM. Barnwell sat on the same dining chair in the Music Room, tidying up the notes he'd been making on the laptop placed precariously on his knees.

Three mugs sat on the floor by the chair, each containing various levels and temperatures of coffee. Mavis happily provided them with regular drinks, knowing the pressure they were under.

However, she wouldn't clean up after them, even if she ran out of crockery.

Mindy took the mugs, along with her own collection, to the kitchen. The room filled with the sound of a food blender and *Bring Your Daughter To The Slaughter* as she did so.

By the time she had washed up and returned with fresh drinks, Barnwell had sent her a copy of the completed contact report from the teleconference. She sat down by the wall, pulled her laptop towards her, and spent the next ten minutes reviewing the document.

Neither said a word until she'd finished.

"Happy with that," she said, although her face told a different story.

"Good," replied her boss, even though he didn't look happy himself.

"Think you'd be happier if you weren't attending tomorrow's news conference?"

Barnwell grimaced.

"What do you think?"

When Mindy laughed, Barnwell had noted over the years, her eyes sparkled and her face lit up, filling everyone near her with warmth and joy. Usually. The laugh didn't reach her eyes today.

The news conference wasn't the worst gig in the world. He wasn't required to say anything or to answer questions. He was the symbol that power had moved on. Reassurance in human form. The first trinket in Crockett's trophy cabinet. Not that he minded. It was an important act at a vital time. He just had higher-priority tasks. A real prime minister to find, for instance.

Mindy watched her boss closely. She understood why he didn't plan to accompany her on the next stage of her journey. Was it the right play, though? She knew he'd always be there if she needed him, but he was giving up his chance of making history. The chance was not of her making, but it didn't matter.

Mart was a craftsman - influencing policy, nurturing talent and making or destroying political careers. She had a knack for recognising opportunities and making the most of them, even when they seemed unlikely to succeed.

The vibration in her right trouser pocket made her jump. She pulled out the mobile, noted the withheld number, and answered.

"White lilies," said the voice she recognised from the previous day's message.

"Who are you? Where is he?"

There was a pause and fumbling at the end of the line.

Mindy used the opportunity to switch the call to speakerphone.

Barnwell leaned forward, grabbed his notepad and pen and started writing.

"Hello Mindy."

"Prime minister." Mindy hesitated as Barnwell stopped writing, looked at her, turned the page and started writing again.

"Are you well?" she continued. "Are you safe?"

"I'm safe."

"Then what are you playing at?"

Barnwell stopped writing again, stared at her, turned the page and wrote again, turning the pad so she could read his note.

CALM DOWN!

She tried again. "We've been so worried about you."

The silence felt interminable until the PM spoke.

"Are you by yourself?"

Barnwell turned the pad again. *YES.*

"No," she said, staring at her boss. "Martin's here."

"Hello Martin. How's Mavis?"

Barnwell put down the pad.

"She's fine, thanks, PM," he said evenly. "Given the circumstances. I'm sure you understand. It would be helpful to know what's happening."

Again. A long three-second silence.

"Long story short, I've had enough. I'm resigning. Not just the premiership. I'm retiring from politics."

People on both ends of the call stared hard at each other. Very hard, with wide eyes and open mouths. Apart from the PM, who was grinning at his host.

Martin Barnwell's political success was built on analysing event outcomes, preparing the correct response, and acting quicker than anybody else. This was a new one on him.

He needed more data. He needed more time.

He forced himself to remain calm and noncommittal.

"Truly, a momentous day," he observed. "Nobody has forced you into these decisions, have they, sir?"

"No."

"The gentleman with you now?"

"A very kind Good Samaritan."

"Before I forget. Your daughter's been in touch. Obviously worried sick. Is there a message I can give her?"

"No. She doesn't exist."

Barnwell hesitated a second, relieved that the PM had answered the safety question correctly. There was no gun at his head.

"How did you end up where you are now? What happened at Grange Brothers?"

"Long story."

"You didn't answer Mindy when she asked if you are well."

"Physically, I'm fine."

Barnwell ignored the omission of the PM's mental state. Recent events plus this most recent revelation told him all he needed to know about that.

"So. Why retirement?"

The PM thought for a moment.

He hadn't quite known what he planned to say on the call, but felt an enormous rush of relief at finally formalising a decision and sharing it a split second later.

The cat was out of the bag and there was no going back. It felt frightening, but it also felt right.

Very right.

"Long story."

"And plans for retirement?"

The PM hesitated.

"None. Yet."

Mindy contemplated what would be required to extricate them all - particularly herself and her boss - from this situation. Before she could speak, a pale-faced Barnwell held up his hand.

"Plenty of time for them, prime minister," he said calmly, "But how do we turn your plans into reality?"

"That, my dear friend," said the PM to his chief-of-staff, "Is an excellent question."

"And you're still in the country?"

The PM looked at Pope, who nodded.

"I'm still in the country. Not going anywhere."

"Give us an hour to work things out, then call us back."

"You won't tell anyone else?"

"We'll let you know before we do."

The phone went dead. Mindy stared at it, urging it to reveal what was left unsaid. Barnwell picked up his coffee; she did the same with hers. They'd been here before. Ten minutes' silence to process the new data. Half an hour of brainstorming thoughts and ideas, then the plan.

Run to the Hills thudded through the wall.

Not a bad idea, she thought.

42

Waist high in the middle of a wheat field, the PM handed the phone back to Pope with a reverence normally reserved for sacred relics or live hand grenades.

Pope accepted it in a similar vein, wondering briefly about its value to a collector of political mementos, assuming he could prove its provenance. He thought about suggesting the PM sign and date it with a permanent marker but decided against it for now.

This was certainly historic.

A man whose arrogance had matched his apparent ignorance over three tortuous years was leaving the government and the country in turmoil. And he, Simon Pope, was right at the centre of events.

Two days ago, he would have exulted at the news of this departure from public office. He would have relished his part in the PM's fall from grace; bathed in the praise of his online community. Vengeance was his. Revenge was his.

Two days.

The PM put his hands in his pockets, then turned and waded off through the wheat towards the car parked under the trees next to the field's gate. Pope followed, stumbling slightly on the rough ground.

"You're serious?" he asked the back in front of him.

"Absolutely."

"So. Where do we go from here?"

The PM stopped and looked around as dusk crept into the surrounds. They were twenty minutes from home and off the beaten track. Not the right time for farmers or doggers to be out.

"Nowhere," he said, opening the passenger door of the car. "We wait."

43

Dave Westlake lived in a modern, three-bed terraced house on a relatively new estate on the edge of East Cumberton. The postage stamp front garden was tidy, covered in grey shale and dotted with several well established but small alpine plants.

Stuart Morris followed his suitcase-carrying host through the pristine white door into a wide hallway. Framed photographs showing family, friends, formal groups and more informal scenes from around the world filled the walls. Most included weapons. A framed set of medals took pride of place. Visitors and interlopers alike would have no illusion about the resident's history and his undoubted ability to do you tremendous harm.

The downstairs had a toilet and kitchen on one side of the hall, facing a dining room and stairs on the other. A large lounge across the back of the house featured patio doors, which opened onto a lawned back garden. Upstairs were a master and guest bedroom, bathroom and an airing cupboard.

Not one item was out of place. Nothing needed cleaning. Morris knew every cupboard and drawer would be just as immaculate.

Immaculate, or psychologically disturbing, depending on your own frame of mind and point of view.

Leaving his friend to put the suitcase in the guest room, Morris took the fish and chips they'd bought en route into the kitchen and prepared dinner.

Half an hour later and comfortably full, both men sat in the lounge armchairs nursing cups of scaldingly hot sweet tea. Here, they engaged in one of their favourite pastimes - criticising police television programmes.

The conversation shifted to how the missing prime minister would be an excellent topic for a similar show and how it would unfold.

"We wouldn't look too good," opined Morris. "Arguably the country's most famous individual goes missing. Surrounded by personal protection officers, the police, and Downing Street staff. Right in front of the nation's media. Nobody knows how he disappeared, where he is, who was involved, or why. Clues comprise a burnt jacket, a damaged mobile phone, and a sausage with a charred corpse in a burning van. 24 hours later, there's no sign of him."

"So," said Westlake. "Either he's dead, kidnapped, hiding, changed identity, or has left the country."

"If he's dead, we'd have found him by now. We searched every ditch, pond, lake, and bin in the land. Twice. He's not in the freezers or slumped in a corner of the warehouse. Hasn't washed up on any shoreline. Not hanging in any woodland. Not in any mortuary or hospital. And nobody's claimed responsibility."

"Not dead then. Or injured. And nobody claims to have him. Absolutely nobody. If they had him, we'd know about it by now."

Both men sipped their drinks and fell silent for a few moments. Morris was exhausted, but the fish and chips, the hot tea and the debate had given him a second wind.

"The event down the road was last minute. Was it the man himself? Spur of the moment?"

"The lads at the farm found the jacket in the changing room. Anything not in a locker is up for grabs, which is why they took it."

"So he says he's off to the loo. Sees a spare cold store jacket and hat lying about. Switches, slips his protection guy and walks out with everyone else, just as the hooter goes."

"Hiding in plain sight. Then what? Walks out of the gate with no cash, no phone, nothing?"

"If it was spur-of-the-moment, what other choice did he have?"

"Few people left before the gates closed."

"Those that did were ID'd, traced and interviewed."

"So. He's wandering around the premises, or he's found another way out."

"Fence is new and secure. He's not the climbing type, anyway."

"So he's nicked a car, grabbed a lift, stowed away…"

"Maybe his own people smuggled him out…?"

"Shit…"

Both men fell silent.

With the television off, the ticking of the kitchen clock added an appropriate sense of drama to the occasion. Finally, Morris broke the silence.

"This isn't a documentary anymore, Dave. It's a movie. A Die-Hard-Mission-Impossible-type movie."

Dave Westlake considered the notion for a while. Something was nagging at him. He just didn't know what.

"I wonder who'll play me?" he mused. He stood up and took their empty cups out of the lounge. "Want anything else?" he called back to his friend.

"To sleep mainly, but I wouldn't mind something sweet if you have it. What've you got?"

Morris stared at the reflection of the haggard man in the black television screen, staring back at him. Shit. He barely recognised himself. It really was time to step down.

There was no answer from the kitchen. Not a sound, in fact. No cupboards being checked, fridge door being opened, no clatter of crockery. Morris decided it was time to stretch his legs anyway, so he stood up and walked back into the hallway.

Westlake stood side on to him, cups still in hand, looking at a framed photograph on the wall. A group of around twenty well-armed soldiers in desert-camouflaged combat gear looked back. Behind them were a couple of slightly battered armoured vehicles. Some soldiers were laughing or smiling, but most looked tense, as they should.

"I knew there was something else," said Westlake. He put the mugs down in the kitchen, then pointed at the picture. One figure stood slightly off to the side, looking at his comrades instead of the camera.

Morris moved forward and focused on the man. There was something different about him. And something very familiar. The soldier - an officer judging by his insignia - wore body armour but carried no weapon or ammunition pouches. He had his hands in his pockets.

Morris leaned forward for a closer look, so his nose almost touched the glass in the frame.

"Well, well, well," he said.

44

After sixty tortuously long minutes watching the evening settle around them, the two men left the parked car. Once again, they made their way back into the middle of the wheat field, taking care to follow the same trail they had blazed earlier. The sounds of the day - even the frantic tones of the search effort - had faded away, as if the world had taken a step back and paused for breath.

The PM hit redial on the mobile phone and his former lover instantly answered the call.

"We have some ideas," Mindy announced without so much as a by-your-leave.

"Right."

The volume added to the PM's voice by the quieter surroundings concerned Pope. He gestured his man to talk more quietly.

"We assume you want to return and resign as PM and MP as soon as possible."

The response was almost too fast. "Correct."

"When you're safe and hidden, the Government will announce your reappearance and stop searching. We'll keep you out of camera range for as long as we can. Medical check-up, debrief, recovery time, and so on."

"How long will that give us?"

"Three days. Possibly three hours. Depends on leaks. Whatever the time period, that's what you'll have to agree everything with your party, the King, and the acting PM. Then you'll need to hold a news conference."

"And that's it?"

"Doubt it."

"When will you tell Crockett?"

"As soon as we have you. Where are you?"

"In a wheat field."

"Sounds great. Do we pick you up from there, your friend's place, or somewhere else?"

"Zero involvement for my friend. He didn't want any of this. What is your plan for picking me up?"

"Tonight. I'll drive up with Curtis as soon as this call ends. Work out where you want to meet us and call me. We'll take you to the safe house, then light the blue touch paper."

"And Martin?"

Barnwell had been quiet so far.

"I'm scheduled to be the show pony at tomorrow morning's news conference with our acting PM. Hopefully, he'll be able to announce your safe return."

"Does anyone else know, Curtis aside?"

"Not even Mavis."

"Let's keep it that way, please. And it's just you and Curtis. No need for a circus."

The phone went dead once more. The PM grimaced. Mindy wasn't a great one for fond farewells. She was the one who had ended their relationship with a text message.

That's your lot. I'm off. X

The men retraced their steps, got in the car, and headed home.

Neither said a word.

45

Trapped underneath the upturned smoking carcass of the patrol vehicle. The acrid smell of burning rubber filling the air.

Deafening tinnitus drowning out the chaotic sounds of the firefight raging around him, while the choking dust made each breath a struggle in itself.

The sticky sensation of blood, both his own and from others, soaking into his clothes, clinging to his skin, dripping into his eyes. Facing his own mortality and unable to raise even one hand to fend off this hell on earth.

Then Dave Westlake jolted awake, drenched in sweat, and found himself in the comfort of his own bed, in the safety of his own house.

He lay still for a moment, getting his bearings and calming his heart rate. A rhythmical snoring from the second bedroom reminded him of his guest.

Stu Morris had struggled to stay awake as the events of the last 24 hours took their toll and he had excused himself not long after a second cup of tea. With an overtime shift starting at eight in the morning, Westlake hadn't been far behind.

He checked his watch and sighed when he realised it wasn't yet nine in the evening.

It had been several weeks since the last flashback, but he knew that sleep would be difficult for the next few hours at least.

He also knew the reason for tonight's nightmare.

"Sod it," he said to himself. "I need to know."

He dressed, then slipped a note onto the bedside table in the next room for his snoring, dribbling guest.

He resisted the temptation to use his phone to record or take photos of the sleeping beauty, but only briefly, then changed his mind.

Two minutes later, he left the house with the framed photograph and got into his car.

He could be about to meet the man who saved lives that day, including his own, thousands of miles away. *They say never meet your heroes*, he thought, but this was an exception.

He'd already met the guy and knew he was a bit of a prick. He needed to know. To say thanks. To share his memories and to learn from someone else's.

It might even help him with his own demons.

46

Even on a Saturday evening, the M1 was busy heading out of London. Curtis kept the anonymous, borrowed estate out of the fast lane and well within the speed limit.

There was no rush. The later the return journey, the smaller the number of drivers on the road, diminishing the chances of the cargo being recognised. His workday suit had gone, replaced by a check shirt and jeans.

Mindy sat alongside him in a T-shirt, chinos, baseball cap and trainers, focused on her laptop.

Along with Barnwell, she had sketched out the process for recovering and securing the prime minister, but she needed an abattoir's worth of meat on the bones.

This included drafting a Plan B, plus a Plan C for when everything went down the pan and they needed to cover their arses no matter what occurred.

"This is ridiculous, you know?"

The kamikaze drivers weaving at crazy speeds through the heavy traffic weren't the subject of the comment, although they could have been.

"Yep."

Mindy kept tapping on the laptop.

Curtis knew when to be quiet.

He had body armour and weapons for them both, plus a special number on speed dial on his mobile. That would have to do. For now.

Both of them jumped slightly when the laptop - linked to Mindy's mobile - rang loudly. Mindy hit the answer button.

"Hello?"

"Hi," said a familiar voice. "Where are you?"

"M1, just south of Luton."

"Take down this number and location share."

Mindy typed the number on the laptop and confirmed the location share on her phone.

"Excellent stuff. Talk later," said the PM, then hung up.

Mindy selected another number on her phone and waited for it to be answered. She didn't have to wait long.

"We have a number," she reported.

47

Back at the house, both dogs were delighted to see their prime food supplier had returned, along with their new treat provider. The joy lasted until Pope finished filling the dog bowls and stepped away. Then both men were dead to them.

The PM opened the fridge door, removed two bottles of beer, and sat down at the kitchen table. Pope grabbed the bottle opener off the draining board and joined him. Both men took a swig as they watched the dogs consume their late tea.

"I'll miss them Simmo. Lovely dogs," said the PM with a touch of regret, followed by a chuckle. "They remind me so much of my Cabinet. They'll be your best mates until they get what they want. Then they're off."

Pope clicked his fingers. Both dogs stopped eating - somewhat reluctantly in Ginger's case - turned and looked straight at him. Pope raised his right arm from the elbow and clenched his fist. The PM jumped and clutched his beer bottle as both dogs barked furiously, hackles raising on their backs. After a few seconds, Pope rested his arm back on the table and silence reigned once more, although Fred and Ginger remained focused on their master.

"Good dogs," he said. "Well done Fred. Good girl Ginger."

Both dogs visibly relaxed and trotted over for a quick fuss before returning to what remained of their food. The PM looked on, gradually recovering his composure.

"I apologise Simmo," he mumbled. "Nothing like my Cabinet. Much better trained."

"And best mates forever, whatever," replied his host, gazing at the most important things in his life.

The steady tick of the wall clock filled the silence, now counting down to zero hour. The extraordinary events of the last couple of days were ending, thought the PM, but the uncertainty continued. He stood on one side of a valley. The life he wanted was on the other. In between was a mist-filled void that had to be negotiated first.

For the first time in a long time, he felt scared and alone. Almost alone. He watched as Pope drank from his bottle, lost in his own thoughts, with his dogs by his side.

The PM's mind drifted back to the golf game, when Coldfront had worked himself into a right state worrying about the location of his ball. "You'll deal with it, whatever it is," Pope had said. "It's not worth worrying about until then."

With a jolt, the PM realised how much he appreciated the change in perspective provided by his host and his location. Away from politics and the backstabbing. Outside the so-called Westminster bubble, where you were never certain who or what you were. Removed from an environment where the largest or smallest of events affect your wellbeing. Well away from the documentation of your words and actions. Often misinterpreted, always judged, until you got to a stage where it wasn't worth the effort of trying to drive the agenda or set the record straight.

It all looked very different from here. It lost its importance. Its value. Unless, of course, it affected you directly. Like the closure of a local hospital. Then, you felt powerless. Weak.

Resentful. Disillusioned with the whole damn system and those within it; especially those who'd taken their eye off the ball, focusing on their own career, their growth in influence, or the development of their power base.

The PM felt uncomfortable thinking about where he sat in that contemptible, complicated web of arrogance, ignorance and hubris.

"I'll grab a shower and get changed," he announced.

Pope nodded.

"I'll take the dogs out and check your people's location," he said, grabbing the leads and burner phone.

My people, the PM thought. *I wish I could be sure about that.*

48

Barnwell sat in his favourite armchair, sipping coffee instead of his usual evening whisky. On the television, a lifeboat rescued yet another hapless sailor who hadn't checked the weather forecast before venturing out.

He checked his personal phone once more to monitor the progress of his protégé and her minder as they headed north-west past Rugby, onto the M6.

The third bedroom was clean and tidy. It was now being swept for bugs by an expert who had carried out similar work for the Foreign & Commonwealth Office for two decades before retiring.

Jenny Barrett now did the same thing for a select group of executives, foreign royalty and celebrities. All were keen to ensure their private affairs remained private. She spent the rest of her retirement in casinos, on racecourses, or in her villa in Cyprus.

"All clear," she announced, emerging with a metal camera case.

The verdict didn't surprise Barnwell, but it made sense to make sure.

"Thanks Jen. What do I owe you?"

"The usual."

Barnwell smiled, stood up and gave her a kiss on both cheeks.

"I shall release Mavis into your good care for a fortnight just as soon as we get the present issue settled," he said. "Just promise me she'll have no hangover when she returns home this time."

"Promise."

"And she won't be penniless when she gets back."

"I promise I'll try."

Barnwell grimaced. "Try harder than last time," he said.

Jenny laughed as she gave him a hug, then turned down the hallway, meeting Mavis at the front door. A quiet word, a comment back and more laughter, followed by a quick hug, and Jenny was gone. Mavis walked into the lounge, tea towel in hand.

"You should come with us," she said. "Cyprus is lovely this time of year."

"Don't think I could cope with you and your sister for two weeks by myself."

Mavis looked him up and down, smiled sympathetically, then walked away.

"No," she said. "I'm not sure you could."

Barnwell shook his head. The truth often hurt, but this wasn't one of those times. He picked up his phone and called Peter Williams.

"Peter? Martin Barnwell here. Let me cut to the chase. Might you be available later tonight?"

49

Curtis cruised towards the motorway slip road they needed for West Cumberton. Just when he wondered for the third time if they were on a fool's errand, Mindy's phone rang again.

"Head for the Grange warehouse," said Pope. "There's a lay-by a half-mile north of the entrance. It's roughly forty minutes away. He'll meet you there."

"Will you be there?"

"No."

"Then, thank you for looking after him."

Pope hesitated.

"Now it's your turn," he said, then ended the call.

Mandy typed the warehouse address into the car's sat nav system.

"Forty minutes," she confirmed. "I'll let Martin know, but that's all."

Curtis nodded in agreement.

No need to rush if they were being tracked. No point getting local assets involved.

Not knowing what direction the delivery was coming from meant that an unusually high police presence in the area may spook the delivery driver.

They'd stop five minutes before the rendezvous and sort themselves out with the stuff in the boot. Just in case.

In the field, a quick five-minute jog from his home, Pope switched off the phone, whistled to his dogs and set off, heart racing as if he'd already run a marathon.

He walked the last couple of hundred yards to get his breath back before entering the house and closing the door behind him.

Thirty seconds later, Dave Westlake drove down the lane and parked outside.

50

Just as Pope removed the dogs' leads in the kitchen, the doorbell rang. He jumped. Almost instantly, he heard the shower upstairs stop.

Walking into the hallway and looking up the stairs, he saw a dripping PM on the landing, anxiously peering from behind a blue bath towel.

Not for the first time, it surprised Pope how calm he felt in times of crisis. His mind took a step back, intrigued by the situation, and wondered, "How do we get out of this, then?"

"It's the front door, Paul," he said just loud enough to be picked up outside, reminding his guest of the day's back story. "Get yourself sorted. We'll be off in about fifteen minutes."

A fleeting look of confusion flitted across the PM's face, followed by sudden realisation.

"Right you are, boyo," he replied. "I'll be down soon."

Pope grabbed the burner phone off the cupboard and put it in his pocket, then switched on the porch light and opened the front door. He recognised but couldn't immediately place the man in front of him.

"Hello again, Mr. Pope," the man said, hands behind his back. "Sorry to disturb you at this late hour."

Westlake noticed the slight frown on Pope's face. "Dave Westlake, sir. Constable Westlake. Visited with Sergeant Morris the other day. In uniform then, of course."

Pope's eyes widened slightly in recognition, and he nodded. "Constable Westlake. Ah, the uniform! Of course. Of course."

Westlake brought his right hand forward. Pope extended his own, relieved to find the man unarmed and without a warrant. They shook hands and Westlake looked earnestly into his face.

"Dave would be fine, sir. This isn't police business. I wondered if we might have a quick chat?"

"It will have to be really quick... Dave... I'm giving a friend a lift shortly. He's just upstairs."

"Understand, sir. I need something confirming. That's all."

Westlake brought out the framed photograph from behind his back and handed it over. Pope moved with it towards the porch light for a better look, then staggered backwards and brought a hand to his mouth. He felt winded, unable to look away from the image. It was all the confirmation Westlake needed.

"It's good to see you, Padre," he said, feeling a lump in his throat.

Pope's mind was no longer leaning against the wall, arms folded while watching events unfold with dispassionate amusement. It was well and truly scrambled.

He didn't remember the photograph being taken, yet there he stood. Part of the group, but not part of it. Some friends. Some strangers. Together, frozen in this moment.

"You're in this?" he asked, trying to find the police officer in the faces gazing at him.

"Crouching down at the front; third from the left."

A maelstrom of memories, smells, feelings, and guilt - especially guilt. Overwhelming sadness. Immense anger.

A feeling of helplessness.

"I'm afraid I don't…"

"Not surprised, sir. First time we'd met, at the briefing."

Pope needed to think. He needed time. The guilt.

"We were the lucky ones," he said, still reeling and unable to tear his eyes from the photograph. "You'd better come in." Lives changed. Lives lost.

Upstairs, the PM clutched the towel and listened hard, trying to envisage what was actually happening. Padre? He heard the two men enter the lounge and close the door.

Simon had called him Paul and had told the officer they were going out. He sat down on the bed and dried his feet. He had to focus on the prepared back story for the golf game and adapt it to the current situation.

For the first time in a long time, he had nobody to help him.

51

Pope slumped down in an armchair. Westlake perched on the settee. Upstairs, they could hear footsteps as the PM made it obvious he was there. Sniffs could be heard from the curious dogs on the other side of the lounge door.

Pope looked up from the photo and into the eyes of his visitor.

"How did you find me? Why?"

"Sheer bloody chance. This PM business. Why? You saved my life that day, sir. My life and at least four others. I've always wanted to say thank you. I find it hard to forget…"

Pope glanced once more at the picture, reluctant to recall the faces he'd spent years trying to forget.

"I spent nine weeks in hospital, sir," Westlake continued. "When I got back to my unit, I tried to get in touch. I know I wasn't the only one. But you'd gone, sir. Disappeared off the face of the earth."

Pope's mind switched away from the nightmare it was reliving, to the aftermath.

"I spent two days in a field hospital. Three days being debriefed at Kandahar. Then I flew back to Brize Norton and left the service. Was kicked out, really."

Westlake looked stunned.

"I was a Chaplain to the Forces, Dave. I wasn't supposed to touch a weapon, never mind fire one."

"You saved lives that day."

"And took them."

Both men fell silent, lost in their own memories of that day.

Four members of a combined patrol had died. Six more sustained serious injuries.

All in an ambush, which wasn't meant for them, in a small town in Helmand province.

The attack's intended target, an armoured American relief column, arrived late but just in the nick of time, resulting in fewer casualties. Fewer, but still bad. In fact, they would have been much worse if not for one man whose involvement was erased from public records.

The footsteps continued overhead as the PM stopped straining to hear the conversation and finished his preparations.

"Three IEDs, two suicide bombers and at least twenty other fighters, Padre. We should all be dead."

Again, each man struggled with his own feelings in silence. Westlake, outraged by the treatment of the man who'd saved his life, but aware of the inner turmoil he must be creating, bit his lip and forced himself to calm down.

"What happened when you got back home?" he asked as calmly as possible.

"I had seconded into the military from the church. Should've been for three years; ended up being nine months. Both organisations gave me the same option - resignation or the sack. And here I am."

"Good God," Westlake muttered without irony. "What did you make of that?"

The former padre thought for a moment.

He heard the PM clump down the stairs and walk into the kitchen.

"War changes people, Dave. You know that. Having a dog collar doesn't make you immune. I'd put every padre in the British Army at risk. The Taliban leadership wanted us targeted, but Intel reported their men were refusing to do so. My action could have changed that."

At that moment, the lounge door burst open. Two dogs charged in, followed by a man in a pink polo shirt and white chinos, carrying three Monk's beer bottles.

"Change of plan Simmo," announced the PM in his best Welsh accent, nodding at Dave Westlake as he distributed the Perms. "Can't go to the pub. Wifey has persuaded brother-in-law to bring her back. He's said he'll pick me up from some lay-by near that new warehouse you work at. Hope you know where it is. I thought it would be fitting to have a quick beer since they'll be there in about half an hour."

He sprinkled some dog treats on the floor, then plonked himself on the settee next to the giant police officer as Fred and Ginger created mayhem in front of them.

"Hello," he said, offering his right hand to Westlake, "I'm Paul."

52

Held up at temporary traffic lights around ten minutes from the meeting point, Mindy read the text message three times.

"What on earth is going on?" she mused, more to herself than anybody else. Curtis was conscious his stress level was increasing as the distance and time to the rendezvous diminished.

"No idea," he said.

"Sorry. Listen to this. *Running a bit late. Lift with off-duty bobby. I'm Paul and Welsh. You wife Karen. Curtis, your brother-in-law. Picking me up after seeing sister in B'ham. Will have golf clubs!*"

"Still no idea."

"Remember improv at school?"

"Improv?"

"Never mind."

The lights changed, and the car moved on. Mindy researched habitats for the fictitious elder sister, up to twenty minutes' drive from the other side of West Cumberton. Curtis considered where to conceal the body protection, which they now couldn't use, and the weapons, which they could.

53

Simon Pope didn't know what to feel. More had occurred in the last hour than in the previous thirty-six. After all the excitement, subterfuge, and shocks, there was silence. Only the gentle breathing of the sleeping dogs, complemented by the occasional treat-induced fart, disturbed it.

The house felt empty. Hollow. A shell. Shell-shocked. That's how he felt. Too much had happened too quickly for it to be absorbed and processed properly.

Credit to the PM. Creating mild mayhem and a sense of urgency broke up the discussion with Dave Westlake. Pope knew they still had more to work through. It wasn't what they wanted, but it was what they needed.

Then Westlake had offered the lift.

It was on his way and would do his friend a favour. The PM had accepted with alacrity. He even remembered to take the golf clubs.

"The secret's basing your story in the truth. In fact. Once they've accepted that part of the story, it's easier for them to accept the rest."

Clearly, the PM had remembered the advice. Had it only been that morning that Pope had given it? He shook his head. So much had happened.

The PM's bedding was in the wash. Pope would remake the bed with those same sheets and give the bedroom a reasonable clean before he finally went to sleep. Only reasonable mind. The PM's fingerprints needed to be there. The bath towel he'd used would still be in the washing basket.

The glass recycling box would contain the beer bottles, complete with the DNA of the three men and Ginger, who loved beer.

He wouldn't touch the car. Leaving the golf course, he'd found Paul Morgan by the side of the road having an argument on the phone with his wife. She'd extended her visit to her youngest sister's until the evening. Having accepted the lift and somewhere to stay until his wife collected him, Morgan had put his set of clubs in the dog hammock on the back seat. Fingerprints, of course, were everywhere.

Pope needed to hide or dispose of the burner phone and any other potentially incriminating items. The next moves were up to the PM and his friends.

He took another look at the framed photograph from Westlake. Was it Cromwell who had urged *Put your faith in God, my boys, but keep your powder dry*?

Well, his powder was dry. The rest was up to God.

54

In the car, the PM centred the conversation on the Westlake and Pope story. By doing so, he could avoid talking too much, answering awkward questions and having to maintain his Welsh accent. He didn't need to try very hard. His chauffeur had a lot to get off his chest.

"If he'd been a normal squaddie, he'd have won a medal, maybe the VC," Westlake remarked. "Five of us were stuck under the lead vehicle in a bloody ditch. It gave us some cover, actually. I couldn't move. Leg was trapped. The first IED badly injured two mates next to me. Others had copped it. Smoke and dust were everywhere, but we could see figures and flashes through it. The two vehicles behind us were taking rounds and returning fire. Hadn't time to worry about us."

Deafened by the blast, Westlake described hearing muffled shots from directly over him, just as he thought his time was up.

It was the padre, blown clear of the vehicle, firing a rifle he'd picked up. Some figures in the smoke crumpled, but flashes showed that the assault continued. Then flame and a deafening noise as a bullet hit a suicide vest on one attacker, killing the wearer and not making life great for several others.

"Shrapnel headed our way, as well as theirs. Popp fell down beside me. Hit in the head, chest and leg. Rifle smashed. Probably saved his life, actually."

"Popp?"

"Yeah. Padre Popp. The lads called him PP. He's changed it. Anyway, Popp falls down..."

The PM listened but didn't hear. Something about dragging a GPMG from the burning vehicle... a failed helicopter rescue... soldiers finally pulled to safety... blah blah blah.

And all that time, Padre Popp provided covering fire.

He identified and neutralised key threats until he ran out of ammunition, the gun barrel red hot and the stock covered in his own blood.

Only then did he allow a medic to check his condition.

"Padre Stephen Popp. He saved my life, you know?" Westlake had tears in his eyes again. The PM genuinely hoped he could still see well enough to drive. "Then they kicked him out. Screwed up his life after he'd saved ours."

They may have kicked him out, thought the PM, *but not everyone had forgotten him*. The box in the wardrobe proved that.

Westlake wiped his eyes and fell silent.

"Thanks for telling me that, Dave. Hard to believe my golfing buddy went through all that."

"I guess we all have our secrets. At least he's come out of the other side."

Both men were uncertain about the statement's accuracy.

"And how are you, Dave?"

Westlake thought long and hard before replying.

"Good days, bad days, but today will help... will help both of us, I think. It's been such a tough weekend."

And so the PM learned how the search for him had developed since he first hid in a car some 36 hours earlier.

The final ten minutes of the journey passed quickly, then Westlake pulled the car into the lay-by near the Grange Brothers warehouse.

"Looks like your taxi's already waiting for you," he observed, halting behind the parked estate car. "Let's get you out and on your way."

The front passenger door of the estate opened, and Mindy emerged, staggering slightly.

"Sorry we're a bit late," she slurred. "Me and sis had so much to talk about."

"And so much to drink?" The PM gave her an awkward hug, the darkness hiding how tightly she gripped him.

Westlake opened the boot of his car and pulled out the golf clubs.

"Want a hand with that, mate?" asked the calm voice behind him.

Westlake spun round.

"Sorry," said Curtis, walking out from nearby bushes. "Just been for a piss. Didn't mean to make you jump."

"I can manage, thanks." Westlake turned and moved off with the golf bag.

Curtis shoved the pistol he was holding behind his back into his waistband, covering it with his shirt, then opened the boot with his remote key.

"Thank you, Dave," said the PM. "I'm glad we had the chance to meet."

"You're welcome, Paul." Westlake looked him in the eye. "Might be best if we keep tonight's chat... you know..."

The PM nodded and, along with his deputy chief of staff and driver, watched the police constable pull out from behind them, make a U-turn and head off.

Silence fell like a blanket over the three of them for a moment, before Curtis took a step forward and put his hand on the PM's shoulder.

"Interesting choice of accent, sir. Good to see you again. Are you well?"

"I'm fine, thank you Curtis."

The driver smiled, nodded, got back into the car and started up the engine. The PM turned to look at Mindy. Even in jeans and a T-shirt, she had never looked so beautiful. He realised how much he had missed her.

"My, don't you look all handsome with your new haircut?" she cooed. He recognised the tone and kept quiet.

"In the back, dickhead," came the follow up. "And why are you dressed like a pimp?"

Moments later, the car crunched out of the lay-by and headed west towards the M40, avoiding all the ANPR number plate cameras it had passed on the way up. The PM lay across the back seat, his head resting on two bulletproof vests.

55

Despite waiting for the call, Barnwell still jumped when his personal phone rang - mostly because he was dozing.

"We have him," said Mindy. "Safe and sound. No problems."

"Is he okay? Has he said anything?"

"Seems fine. Gone to sleep."

"ETA?"

"Two hours max."

Lying on the sofa, he set an alarm on his phone for an hour's time and pulled up the blanket. Mavis was already in bed, and he didn't want to wake her yet. Within three minutes, Martin Barnwell was also asleep.

Catnapping was a talent he had discovered early, then practised regularly throughout his career. It had helped him through elections, wars, global catastrophes, international summits and cabinet meetings.

The prime minister's disappearance and the consequent crisis wouldn't change this beloved habit of a lifetime.

56

The prime minister woke when his body gently lurched as the car slowed, then turned left into an alleyway between two large buildings and came to a halt.

In the early hours of the morning, it was as dark outside as the streetlights allowed.

"Where are we?" he asked, cautiously lifting his aching body to a sitting position.

"London," replied Mindy.

"And where are we going?"

"You're two minutes from here to the Barnwells. Walk to the end of the alley, turn right, cross one road, then turn right again. First building on your right, apartment 10 - as in Downing Street. Martin and Mavis are waiting for you. He's breaking the news to her now, along with Doctor Williams."

The PM was pretty sure Mavis had known for quite a while. Barnwell wouldn't spring a surprise like this on her.

He valued his life too much.

"Why can't you drop me off?"

"Because the walk will do you good. Besides, we want nothing to do with your return. A noble citizen took pity on you, gave you a lift and dropped you off."

The PM fumbled for the door handle and left quietly.

He waved a thank you and shuffled off towards the far end of the alley.

"Are you sure we shouldn't be taking him to Downing Street? Chequers? A hospital? He's the prime minister after all…"

"For all we know, he's a ticking time bomb. We keep this as quiet as possible until we know what we - and the PM - are dealing with."

They watched the silhouetted figure in front of them reach the end of the alley, hesitate a moment, and then turn right.

Mindy sent a quick heads up text to Barnwell.

"Right then. Let's go. Make sure you ditch the clubs and change the plates again before you hand this back."

Curtis drove slowly down the alleyway, careful to avoid the occasional bin, and turned left at the end.

57

Conscious of the CCTV system that covered his building, Barnwell waited half a minute before answering the buzz of the intercom system.

"Sorry to disturb you at this late hour, Martin," said the PM. "It's me."

"Good Lord," said Barnwell, "Come in. Come in."

He pressed the access button and, dressed in pyjamas and dressing gown, hurried out to the lift doors in the second floor access hall.

Back in the apartment, Mavis made a quick call to Dr. Peter Williams, the PM's private physician, then walked into the kitchen to put the kettle on.

58

That he'd fallen asleep quickly would have been a pleasant surprise for Dave Westlake, had he been awake to appreciate it.

By the time he returned home, dropping off Paul Morgan was already a hazy memory. The exact opposite of his encounter with the padre.

Miraculously, he had found him. Just the same as he remembered him. Eyes filled with panic, fear, and defiance.

Westlake finally found closure, despite no support from the military or church over the years.

He collapsed fully clothed on his bed and dropped into a deep sleep, undisturbed by nightmares of the past.

59

Martin and Mavis Barnwell sat in their usual armchairs at this most unusual time of the night, each with a tumbler of whisky. The scent of the alcohol wafted through the air, mingling with anticipation that hung heavy. As they swirled their glasses, the clinking of ice echoed softly, a melodic reminder of the uncertainty that loomed. The couple wondered about the outcome of the medical in the guest room and what would happen next. They had had their share of unusual days, Mavis thought to herself, but this one took the biscuit.

She observed her husband, focused on swirling his drink with no spillage. He had aged a lot over the past few months; over the past 48 hours, in fact, and that tugged at her heart. His facial wrinkles were more pronounced. His eyes looked more sad than usual. There was usually a discernible twinkle in them when he was home, but it was a while since she'd seen it.

"What a day," she said.

He looked at her, smiled, and shook his head slightly.

"How are you feeling?"

"Like a holiday… but not Cyprus," he added, as he saw her eyes widen. Mavis laughed. Martin felt his spirits lift.

It was her laugh that had first attracted him to her, across the hall where ballot papers for a dim and distant local election were being counted. Their eyes locked, and both had fallen in love straightaway, although neither had said anything for several weeks. Mavis used the time to extricate herself from a recent engagement to a childhood sweetheart. Martin finished his political science degree at a local college of higher education.

Forty-five years, they'd been together. Married for forty-three of them. *Forty-three. Shit.* A look of horror spread across Martin's face.

"I promised you a memorable holiday for our ruby anniversary."

She smiled. "You did."

"Three years ago."

"Correct."

"I'm assuming the conference weekend in Llandudno didn't count…"

Mavis simply smiled at her husband.

"But you've never mentioned it."

"You've been busy."

"I'm so sorry…"

"You can make it up to me."

"How?"

"World cruise? No laptops or mobile phones?"

"Agreed."

Neither knew who was the most shocked. Then the guest room door opened and Doctor Williams emerged, followed by the prime minister, who wandered off to the kitchen.

"I'll get the bloods analysed in the morning. Physically he's fine," announced the doctor with total disregard for patient confidentiality. "Mentally, he's a nut job - although frankly, that's always been the case. Most politicians are." Both Barnwells nodded subconsciously. "Emotionally however…"

"Emotionally, I'm a wreck," announced the PM, leaning against the kitchen door with a large scotch in hand and a tired smile on his face. "And I have no intention of changing."

He sat in the middle of the settee and motioned for the doctor to join him. Instead, Peter Williams drew a chair from the dining table and set it between the two armchairs, happy to let his patient have the stage to himself.

Martin picked up his phone and called his assistant, then left the mobile in conference mode on the coffee table to his right.

Two miles away, in her apartment, Mindy moved the dictaphone closer to her phone and pressed record. It was vital to ensure every detail, every nuance of the prime minister's account was available for future reference. Plus, it might be useful for her book.

"Thank you, everybody, for your help today. Sincere apologies for the events of the last couple of days. It's been a difficult time, I know."

And with that, the prime minister launched into an edited, slightly amended account of events since he had disappeared from the warehouse.

Base your story on the truth, Pope had said, so that's what he did.

Once he was done, everyone knew that the man's political career was over, at least for the time being, and he needed professional support. Similarly, everybody realised he didn't give a stuff. And two audience members knew parts were untrue.

"I didn't know you played golf," said Mavis. "A strange thing to do during a breakdown."

"Many golfers play in the middle of a breakdown. You just can't tell who they are."

"And the couple who took you in?"

"They play. I spent hours swinging clubs in their garden. Kept me occupied. Calmed me down. Helped me think."

"They dumped you yesterday."

"They suggested I should move on. Can't blame them. Dropped me at a local course. I reckon he was happy to donate an old set just to get rid of me."

"And the plan…"

"Have a game, enjoy my freedom, then bite the bullet and call the police. Funnily enough, police were at the clubhouse when I was halfway round but had disappeared a bit later."

"So you panicked…"

"No. I played with two members at the club. Wanted to keep them out of this. Made my excuses and left. One drove by as I was about to make the call. To my sister, I told him. He suggested I call and arrange the pickup from his place. I had no reason to decline."

"Then you ended up here."

"Indeed, I did," smiled the PM.

Mindy stared at the timeline and notes she had written during the phone call. The PM knew that she and Mart could pick huge holes in his story. He also knew they wouldn't, at least not publicly, having been involved over the weekend much more than they were letting on. Her job now was to make the account watertight, from start to finish.

She continued to listen as Peter Williams announced his taxi's arrival. Mavis escorted him to the elevator, then made her excuses and went to bed. Once all was quiet, Martin spoke.

"We need a plan and a plausible account that will withstand scrutiny."

"I have incontrovertible third-party evidence," interrupted the PM.

Oh, I'm sure you do, thought Mindy, rolling her eyes and resigning herself to a sleepless night.

60

At six-fifteen in the morning, Damien Crockett's mobile started ringing on the table next to his bed. Normally, the 48-year-old divorcee would continue to enjoy his regular early morning shower. Not today, though. Not after the text he'd received from Mindy half an hour earlier.

PM safe. Talking now. Will call ASAP.

Crockett raced from the bathroom butt-naked and grabbed the phone. He didn't notice the withheld number. Neither did he expect the PM's rather drained voice at the other end. He certainly didn't prepare for the mix of relief, excitement, and trepidation he felt during the call.

Still dripping onto his damp bed after the conversation ended, he forced himself to breathe slowly and deeply until his raging brain and his pounding heart settled down. Time paused briefly and then continued.

First, he called Barnwell to verify the PM's account and location.

"Yes, he's here. You can call off the dogs," Barnwell confirmed. "Turned up in the small hours. He's shattered. Mavis called his doctor, who came out straightaway. Physically, he's fine; mentally less so. He's asleep at the moment."

Barnwell looked across at the PM, sat on the settee, cradling another large whisky. The PM grinned and gave him the thumbs up, splashing his drink onto himself as he did so.

"Doctor is coming back later with a mental health specialist."

"Has the PM talked about his plans?"

"Dead set on resigning. I imagine he said the same to you. Frankly, I doubt anybody would want him to stay on anyway, given the last couple of days."

The PM nodded soberly.

Crockett fell silent a moment, letting the significance of that confirmation sink in.

"When's he coming back to Number 10?"

"He wants to stay here for now. Needs as much time as we can give him." Both men on the call, plus the tipsy eavesdropper, knew that wouldn't be very long.

"We'll need at least a statement from him for the news conference. Something to keep the dogs at bay. Maybe a pic or some video."

"Mindy's on it."

Crockett's next call was to Sir Michael Stanfield. The Commissioner of the Metropolitan Police commanded the search operation. As luck would have it, the Royalty and Specialist Protection branch was also under his remit.

"He's back with us, Micky. Nobody else involved," Crockett informed him, conscious of the embarrassment this news may bring to the head of RaSP.

"Damn," said Sir Michael, watching his hopes of a well-organised kidnapping replaced by a man slipping his experienced minder by walking out of a toilet. "That's a bit of a pisser. How is he?"

"Good physical health, but there are doubts about his mental state. We're keeping him out of the spotlight at Barnwell's. We'll need a team there. Low profile."

"We'll increase presence at Chequers at the same time."

Good idea, but an unwelcome one, thought Crockett. He wanted the resignation story out there and set in stone before the idiot changed his mind.

"It's important this doesn't get out until the PM feels ready," he said. "Keep the numbers involved to a minimum. Reduce the risk of someone blabbing."

His last call was to his new chief-of-staff, who had attempted to call him a minute earlier.

"I'm going over to Martin's shortly," Mindy told her new boss. "If the PM'll make a statement, I'll video it. Otherwise, I'll get a signed letter and a couple of shots we can use at the news conference."

"I just want something we can use. We should celebrate his return, hope for his full recovery, recognise his contribution to the country, and then get on with the job."

We can try, thought Mindy, although throwing a sandwich to ravenous wolves rarely prevented a bloody attack in her experience.

61

Pope had struggled to sleep overnight; understandably so, given recent events.

He lay on top of his mess of a bed and continued to stare at the ceiling. Today, he could only carry on as normal and wait for whatever came.

Familiar sounds downstairs suggested the dogs were getting hungry and wanted at least a brief meander around the garden, if not a longer walk.

He dragged himself to the bathroom, had a quick shave and shower, dried, dressed and set off down the stairs, only to stop halfway and retrace his steps.

He opened the wardrobe in the guest room, pulled out the weighty memento box, and removed the gun and ammunition. *Not helpful if someone discovered them in a search*, he thought. He would hide them, along with the burner phone.

Pope held the gun and felt its weight.

He hadn't touched it in three years, and he felt uncomfortable holding it. Guilty.

The Regimental Sergeant Major presented him with the parting gift before he left the barracks for the last time. "From me and the lads, sir. Just in case."

The RSM saluted, then left the room. Pope was considering what to do with the weapon when the RSM came back and handed over a business card. Printed on it were three words - The Garden Club - and a telephone number.

"If you ever need anything…"

Pope looked at it and nodded.

"You did what needed to be done, Padre. You saved lives."

"And took them."

Only a ticking clock disturbed the silence. Each tick, enough time to decide. To point a weapon. To fire. Just a few ticks for lives to change forever.

"You looked the devil in the eyes that day, sir. You'll deal with it. Maybe one day you'll be at peace with it."

"What about you, RSM?"

The man at the door struggled to find words, as the ticks persisted.

"Still looking sir."

With a nod, the RSM was gone.

You looked the devil in the eyes. Had that really been seven years ago? It still felt like yesterday.

Pope pulled an old pillowcase from the drawer underneath the bed, wrapped the gun and ammo box in it, and took the package downstairs. He turned on the TV and let the dogs out before making tea.

By the time the kettle boiled, the outside world had moved on. Pope's world had to as well.

62

As proud as he was of his uniform, Dave Westlake wasn't keen on wearing it when driving to work. He wanted to avoid making himself a target or a source of help when not on duty. The uniform travelled in a suit holder, with his belongings in a sports bag.

He'd woken early and felt refreshed, as if someone had lifted a weight off his shoulders. A quick jog and a shower, then breakfast. He served tea and hot buttered toast to his guest. Stu Morris had enjoyed a deep sleep all night.

Now, he planned a quiet day watching television before his early evening check-up back at the hospital. Dave would take him.

Westlake was changing in the police station locker room when word came through of 'developments'. In the packed briefing room, all soon became clear.

"The prime minister is safe and well," announced Superintendent Pamela Whitwell. "He turned up in London overnight and is currently being examined and debriefed at a secure location. We've been told to stand down."

There was a mixed reaction from the assembled throng. Relief on the one hand. Dejection on the other. The man was safe, but the chase and overtime were both over.

"Any news on the abductors?" asked a voice from the crowd, desperate for consolation arrests or even a shoot-out.

Whitwell cleared her throat before replying.

"There don't appear to have been any," she replied, anticipating the groans of disappointment from her team. "That's all I have for now. I suspect we'll learn more during the day. Day shift will remain here for their morning briefing. The rest of you come with me. Thank you for your efforts."

Whitwell walked out of the room and led eight personnel, including Westlake, into her office. Everybody fell silent while their boss adjusted her glasses on her nose and gathered her thoughts. Eventually, she looked at them with a slight smile on her face.

"I understand RaSP is looking into the possibility of the PM having early-onset Stockholm Syndrome."

"Is that actually a thing?" asked Westlake, incredulous that anybody could develop positive feelings for their captors in such a short timeframe. The PM didn't have those feelings for people he'd known and worked alongside for years, for God's sake.

"RaSP want a way out of this mess," said Whitwell, "They had one job and look what happened. But there'll be an inquiry and remember, they have a close ally in the home secretary stroke acting PM."

"So they still think there's the possibility of third party involvement?"

"They might look for a scapegoat. My bet is they finger someone else for this mess. That could be some poor local who's inadvertently become involved, or it could be a bigger target."

"Like us?"

Superintendent Whitwell took a sip of water from the glass on her desk.

"Like us."

63

The Barnwell residence was unusually quiet for this time of day.

Martin was heading to Downing Street to meet the acting prime minister before the news conference in the media room.

Mavis had embarked on a holiday research trip, intending to strike while her husband was in a rare mood for a long vacation.

That left the apartment totally empty, apart from the country's current prime minister and his deputy chief-of-staff.

They analysed the PM's account of his disappearance, fixed its weaknesses, and refined the entire narrative. Mindy read through the draft she'd been writing and amending throughout the discussion.

"Introducing the locals who looked after you would be beneficial. It'll give credibility to what you say."

"That's not happening."

She took a breath and tried a different approach.

"You're sure about resigning. Leaving Parliament?"

The prime minister continued to stare at the Persian rug on the carpet and nodded.

"And the episode at the warehouse? You just decided you'd had enough and walked out?"

"That's what happened. One hundred percent."

"That will be the headline. They'll view anyone else involved as good people who did their bit for somebody in trouble. Two minutes of fame and they'll disappear back to obscurity."

"You know that's not how this works. They'll have reporters crawling all over them, their families, friends, enemies…"

Mindy lifted her eyes from the screen and looked at her former boyfriend.

The dynamism, charisma, idealism, and passion that initially attracted her to him had all but faded away. Maybe he felt the same when he looked at her.

Perhaps that was the price of power.

You didn't gain it. It gained you. Changed you.

"Remember the conference in Brighton?" she asked, thinking of the first time they'd met.

He smiled and nodded, still looking at the rug. They dined, drank, debated, and danced all week, and were always ready for the next day. It was a magical time, but now a distant memory.

"We had plans to change the world," she said.

"We did," he replied. "Look how that turned out."

Neither needed to say anything else. They'd ridden the crest of a wave but playing the game had sapped their energy. Winning the battles had become paramount. No time for war or the endgame.

"I miss you," he said, still looking at the rug.

Before Mindy could respond or think of a response, her phone rang.

"Yes?"

"Doctor and friend on their way up."

The misplacement of a key government member had unsettled the usually impeccably polite RaSP officers.

She ended the call, walked to the door, and opened it just as the lift stopped.

"Gentlemen," she said to the still flustered figures, searched thoroughly on their entry to the building. "Welcome to the madhouse."

64

Unusually for the weekend, Pope decided against a full English breakfast. He settled for tea and a couple of slices of buttered toast in front of the television.

Both dogs sat facing him, watching every move of the toast from the plate to his mouth. Between their heads, he watched as the news presenter announced the prime minister's reappearance.

The broadcaster used footage of government officials and the PM at the warehouse for the major event, despite having little to say. Even when the programme cut to interview the political editor standing outside Downing Street, there was nothing new to add.

After giving the coverage a couple more minutes, Pope decided it was time for Fred and Ginger's long walk. Plus, he'd feel happier once he had removed the incriminating evidence from the house.

The forecast was 'mostly' cloudy and dry - typical weather presenter-speak when trying to cover all bases. He took a flask of tea and a light rain jacket alongside the dogs' stuff and the weapon to justify the rucksack.

The burner phone could go as well. He'd already made a mental note of the number he'd called from it. Just in case.

Once he'd packed everything - no mean feat with two excitable dogs getting in the way - Pope left the house and walked down the lane, away from the village. The absence of helicopters, drones and police sirens made wandering in the fields and woods a peaceful delight.

About half a mile away from his house, with the dogs contentedly mooching around the trees, he removed the phone and a small notebook from the rucksack.

He switched on the phone to remove the last number called when a text message appeared.

Back safe and sound. Million thanks for your help. Hopefully meet up again for a beer. Reach me on this number. Paul.

He noted the number, reversing the last six digits. Then he deleted everything on the phone, switched it off and wiped it clean before wrapping it in a small plastic bag.

Using the trowel he'd brought, he buried the bag in the roots of a tree one hundred paces from another, which marked the resting place of the gun.

Happy with his work and feeling more confident about the next day or two, he set off with the dogs towards the top of a nearby hill. It offered great valley views - an ideal place for a mug of tea and dog treats.

65

Barnwell and Curtis entered 10 Downing Street via the passage from the Treasury building. By doing so, they avoided the questions shouted by journalists stationed across the road from the famous black door.

Even for a Sunday, the entrance lobby was unusually empty. The entire building was listless, unsure and reluctant to make a move, fearing it could be wrong.

The two men walked up the stone staircase to the prime minister's private quarters on the third floor.

The four-bedroom apartment didn't meet Curtis's expectations on this, his first visit. For a prime minister with such a reputation for grand gestures it was spartan and, well, boring.

Barnwell, having been here often, was stunned. He had never seen the rooms looking so tidy. The PM's absence had given the cleaners the chance to remove a significant amount of the usual, almost traditional, detritus. They had given everything a good going-over.

Barnwell was sure their reaction to the PM's return would be mixed. He grabbed a holdall and threw it across to Curtis, who opened a chest of drawers and gingerly removed some underwear, pyjamas, and several pairs of socks.

The driver then went to the bathroom and came back with the PM's shaver and toiletries in a bag.

Meanwhile, Barnwell had put two suits, several shirts and a couple of ties in a suit bag. He went into the bedroom and came out with the PM's personal organiser and shoes, which he put in the holdall.

With everything zipped up, the two men retraced their steps down to the lobby, where they parted company.

Curtis took the bags and headed back through the Treasury building to his car.

Barnwell made a coffee in the basement kitchen, then headed to his office.

66

The PM felt 'sullied' by the recent 'interrogation' and was in the shower. Mindy sat down to debrief Peter Williams and psychologist Professor David Maugham.

The professor initially protested, citing patient confidentiality. He finally agreed to take part when forcibly reminded that a national emergency took precedence over the sensitivities of a potential lunatic.

"Some may view his current state as some form of mental illness, perhaps a nervous breakdown," opined the professor. "Obviously there has been a huge recent change in behaviour. Did anybody observe earlier changes - physical, verbal, emotional?"

Mindy shook her head. Over several years, the PM had appeared as mad as a box of frogs, but people viewed this as his way of coping with the pressures of the job.

Significant events caused stress for many in the government, not just their leader. People dealt with it in different ways. He was the way he was and, yes, carrying a sausage to wave at the nation's media was par for the course.

"So he hasn't sought support or help from anyone else? Talked to anybody about how he's feeling? Friends? Family? Partner?"

Again, a shake of the head.

"Is he taking any medications or undergoing medical treatments other than those prescribed or arranged by Peter? Illegal substances perhaps?"

Another shake of the head.

With the weight of the situation bearing down on him, Maugham was suddenly aware of the importance of his words.

It felt as if the entire system couldn't move on until he had come to an initial diagnosis and a prognosis of the PM's condition.

At that moment, he felt the constant responsibility his patient had.

And he didn't like it. Not one iota.

"This is my first meeting with the PM. I've spent less than an hour assessing his mood, thought processes, cognition and perception."

Mindy couldn't help herself.

"Consider your arse covered."

The professor blanched slightly as Peter Williams studied a lampshade, trying hard not to laugh.

"Then... my early assessment is... he's come to his senses."

He looked with quiet satisfaction at the blank stares and waited for his words to sink in.

"And my prognosis - subject to further assessment - is that he'll be absolutely fine once he's looking after his wellbeing properly."

"Which means?"

"This job nearly killed him. It may be the death of you, eventually. Dear God, how do you all cope?"

The outburst surprised even the professor.

He took a moment to contemplate a study on deteriorating mental health within the Whitehall bubble. Then he shifted his attention back to the present situation.

"The occasional craziness has been his coping mechanism. But even that's breaking down. It's why he went AWOL without realising what was actually happening. Frankly, it's the best thing that could have happened to him. Brought things to a head."

"He's definitely going then."

"It's what I would prescribe."

"But politics is his life."

"Was his life."

All three of them turned.

A semi-naked, damp prime minister stood in the hallway, wrapped in a bath sheet and clutching a small, yellow plastic duck.

67

The prime minister had been unusually quiet after the inquisition had left the apartment. He had thanked and said farewell to the guests in his shower regalia, then changed into a borrowed dressing gown. Now, he sat at the kitchen table, nursing a mug of coffee and reading through the revised account of his disappearance, or adventure, as Mavis had called it.

Mindy was just finishing a message to Barnwell, prior to his delayed meeting with Crockett.

"I'd like you to do something for me please, Mindy, while I'm still the prime minister. If that's okay?"

Mindy resisted the temptation to comment on a politeness she rarely saw in her boss. Maybe she should report the significant change in behaviour to the psychologist.

"What do you need?"

"There was a kerfuffle in Helmand seven years ago. We lost men. The cavalry's arrival saved us from losing more."

"There were many kerfuffles."

"A Chaplain to the Forces played a significant role in the action. As a result, they pulled him from Afghan and kicked him out. There must be an official account somewhere. I'd like a copy please, or at least sight of it."

Mindy resisted the temptation to ask why the sudden interest in military history.

"I've a couple of friends at Defence."

"Thank you." The PM returned to his coffee and the newspapers.

Mindy messaged Mart, then went to the lounge to make a call and ask for a favour.

Ten minutes later, she walked back into the kitchen, looking pensive. The prime minister barely noticed her and jumped slightly when she spoke.

"Why did you ask about that specific action?"

He knew he couldn't lie to her. She always knew. Besides, that was the old him.

"I met a couple of people. What happened that day is important to them, but I didn't hear the entire story and I'm intrigued."

"The man who dropped you off?"

The PM briefly stared at her before nodding, trusting her with the information.

"And the other?"

"His friend. How did you get on?"

She decided not to push the issue.

"She immediately understood what I meant. Quite touchy about it. She'll send what she can - probably war diaries - but there will be redactions."

The PM added his signature to the bottom of two documents, then pushed the papers in front of him across to her.

"That's good to go," he said. "Light the blue touch paper and stand well back."

"Oh, I think you did that a while ago," she smiled.

A brief phone call from the security detail announced Curtis. Shortly after, the prime minister was looking like the prime minister again. For the moment, at least.

217

It took several attempts for Mindy to capture a photograph of him looking reasonably serious.

She sent that across to Barnwell, then deleted the pictures of him with a big grin on his face apart from one.

She'd keep that one. It might make it into the book one day.

Besides, seeing him genuinely happy made a welcome change.

68

Barnwell walked into Crockett's office and placed the innocuous looking A4 envelope on his desk.

He pulled up a nearby chair and sat down while the acting prime minister opened the seal and gently removed the contents.

Crockett first looked at the enclosed photograph, resisting the temptation to read through the paperwork.

"He's looking good," he said, "More statesmanlike than I've seen him in a long while. Are you sure he's not mounting a comeback before he's even gone?"

Barnwell smiled indulgently.

Crockett tossed the print onto the desk and looked through the paperwork, finally arriving at the note with the appended signature. He sat behind the desk, holding the letter and trying to remain steady.

"This makes it official?"

"Not quite. Usually a prime minister makes a statement. This triggers a leadership contest. The King invites the winner to form a new government. There's a confirmation vote in Parliament. The outgoing PM then formally resigns, and the incoming PM takes office."

"This isn't usual, though."

"Mid-term resignations are rare. This one's unique. Nobody saw it coming. The ruling party already has an existing leadership structure. That structure has already nominated you as the prime minister."

"So we can jump to the Palace."

"Which could be tomorrow, depending on the King's diary. The letter is good enough for what you need. Once it's public, there's no going back."

Crockett placed the letter on the photograph and leaned back, gazing at the ceiling.

The position was his. The incumbent was resigning because he thought Crockett would be an excellent replacement.

Barnwell observed the new leader's moment of euphoria turn to panic.

Normally, the chief-of-staff would enjoy this moment, watching the joy dissolve to reveal the start of the harsh reality, but not today. It was important that this went well. His last important act in his current role. Before Crockett knew what he wanted to ask, Barnwell gave him the answers.

"You should have two years at least. I can't see anyone objecting. Your colleagues could have put themselves forward. They failed to do so."

"Two years, Martin," mused Crockett, closing his eyes for a moment, then opening them and sitting up straight. "No time to waste." He grabbed a pad of lined notepaper. For the next thirty minutes, he took notes as the country's leading political operator lectured him on how to succeed as prime minister.

By the end, Crockett realised how little he really knew about politics and how much he would miss this old curmudgeon. They had clashed a few times during the former police commissioner's tenure as an MP and in office. In every instance, Crockett always believed he had won, only to realise later that he hadn't.

Resentment of that fact had gradually turned to an arms-length respect. Now, he believed he was in the presence of a true guru, perhaps even a deity.

"You sure I can't persuade you to stay on? Maybe as a special adviser for a couple of years?"

"Did you see what happened to the latest Spad?"

Crockett had and had a good idea of who caused the humiliating exit.

"This is a vital time for the country, Martin. It needs you. I need you."

"You'll have Mindy. Trust her. She won't let you down."

"She's not you."

"She's better."

Crockett gave up. For the moment, at least. The most important news conference of his life was in ninety minutes. He needed to rewrite a speech and reach out to favourite journalists.

It was almost his time.

69

The security control centre at Grange Brothers' distribution centre would have fitted in well in NASA, a Las Vegas casino or a South African diamond mine. It was light, air-conditioned and state-of-the-art. Five desks, each with a black gaming chair and a large 4k monitor, sat in front of a large, high-resolution video wall. The display wall could show images from up to sixteen cameras.

A larger desk on a raised platform held three 4k monitors side-by-side. Security manager Gail Hardy sat behind the console in another gaming chair.

Hardy was a former senior prison officer who now had a role that didn't involve daily fights, drugs, blood, and suicide attempts. At least, not yet. Beside her, perched on a smaller, standard office chair but still the same height, sat Dave Westlake.

"You haven't seen the footage from the warehouse yet, Westlake," Superintendent Whitwell had said. "A new perspective would be helpful. Not here, though. Go to the warehouse security room. Marvellous place. Totally over-the-top for the job. Talk to their security guys at the same time. You never know."

Whitwell had been right about the setup.

"When we're done, we'll have twenty-six cameras across the site," said Hardy. "Currently, we have ten operational."

The manager showed him the footage compiled by her team for the security agencies, which focused primarily on the prime minister in the facility.

Occasionally, Westlake asked for the images to be paused. He marvelled as Hardy zoomed in on the high-definition faces of specific visitors or employees. He recognised some from the television; others he recognised from his time on duty in the surrounding area.

In the army, Westlake unearthed a talent for facial recognition and spotting when somebody behaved unnaturally.

Those abilities saved no lives but provided valuable information to the intelligence stream and had led to several arrests. Now, in the police force, his skills had proven to be transferable and equally valuable.

A figure caught his attention on the video footage. It was some considerable distance beyond the group of visitors, who were watching the prime minister trying to shrink-wrap cartons on a pallet. The figure glanced at the group and then paused briefly.

Something and nothing, Westlake thought, putting the image to the back of his mind.

Half an hour later, the montage of footage was at an end. He had identified two employees who he remembered from the council's CCTV footage, pinching a charity collection box from a local pub, but that was all.

"Could I see the footage that didn't make the final showreel?" he asked.

The team put the synchronised, recorded images from all ten cameras on the video wall. All played in real time, from the prime minister's arrival to ten minutes after he had disappeared.

Gail Hardy ordered a couple more coffees and some sandwiches from the canteen, then settled back into her gaming chair.

So much nicer than working with criminals, she thought.

One hour later, she was changing her mind. There were only so many indistinct, foggy images one could view, then review, then review again before one questioned one's own sanity.

Images from four exterior cameras showed small, unidentifiable workers dispersing across the car park.

On one screen, someone emerged from the mist, jogging against the flow and into the building.

"What's he doing?"

"Probably late for his shift," said Hardy. "Team members clock in and attend a briefing fifteen minutes before the previous shift clocks off. He's late."

"Can we check who he is?" Westlake asked and then, seeing a look of fleeting exasperation cross his host's face, added, "The previous shift has gone. His mates are already at work. He's late so isn't where he should have been. He could have seen something everyone else would have missed."

"I'll make a call."

One minute later, Westlake had his answer, or rather, he didn't. Human Resources was adamant that nobody had clocked in late for the following shift. A CCTV operator matched the number of team members for that shift to the number of personnel who entered the actual warehouse after their briefing.

None of the operational cameras captured the individual inside the facility. Hardy programmed the system to detect movement at the door the mystery man had entered. Shortly after the entry time, a figure resembling the previous one emerged from the door. He walked a few steps, inspecting the two bags he held, then jogged and disappeared into the fog.

"Show the walking bit again," asked Westlake, failing to hide the excitement of the hunt. "Now find the coverage of the PM shrink-wrapping the pallet."

Hardy displayed the two images side by side on the big screen and zoomed in on the worker in the pallet footage. The man in both recordings had the same clothing and a slight limp.

"Can you pick him up inside with another camera?"

The security manager brought up images from a camera covering the goods-out area to the large screen. She entered the date and time shown on the inside image already featured, then pressed play. Moments later, the man emerged from an aisle and deposited a barcode reader into a charging unit before disappearing through a nearby door.

Hardy zeroed in on the man's face.

"I can send the image to HR and get you a name," she offered.

"Thanks Gail, but I already have it," said Westlake, silently kicking himself. "I know the guy. I'll have a chat."

He scribbled some details into his notepad and checked the notes he'd made back at the station.

"We're just about done," he said.

Hardy breathed a quiet sigh of relief.

"I just need to check the time before the PM's arrival. Let's say half an hour before. Anything that features people who aren't Grange employees - media, officials, guests, deliveries, etcetera."

"Of course you do."

Hardy had spent years in the prison service, presenting a calm exterior that hid the frustration, impatience, anger, fear or shock she was feeling at the time. She did so again now, although it was a close-run thing.

70

Back home after his enjoyable and invigorating walk, Pope settled both tired dogs on their beds for the afternoon. They looked at him expectantly and were each rewarded with a pig's ear.

Pope poured the rest of the tea from his flask into a mug, sat down at the kitchen table, opened his laptop and fired up his web browser. The news headlines told him all he needed to know and, thirty seconds later, he was in the lounge, sat in front of the television.

The screen showed an empty podium emblazoned with the UK coat of arms, in front of an oak-panelled backdrop. Movement in the briefing room signalled the imminent start of the event, relieving the off-camera presenter. A disembodied voice whispered, "About bloody time," thus labelling the moment forever as the bloody time resignation.

Flanked by the Metropolitan Police Commissioner and the Chair of his political party, Damien Crockett walked to the podium.

"Good afternoon," he said. "I am delighted to announce that the prime minister is back with us and resting. He has received a full medical check-up and is physically fit and well."

Mindy's photo of the prime minister appeared on two large screens. The broadcasting cameras immediately latched onto them. The photograph impressed Pope. Smart clothes and clever lighting meant the PM might look vaguely familiar to anybody who had seen him over the weekend. But he also looked different to the rest of the world. All viewers, therefore, would feel unsettled by the image, without knowing why.

As he started to hope his involvement in the whole sorry episode would never come to light, the fates started to conspire against him.

71

Viewing a screen in the warehouse control centre, Westlake watched the prime minister's advance team step into the fog from two vehicles. He recognised Marcus Michaels from his ignominious exit in Downing Street the previous morning.

How the mighty have fallen, he thought, then noticed a woman in a bright red coat, part hidden by the cloaking mist. She turned to talk to a member of the Grange team, and Westlake's heart missed a beat.

"Can we zoom on the lady in the red coat please?" he asked, hoping against hope that the action wouldn't confirm his suspicions. If it wasn't the tipsy wife of the man who'd been at Pope's house, it must be her twin sister. The zoom confirmed the likeness. "Do we know who she is?"

Hardy opened a briefing document hastily written and distributed by the Grange marketing office on the morning of the visit.

"Amanda Abbott. Deputy chief of staff in the prime minister's office."

Westlake made a couple of additions to his notes, closed his book, and then shut his eyes for a few moments. He pictured what he could remember from the scrambled, emotional night before.

Paul's wife had acted as if she'd been drinking, but he couldn't smell any drink. He had an opinion on her attire for a day out with her sister, but what did he know about fashion and personal preferences? She was the spitting image of the woman on the big screen. As for the brother-in-law, he looked as if he could handle himself, but that was about it. There were no clues there.

But if both women were really the same woman, then who was Paul?

Westlake opened his eyes, expecting to see Gail Hardy staring at him, wondering what was going on. In fact, her attention was elsewhere. One of her team had put the live news conference on the video wall. The screen showed the photograph of the prime minister over the headline 'PM to resign'.

"Can I have a printout of that image, please?" the police officer asked with a strong sense of urgency.

The security guard put down his sandwich and hit the buttons on his console.

"I'm done here," Westlake said, turning to Ms. Hardy whilst trying to hide the mix of confusion, embarrassment and excitement in his brain. "Many thanks for your help."

72

"Well, Crockett's not hanging about, is he?"

The prime minister hunched on the sofa, watching himself on TV, appearing more prime minister-like than ever.

"What is there to wait for?" Mindy's eyes never left her laptop, as she scanned through the documents just received from her contact in Defence.

On the television, Crockett read out the letter of resignation. He failed miserably to show even a modicum of modesty at the key moment.

"In its choice of acting prime minister, my party has already shown itself ready to move forward with a leader who is just as, if not more, capable than myself. With this in mind, I resign from my position in the Government and as the Member of Parliament for my constituency."

Professionally obliged to record the moment for posterity, the photographers unleashed a barrage of flashes at the podium. Crockett struggled to overcome his feeling of smugness with a countenance of levity.

"Dear God. He looks like he's just broken wind."

"He'll get over it," said Mindy, eyes still on the laptop.

The screens in the briefing room switched to a close-up of the letter's end, including the PM's signature.

"That's it then," said the PM, leaning back into the sofa cushions and switching off the television as Damien Crockett continued to talk. Mindy looked up for a moment.

"How are you feeling?"

The PM looked up at the ceiling, then broke into a smile.

"I feel as if I've hit a great golf shot, but I don't know where the ball's landed," he said.

Mindy's eyebrows furrowed briefly. Then she changed the subject.

"The Afghan information has arrived," she stated. "It was certainly more than a kerfuffle."

She handed over her laptop, then made coffees in the kitchen, adding a shot of whisky to each. She put the PM's drink on the coffee table and sat back in her armchair, watching as he read.

Fifteen minutes later, he had read enough, struggling emotionally to take in all the detail. He handed the laptop back to her.

"It happened then, just like he said," he sighed. "I was hoping it hadn't been as bad."

He picked up his coffee and took a sip, oblivious to the added alcohol, and lapsed into silence. Mindy gave him a minute before trying a bit of fishing.

"It's a pity they have redacted the names. You can't be sure what your friends' involvements were without the names."

The prime minister stared at the coffee mug.

"I'm pretty sure one of them wrote one diary. It was his story," he said. "There was no diary from the padre. Stephen Popp his name. Dear me, what a brave man."

"Padre Popp…"

"That's what the squaddies called him."

"And is he your other friend?"

The PM's eyes never strayed from the mug. He shook his head.

"The army kicked out Stephen Popp. His church did the same. Then he disappeared off the face of the earth," he said. He turned the television back on, now eager to hear the pundits' thoughts on his resignation, his legacy and the potential of his likely successor.

Mindy quit all the documents, logged out of the defence server to which she'd had temporary access, and sent confirmation and her thanks to the provider.

Stephen Popp, she mused. An unusual name and one she'd never heard before; so why was it clanging such a huge bell in her head? The answer arrived twelve minutes later as she opened the fridge door and took out the milk for another special coffee. Three cans of pop on the top shelf caught her eye - particularly the logo on the orange soda.

It couldn't be, could it?

Stephen Popp. Esteban Canafanta?

Without waiting for the kettle to boil, she marched back into the lounge, switched off the television and sat on the coffee table facing the PM. His startled expression made her pause for thought. Was now the right time to bring this up? Might he warn Popp out of a misguided sense of loyalty?

Instead, she asked, "There was a whisky in that last mug. Do you want another?"

The PM nodded. She nodded back, stood up, turned the television back on, and marched back into the kitchen.

73

Barnwell welcomed the chance to escape the media throng in the briefing room at number 12 and almost ran down the corridor back to his office in number 10. He closed the door and put his mobile on speakerphone to take notes while listening.

"Sorry," he said, "Thanks for rescuing me. Where are you?"

"Outside your block. Said I needed some fresh air," replied Mindy against a backdrop of birdsong and the occasional car engine. "Not sure you'll be thanking me in a minute."

She told him about the PM's request, the War Diaries and the subsequent discussion, ending with the potential, admittedly tenuous link between Popp and Canafanta.

"One of the lads I did Spanish with at school was called Stephen. The teacher always called him Esteban - even out of the lessons," she said. "And to think I never imagined Spanish would be useful for anything other than ordering a holiday beer."

She recounted her call with Noel Sutcliffe at Greater Manchester Police and the zero progress he had made tracing the missing contributor.

She expressed her fear that there could actually have been some level of terrorist involvement over the weekend.

Or that somebody could make it seem like there had been. Perhaps the PM didn't go AWOL because of a breakdown and then reappear after feeling better.

"Even if our story is accurate and no third party was involved, we must stop other versions from becoming public. It'd damage him, us, the Government, the people who actually helped him, everyone."

The phone went silent, apart from Mindy's breathing, the song of a blackbird and the whine of a passing electric car.

"What do we do, Martin?"

"Let's give ourselves a minute."

He added more doodles to the paper in front of him. They helped him to think.

Plus, he'd known not to make any notes as soon as Mindy started talking, such was the urgency in her voice.

Two minutes later, her breathing calmed and even the traffic noise reduced.

"Are you in the park?" he asked.

"I am. Found a bench without bird shit on it."

He smiled to himself.

"Right then," he said, "Tell me what you're thinking."

74

Stuart Morris had just finished a late, light lunch and was watching crown green bowls on a sports channel. It was about all the excitement he could take in his current condition.

He heard the key turn in the front door. Moments later, his host and good friend appeared in the lounge doorway, still in his police uniform and still technically on duty, looking flushed.

"Didn't expect you for another three hours."

"Didn't expect it either," said Westlake, "But I need to talk to you. Bit of advice needed."

He went into the kitchen and came back with two mugs of tea, spilling them slightly while placing them on a side table. Morris waited, keeping half an eye on the bowls match, while his mate decided what he wanted to say.

"After you'd gone to bed, I visited our friend Simon Pope to see if he is the guy in the photo. Turns out he is."

"Wow."

"I know. How freaky is that?"

"No. I meant wow, you left someone recovering from a serious operation with no support or means of help if he took a turn for the worse."

"You were snoring your head off. Piss off."

Morris considered the robust defence and conceded with a thoughtful nod. After all, he had survived the night. More to the point, he hoped he'd lightened his mate's mood a little.

"Had a decent chat with him, but he had someone round there he'd met at golf earlier - a guy called Paul. His lift from the club had fallen through. Something to do with his missus seeing her sister in Birmingham. Anyway, Paul comes in and says his sister and her brother-in-law have called and are picking him up from a lay-by close to Grange Brothers. It's on my way back, kind of, so I offered to take him. Pope said he was happy for us to continue our chat another time."

"Did he get his lift?"

"Yeah. His wife and her brother-in-law were waiting for him. Then I came home."

"So?"

Westlake removed a couple of folded sheets of paper from his back pocket and handed one over. Morris unfolded and smoothed out a print of a woman in a red coat.

"Your new girlfriend?" he asked.

"Amanda Abbott. She's the deputy chief-of-staff in the prime minister's office. This CCTV image is from Grange Brothers, ten minutes before the PM's visit. I thought she was the woman I saw in the lay-by last night."

"But..?"

Westlake handed over the screen grab of the prime minister from the morning's television coverage.

"Now I'm certain. Here's the golfer I dropped off."

Morris felt a slight tightening of his chest. Westlake noticed his friend's face changing colour.

He reached for the spray bottle provided by the hospital and sprayed its contents underneath his friend's tongue.

Thirty seconds later, Morris felt well enough to review the two images and his friend's account.

"I don't know," he said, "I leave you alone for just ten minutes…"

Westlake grinned, but Morris noted the grin merely emphasised the strain in his face.

"What should I do now, Stu?"

75

Simon Pope had enjoyed his afternoon in the garden. Work always helped him to relax when his mind was over-busy. The recent news of the prime minister's resignation had his synapses firing on all cylinders.

The bugger had only gone and done it. Good. Good for both the country and the man.

Pope celebrated by mowing, trimming, and weeding. He even removed some overhanging branches from the tree in the jungle next door. Pope saw the lack of close neighbours as a good thing, but there were downsides.

Grabbing a second bottle of beer, a bag of crisps and some dog treats, he settled in a deck chair on his now-pristine lawn. It wasn't the warmest of days, but the sun was always welcome when you spent most of them indoors.

He took a couple of swigs from the bottle, threw the treats for the waiting hounds, closed his eyes and promptly fell asleep.

About an hour later, he woke in the growing shadow of the house to the sound of a gentle growl. Both dogs were on their feet - Fred with hackles raised - looking at the wall next to the garage. Beyond was the not-so-subtle sound of boots on gravel.

Pope stood up quietly, clicked his fingers once, then raised his arm and clenched his fist. Immediately, canine hell broke loose. Both greyhounds emulated their ancestors in wars of ages past by scaring the shit out of their currently invisible enemies.

After twenty seconds, Pope dropped his arm, and both dogs fell silent. He stood still, waiting for the person on the other side of the wall to act. When he heard a soft crunch on the gravel, he raised his arm again and raised canine hell, volume two.

The commotion caused a hasty retreat and an indistinct radio message.

Pope walked inside, waited for the dogs to follow him, then locked the back door. Each dog happily accepted a well-earned digestive biscuit for their impressive performance, then lay on their beds.

Pope switched on the kettle, then wandered into the lounge. He glanced out the window, as if looking for what was disturbing his dogs.

His sudden appearance made three of the six police officers in conference on the road jump in alarm. Pope waved at them, then disappeared, only to appear moments later at his front door.

"For goodness' sake," he said, "You scared the wits out of my poor dogs. I was just about to phone you. You'd better come in."

He turned and went back inside the house.

Pamela Whitwell looked at her team.

"You two, round the back just in case he does a runner. You three, wait here. I'll call if I need you." She followed Pope into the house and found him in the kitchen.

"Tea, officer?"

"Superintendent Whitwell, Mister Pope. Thank you. White without, please. I think you know why we're here."

Waiting for the suspect to 'cough' and keeping a wary eye on the dogs, she sat at the table and pulled out a notebook.

"Simon, please. I imagine it's regarding the prime minister, or the ex-prime minister. I don't know what he is right now."

"Still the prime minister, sir. I understand you have a connection to him…"

Pope had worked through his story and what he would say. The aim was to make it seem unplanned. He laughed as he handed over the mug of tea to his guest.

"Not sure 'connection' is accurate," he said.

He recounted the meeting at the golf club, the game, and the aftermath.

Then he described the surprise evening visit from an old acquaintance, who offered his visitor a lift to the rendezvous point with his family.

"It was only when I saw the news coverage this afternoon that I realised who he was," said Pope. "He looked quite different in real life. Much shorter, in hair and stature. Plus, he had a Welsh accent."

Whitwell finished writing and looked up.

"I'd like to verify a couple of things, if that's okay. Also, would you mind if my officers have a look round your house?"

Pope took a slurp from his mug of tea.

"Not a problem, Superintendent. Just one question. How did you know to come here?"

"You know David Westlake?"

Pope nodded.

"He's one of my lads. Recognised the PM much like you did and got onto me straightaway. Unlike you, Mr. Pope."

"Dave doesn't have dogs, does he?"

Whitwell shook her head.

"Ah," said Pope, trying his best to look enigmatic, "There's your answer."

Not having dogs herself, Whitwell wasn't sure what to make of the comment, so left it for now.

She walked outside, issued her orders and, within seconds, a team in white forensic boiler suits started a methodical sweep of the premises.

Whitwell walked back into the kitchen, sat down and picked up her mug. Pope looked at her over the rim of his own, and asked quietly, "Am I in trouble? Do I need a lawyer?"

Whitwell shrugged.

"You're just helping us with our enquiries. At this stage you don't need a lawyer, but you might need somebody to look after those two."

She nodded towards the hounds of hell, curled up asleep on their beds and totally oblivious to the mayhem just starting around them. "I'll need you at the station for a formal interview."

With quiet satisfaction, the policewoman watched as Pope blanched behind his mug. The thought of being invited to the station made people uncomfortable. That's when they made mistakes.

This man was no different and Whitwell was determined to get to the truth - especially when the reputation of herself and her team was on the line.

Pope, however, had realised there was only one person he could trust with his dogs and who lived close enough to get to them if required.

He couldn't avoid talking to her any longer.

76

Philippa Mills almost swerved off the road when she saw who was calling her.

The shopping bags on the back seat slumped to their right and then steadied themselves as she regained full control of the vehicle. She pressed 'answer' on her steering column.

"Hang on," she said calmly, hiding her surprise. "I'm driving."

Pope hung on silently as she navigated her way onto a suburban side road and parked up underneath a tree outside a nursing home.

She switched off the engine, glanced at the handset, and tried to calm her breathing.

"Back again," she said. "It's been a while."

"Sorry about that. And I haven't time to chat, unfortunately. I need a big favour."

She took her cue from the urgency she sensed in his voice.

"Are you okay?"

"I'm fine, but the police are here."

"Oh crikey. You've not killed anybody, have you?"

As soon as the words came out, she regretted every one of them.

"So, so sorry," she blurted. "Such a poor joke."

"Like I said, the police are here. I may need to give a full statement at the police station."

"What's happened?"

"Can't really say at the moment. Nothing bad, though. Can you watch Fred and Ginger for a little while? Might only be a couple of hours."

"I can do that. When?"

The phone briefly went silent. Pippa heard a muffled voice before her ex resumed the call.

"They need another hour here."

"I can be round in forty minutes. I'll just dump the shopping and grab a bag."

Again, the muffled voice.

"I'll text you when I'm leaving. I'll put a key in the usual place."

Pippa bit her lip to stop herself from telling him she already had one. Then she would need to explain her weekly visits to the dogs while he was at work. Soaking up warm memories of her old life. Now certainly wasn't the time.

"You haven't found another one?"

"Another what?"

"Place. For the key."

"There's been no need. Thanks for doing this, Pip."

"No problem Pop. You take care. If you need anything, like breaking out from the penitentiary, just let me know."

Before she could bite her lip and apologise yet again, he'd hung up.

"ILY," she said automatically, looking at the phone. Old habits died hard, even though it was years since she'd last told Pope she loved him. She started the car, turned around, and headed home. Meghan would be on her way to work. She'd leave a note for her just in case. No sense in risking setting her off again.

77

Morris and a uniformed Westlake walked into outpatients, registered at reception, and made their way to the public cafeteria.

They were early and had time to kill.

Unsure of what would happen at the station, Westlake had taken Morris along.

The old boy could catch up with his mates while he had a chat with the superintendent. Then, if Westlake was late, interrogated, or arrested, Morris could grab a lift to the hospital from someone else.

The chat with Whitwell had gone better than expected.

"You reacted quickly to a rapidly developing situation. You recognised and recovered the prime minister, then helped him to a place of safety. Government officials took him from there. I wouldn't be surprised if you ended up with an MBE," she commented, taking off her glasses and giving them a clean with a handkerchief.

Westlake had shifted uncomfortably in his seat.

"It wasn't quite like that, ma'am."

"When you write your report, it will be. Much better than the alternative."

Westlake understood the implication.

"Look Dave," said his boss, "Hopefully, your account will never see the light of day, but it provides us with leverage if the Met has a pop at us. It shows the government was more complicit than they're letting on. Get it written. Now. I'm going to meet your mate, Pope."

The report had taken an hour to write, then another twenty minutes to edit.

Westlake was pretty sure it fit the bill without implicating Pope as anything other than an innocent, helpful bystander.

Morris had listened to his friend's account all the way to the hospital without comment. After Westlake arrived at the cafeteria table with a tray of teas and biscuits, he finally spoke.

"At this moment, only Whitwell will read that report. It says what Whitwell wants it to say. It doesn't implicate your mate, other than he played a round of golf with a stranger and did him a favour."

Westlake nodded and took a bite of his chocolate biscuit.

"Our lads at Pope's house will wonder where the tip-off came from," he said. "They'll find out."

"How? It's in nobody's interest for this story to get out. They'll turn the house over, maybe bring him in for a chat, satisfy themselves he's not part of a terrorist cell and turn him loose."

"He'll know it was me."

"If he saw the same coverage earlier, he probably expected someone to turn up. Possibly you, but he'll understand when it isn't."

"He could be in serious trouble."

"For what? Harbouring a stupid politician? Imprisoning a guy by giving him the run of his house, letting him shower, drink his beer and feed his dogs? Failing to recognise someone he'd never seen in real life before?"

"Accessory after the fact…"

"What fact? There's been no crime. And he actually opened his door and let us search his place without a warrant just two days ago."

Westlake knew Morris was right, plus he could tell he was agitating his friend. Before he could say anything else, Dr. Meghan Mills burst through the door and walked over to them.

"Mr. Morris. You're early. Good to see you're still alive though, despite the chocolate biscuits."

She glared at Westlake, who checked his watch.

"Come with me please, Stuart. Leave your friend here. We'll check you over, then talk to you about finding other friends who won't try to kill you."

Westlake watched as the woman he'd like to see-if-she-was-so-inclined stormed off with his best friend in her choppy wake. Then he settled back in his chair with biscuits, two cups of tea and a whole load of heartache.

At least I'm in the right place if the heartache gets worse, he thought.

78

It was seven-thirty in the evening before forensics had finished their work. Pope sent a text to Pippa before accepting a lift with the superintendent to the police station. They bypassed the reception area and went directly to the superintendent's office, rather than an interview room.

"No need for that, Mr. Pope," explained Whitwell, pushing her glasses up the bridge of her nose for the third time. "It's not like you're a criminal." She smiled a tight smile.

An officer brought in recording equipment and connected it on the superintendent's desk. Immediately after the door closed, another officer arrived with a note. Whitwell read it carefully, then folded it and put it in her pocket.

"Would you excuse me? I just need to take a quick phone call. I'll order some tea while I'm out."

She left the room, leaving Pope to his own devices. First, he checked his messages and saw that Pippa had arrived at the house. She was delighted to see the dogs but was fuming at the mess the forensics team had left behind. Pope didn't care. He'd overheard the brief conversation between the forensics lead and the superintendent. Both seemed pleased with what they had found, but their findings only amounted to what Pope had left to corroborate his version of events.

He stood up and walked to the other side of the desk to stretch his legs. A tidy desk was a sign of a sick mind, in his opinion. Superintendent Whitwell was obviously very sick. The only thing out of place was a manilla folder, askew on the desktop. Pope flipped open the cover and looked at the report by Constable Westlake on the previous evening's activities.

Three minutes later, a police sergeant entered the office, pushing the door open with his backside and holding a tray. Pope hurriedly helped with the door while the sergeant placed the tray of tea and cakes on the desk. He left without a word. Just a nod and a wink. Staff had apparently been told not to engage with the senior officer's guest.

Pope made himself a cup, grabbed a couple of cakes and sat back down on his chair. There hadn't been time to read the entire report, but the main points were clear even if some of the account was opaque. Time dragged, but only two more minutes passed before the superintendent returned, full of apologies for the delay.

"That was a member of the prime minister's office on the line," she explained. "She was after the officer who aided the PM, but Constable Westlake isn't currently available. She's coming up first thing tomorrow morning to see him. And you."

"Really? Why?"

Whitwell leaned forward and switched on the recorder.

"Interview with Mr. Simon Pope. Led by Superintendent Pamela Whitwell," she said. She made herself a cup of tea and took it, along with a cake, to her side of the desk, quietly pleased to notice the folder was no longer askew.

"Mr. Pope is not under caution and is providing a voluntary statement to assist with our enquiries into the recent disappearance of the prime minister. I have just informed Mr. Pope that a member of the prime minister's office has asked to meet with him tomorrow morning."

Whitwell paused and pushed the second microphone towards her guest.

"Mr. Pope. Why does this representative of the prime minister want to see you?"

Pope stared at the microphone in front of him for a few seconds. He struggled to focus on anything else. He wasn't under caution, but every word he said might be used against him at some stage in the future. He almost asked for a lawyer. Whitwell was expecting it. He knew it.

Then, just like that day all those years ago, a bucket of calm doused the panic and fear he was feeling. He looked up and smiled.

"I expect they want to thank me for looking after their boss, even though I didn't know that's what I was doing," he said.

79

Mindy Abbott hung up on the superintendent, checked through her notes, then called Barnwell at Downing Street.

"Spoke to the local superintendent. The man who delivered the PM to us was PC David Westlake, who had met the PM - calling himself Paul Morgan - at the home of one Simon Pope. Westlake has filed a report on what happened. The superintendent hasn't read it yet but will send me a copy when she has. She's just had forensics around at the house. They found evidence the PM had been there, but there was nothing untoward. Pope's at the station now, helping the police with their enquiries."

"So we have an address?"

"We do. They won't be holding Pope. They doubt he's committed a crime, plus he's been very helpful and is a little bemused by it all. He was just about to call them, having finally recognised who his guest had been from the television coverage. He hadn't called earlier because he'd been out with his dogs and not seen the news."

She explained Pope's employment at Grange Brothers and his presence there at the time of the disappearance. Westlake and a sergeant had searched his home as part of the immediate police response.

They found nothing.

Westlake thought he knew Pope from somewhere, but it took him a while to realise it was from his army days. Only then, he wasn't called Simon Pope.

"Stephen Popp?"

"Yep."

"So, what happened from there?"

"We need the report for detail, but it sounds like Westlake dropped by to see him. Pope told him he only had a few minutes to talk as he was taking a friend home. When our man finally appeared, Westlake recognised him as the PM and offered to take him where he wanted to go. He elected to hand him over at the lay-by when he recognised me. He wasn't sure of the PM's emotional or mental state and so stayed with the PM's story, even after giving him to us."

"And waited until he'd had a sleep, eaten breakfast and gone to work the next day before telling anyone?"

"I don't think he recognised his passenger until he saw the news conference photograph today. But his report drags us into the story much earlier than people are aware. I suspect we're being warned to leave the local police well alone if we're looking for a scapegoat."

"Fair point. Plans?"

"Curtis is on his way. The superintendent is arranging for me to meet Pope and the constable tomorrow morning at Pope's house."

"And the Canafanta link?"

"I'll see how things go."

Barnwell hung up, called Crockett, and gave him most of the story.

"Mindy's meeting should confirm the PM's account and rubber stamp his decision to resign," he told him. "Request two appointments with His Majesty for Tuesday. I'll inform the PM. Then you can get on with running the country."

The future prime minister instructed his PA to contact the Palace, then shared the good news with one of his closest allies.

Over-excited by the position within his reach and grossly over-estimating the power that came with it, he encouraged his friend to 'think the unthinkable' if required in order to stabilise the reputation of his own services.

His full support was guaranteed, if it meant his law and order objectives could be met.

"You need to break eggs to make an omelette, after all."

Sir Michael Stanfield offered his congratulations and best wishes. Then he sent urgent instructions to the deputy director of RaSP and made another call.

80

Stuart Morris walked back into the waiting area carrying several pieces of paper. Dr. Mills showed him through the door, threw what could have been a glare at Westlake, then returned to her lair. Westlake's heart interpreted the glare as a lingering look and fluttered a little.

Both men went to the pharmacy, handed over the prescriptions, and joined the patients in the waiting area.

Morris read through the advice notes, diet sheet, and his copy of the report being sent to his GP. He passed each to his friend once he'd read it, out of politeness more than anything else.

"That's it then," said Westlake. "Happy retirement, you lucky bastard. Hope you have plans for all that time."

"Don't you worry. I'll think of something."

Something, thought Westlake. *Takes more than something to replace decades of long hours in the police force.*

"Pope's at the station, helping with our enquiries," he said.

"Nothing that we didn't expect."

"Whitwell tells me I've got to be at Pope's house just before nine tomorrow morning."

"Because?"

"Amanda Abbott is coming to visit and talk with us both."

"Sounds like fun. Maybe I should come along."

Westlake laughed. "No chance. You've only just retired."

Morris took the papers back and examined them but saw nothing. Retirement made him feel more scared than he had felt in a long time.

He'd walked along one clear path for an age. Now, he discovered himself in a thick fog, alone and unable to see any way forward. Uncertain of what lay ahead, with only memories for company.

He took a sidelong look at his friend and felt jealous. Jealous of the certainty he still had in his life; the camaraderie and experiences he'd share; even the stresses and strains of life in the force. He sat back in his chair with an enormous sigh.

"What am I going to do?" he asked nobody in particular.

"You'll be fine, mate."

"I'm losing a lot of who I am, Dave. What I am. I'm used to looking after you all. Now? The big decisions will be ring doughnuts or jam doughnuts and setting the alarm time."

Westlake took the words on board and tried to put himself in his friend's position. What happened to Stu Morris could happen to any of them, perhaps even more violently and with greater finality.

This job could ruin your life, as his own divorce had shown. It became your reason to get up in the morning. The wins could be big; the losses were traumatic. It was hard to value or recognise anything beyond work. Yet, one day, it would be gone.

If you had the energy, you'd have to start again by reinventing yourself; reintroducing yourself to an alien lifestyle; building new relationships; adopting broader interests; accustoming yourself to a loss of respect and recognition.

Maybe losing your own self-respect.

But how to respond to the despondency his friend was experiencing? How to assure him that everyone would support him, and this feeling would fade? That he'd find his new life to be dynamic, exciting and enjoyable, but without the death, the gore, the threats and the violence? *Small steps, Dave. Small steps.*

"Jam doughnuts and eight-thirty a.m., unless you take up fishing or golf."

Morris resisted the urge to smile, nodding thoughtfully and appearing to consider the suggestion. It knocked him out of his reverie and reminded him he had something else to mention.

"I have some news about your unrequited love interest."

Westlake sat up. "Go on?"

"She left the room for a couple of minutes while I was being rigged up for the ECG. The two nurses chatted as if I wasn't there. All is not as it should be in the Mills household. She was certainly in a bit of a mood. Just thought I'd mention it."

Maybe there was hope after all. He who dares and all that. Westlake looked at the papers in Morris's hand.

"When's your next appointment?" he asked.

81

Pippa Mills sat cross-legged on the soft carpet in the front room, gently stroking the two dogs. A faint sound caught her attention. The distant hum of a car engine approaching, followed by the sharp clunk of a car door closing and the fading rumble as the vehicle drove away.

Her heart quickened as she heard the familiar jingle of keys in the front door lock. The dogs, sensing their owner's imminent arrival, leapt to their feet and dashed towards the entrance, tails wagging with excitement.

Pippa stole a glance at her reflection in the glossy black television screen, fixing her disheveled appearance with a swift brush with her hand. Composing herself, she walked into the hallway, the coolness of the polished wooden floor a slight shock to the soles of her feet.

Pope was hanging his coat on the wall hook. Pippa couldn't help but notice the subtle signs of time's passage on his face. His features appeared more weathered and pallid than she remembered, his unkempt hair in need of a trim.

He didn't look any heavier, the lucky sod, but his presence seemed to carry a weight, a weariness that she hadn't noticed before.

"They didn't keep you in then."

He turned to look at her and managed a tired smile.

All his plans for what to say and how to act when he saw her went out the window. After three hours of gentle and not-so-gentle questioning, plus a half-hour wait for a taxi to get him home, he was delighted to see her.

"That place wasn't big enough to hold me see," he boasted, affecting a poor New York accent. "Even though they tried pretty hard."

She rushed up to him and they hugged like they used to, a warm and comfortable squeeze that neither wanted to break. He hadn't realised how much he had missed it. Missed her. She hadn't realised how badly stressed he was. Until he deployed that crappy accent.

"You can't fool me, big guy," she said with an accent as New York as the Bronx. "You is hurting."

They stood there and hugged, and she held him even tighter when she felt his tears moisten her cheek.

Both cherished the moment and held on to it and each other for as long as possible, knowing how it would end. With two dogs staring at them, whining for a biscuit.

Pope sorted out the dogs and washed his face while Pippa boiled the kettle and made two mugs of tea. She sat at the kitchen table in her usual place and watched as he slumped down in his.

"Thanks for coming round, Pip."

"Any time," she said, holding her mug with both hands. "Can you fill me in?"

"I would love to, believe me."

"Is it serious?"

"Might be. Not sure." He took a slurp of his drink. "There's a meeting here tomorrow morning. Maybe I'll know more after that."

"Is it to do with Afghan?"

He frowned slightly. "No. Why?"

She stood and walked into the lounge, returning with the framed group photograph.

"I came across this tidying up. Hope you don't mind."

He didn't have to see the picture.

"One of those guys looked me up and left it for me. He'll be back for it, but no," he added quickly, seeing the worry wrinkles creeping across her forehead, "This is nothing to do with Afghan."

"So where's the gun?"

He didn't want to swallow at that moment, but he did.

"The box was out on the guest bed," she continued. "I thought they'd found the gun. Taken it as evidence for something."

He shook his head. "It's gone."

She decided not to push, even though having a loaded weapon in a quiet, fairly remote house had always been a comfort to her.

"The police were here because I played golf at the club with a guy called Paul Morgan yesterday afternoon. Coldfront introduced me to him," said Pope, keen to put her mind at some sort of rest.

"To be fair, Coldfront had only just met him as well. Paul's ride didn't show up after the game, so he came back here for a bit and then left."

Pippa locked eyes with him, anticipating a mischievous sparkle that would confirm a joke - albeit a poor one. She waited for quite a while.

"That's it?" she asked.

"That's it."

"So," she summarised, "Police and forensics crawling all over the house. Turning it upside down. Dragging you down to the station. Interviewing you for hours. Because you played golf?"

"Yes."

She stared at him again, waiting for the sparkle. When it didn't appear, she shook her head slowly.

"I always said golf would be your downfall."

He smiled at her, received a smile back, and changed the subject.

"How's the new job? I heard you got a promotion. Deputy CEO? Congratulations."

"That was a year ago but thank you. It's tough but good. Times are tight. Charities are feeling the squeeze, even when kids are involved."

"I'm sorry to hear that," he said, quietly determining to double his monthly anonymous donation to her organisation.

"I can understand people and businesses tightening the purse strings, but the government's doing the same. Our work takes a lot of pressure off public services. If we stop, it'll cost them an awful lot more. They just have their head in the sand."

Pope took another drink from his mug and shook his head.

"Tell me everything," he said, walking to the fridge and returning with two bottles of Monk's Perm. Pippa looked at him curiously, then decided bouncing some ideas around might take his mind off things and even help both of them.

"I'll give you half an hour, then I must go. I've a big meeting in the morning," she said and then risked, "I can always come back if we haven't finished."

Pope reached into the table drawer and pulled out a notepad and pen.

"Sounds good to me," he smiled. "Shoot."

82

The late night, the chat with Pippa and concerns about the morning made it tricky for Pope to sleep and even more difficult to get up.

He dragged himself out of bed just after seven and was making his breakfast, having fed the dogs, when he heard a gentle, barely discernible knock at the front door.

A smiling middle-aged lady dressed in a plaid suit stood outside on the small lawn, holding a large white card and with a large briefcase at her feet.

On the card were four printed words and one written one:

SAY NOTHING.
COME HERE.
Please!

Pope saw a car parked up the lane with its engine running. He walked out onto his front lawn and took the business card proffered by the stranger.

"Hello Mr. Pope," she murmured. "My name is Jenny Barrett. I am a highly experienced security specialist formerly employed by the Foreign & Commonwealth Office. Martin Barnwell, chief-of-staff to the current prime minister - though goodness knows for how much longer - asked me to visit you at this ungodly hour. I'm to carry out a quick bug sweep of your home. You have a meeting with Amanda Abbott at nine and both she and Martin are keen to ensure the conversation just remains between the participants. It shouldn't take me more than half an hour."

"I'm pretty sure the house is clear," said Pope.

"I'm sure you are dear," replied Ms. Barrett soothingly. "But I understand the police and a forensic team were here yesterday evening. Heaven forbid that they planted a device, you being a suspect in a potential kidnapping investigation and all."

Pope thought about the team's unsupervised time in the house, as the superintendent kept him occupied in the kitchen.

"It would be a shame if you declined my help after I've come all the way from London this morning," she added.

"How do I know you won't plant something yourself?" Pope asked.

"Because you'll be with me, dear," she replied. "Half an hour, max, then I'll be on my way. That taxi costs serious money. And no talking."

83

Menzies 'Ming' Murdoch, deputy director of RaSP and known as Ming the Merciless to his minions, looked as if he was about to explode.

Here we go again, thought the driver, catching sight of his boss in the rear-view mirror and rolling his eyes at his colleague in the front passenger seat.

The SUV and the specially adapted van tagging along behind it dawdled along in heavy traffic on the M1 northbound.

"This is bloody overkill, sir," moaned Ming on speakerphone to his boss. "An MI5 support team? There's already three of us, plus the local police. The suspect works in a warehouse, for God's sake. It's ridiculous."

"Home secretary's decision, Ming. Can't do anything about it. But they're your support. It's still your show."

"He should focus on his new job. This'll be a waste of everyone's time, especially if this bloody traffic doesn't clear soon."

Sir Michael Stanfield thought back to the call with Crockett. The future PM had suggested that the only chance of exoneration for RaSP rested on a terrorist link and the Official Secrets Act.

If, god willing, there was a terrorist link, the country's counter-terrorism service had to be involved from the start. Murdoch understood the reason for the backup.

He was just blowing off steam and letting the two armed officers in his vehicle know he had total confidence in them to handle whatever came their way. Even if one of them had actually misplaced the prime minister.

"We might need to delay the meeting. It could finish before we arrive at this rate."

"Not possible. Nobody knows you're coming."

The driver and front passenger held their breath as their boss turned a violent shade of puce.

"Seriously? We're rocking up, locked and loaded and nobody will know why? Or who we are?"

"There was a concern that they may bring the meeting forward. We're not the only ones in this game."

"Russia? Iran? The Israelis?"

"The local constabulary. The PM's office. Even Grange Brothers. Nobody wants responsibility for this shitshow on their CV."

Murdoch counted to twenty before responding. Ten was nowhere near long enough for him to regain a semblance of self-control.

"I'll call you when we're there," he said.

He put down his phone and scowled out of the side window, causing a child in the car next to him to scream loudly and frighten its unprepared parents.

Feeling slightly better, he tapped Freddie Jackson, the former close protection officer for the prime minister, on the shoulder.

"Call those superheroes behind us. Let them know we're not expected and may have some explaining to do."

Jackson followed instructions, but the conversation lasted longer than expected in the SUV.

Once it ended, Murdoch and his men felt the day had worsened considerably, particularly for Simon Pope, who was unaware of the approaching storm and would likely be dead very shortly.

Murdoch slumped back in his seat and closed his eyes. Very senior people in government and the security services had lost their collective mind. The MI5 couple in the minivan were chauffeuring a black ops team from E Squadron. Their mission was to eliminate the target; not to help bring him in.

Whether Pope was a warehouse worker or a terrorist was irrelevant. He'd be the latter by the end of the day, and unable to protest his innocence. The terror-linked inquiry would be too sensitive for the public domain. Case closed.

Every person in that convoy was as miserable as he was. Murdoch needed time to think. As luck would have it, the queue in front of them broke up, and the vehicles increased their speed.

"Oh, dear God," said Ming, his voice drenched in exasperation, "Is anything actually going to go right today?"

84

At the Barnwell residence, Martin and Mavis hunched together on the sofa. Both looked at a brochure with smiling passengers on the cover, holding cocktails on board a cruise ship as it passed a small tropical paradise.

It was the third brochure to be reviewed. Martin was struggling to tell them apart and looked warily at the remaining five. If a task needed doing, Mavis had opined, it had to be done well.

As she had waited several years for this task to come up, she would do it very well indeed.

Martin's attempts to encourage her to decide for both of them had fallen on deaf ears. She didn't want to take all the blame for the final selection.

Fortunately for her husband, the guest bedroom door opened, then the guest bathroom door closed, bringing him some temporary respite.

"I'll sort breakfast today, Mave," he offered. "I'd be happy with the six-week cruise we've just looked at. See if you can find anything better in the others. I'll look at them later."

"But deciding on this together is such fun," Mavis said, giving her beloved an excited, radiant smile, "I'll wait, but I wouldn't mind a coffee."

Martin's smile turned into a grimace as he stood and headed for the kitchen. The attempt had been worthwhile, despite the predictable outcome.

He put the kettle on, then checked the wall clock whilst removing the bacon, eggs, and tomatoes from the fridge. He wondered about the day's events in the Midlands and the stability of their current plan. An insistent buzz interrupted him, and he picked up the intercom extension next to the oven.

"A quick heads up sir," said the RaSP man, currently keeping the porter company in the downstairs reception area. "Our outside team reports a couple of photographers and a television van have arrived. Looks like the cat's out of the bag."

"We've done well to last this long," said Barnwell. "Thanks."

The appearance of the media didn't surprise him. Mindy had made the calls an hour earlier.

Now, the police would implement Operation Sausage and shut half the street, much to the annoyance of his neighbours.

However, it would ensure all eyes were on London. His assistant could get what she needed from Pope in peace.

Half an hour later and after filling the dishwasher, the prime minister was in the lounge with his chief-of-staff.

Mavis opted for the kitchen.

She tuned the radio into a heavy metal station, rearranged the items in the dishwasher, then settled down with her laptop to read the morning's news. Most of the websites featured her own home.

"Do you want me to leave?" the PM asked, peaking from behind a net curtain at the chaos being transformed into order on the street below.

"My home, the government or politics?"

"Your home."

"Tomorrow, you'll visit the Palace and then return to Downing Street for farewells and a media statement. Crockett is happy for you to have your moment at Number 10 after you've met the King. It's an unconventional but fitting conclusion to the last few days. He'll leave for the Palace from the Party head office. Once the new PM returns to Downing Street, you'll be back home, consigned to history."

Both men knew that wouldn't be the case, but it felt the right thing to say.

"Where is Mindy anyway? Helping Crockett to tie his shoelaces?"

"She's tying up some loose ends in the Midlands. Should be back around lunchtime."

The PM tried not to look shocked but failed miserably.

"What loose ends?"

Barnwell had planned his words but reconsidered.

"Mindy tracked down the police officer, who gave you a lift the other night. She's meeting him at Pope's house this morning. We want to corroborate your account of events."

"I didn't want either of them dragged into this."

"We know. You also told Mindy that Pope had a previous life and had changed his name from Stephen Popp."

"He's a hero."

"He was. Undoubtedly. Now, he could also be a terrorist or have links to terrorism."

Barnwell explained the potential link to Esteban Canafanta.

He marvelled at the speed with which the human complexion could change colour under stress.

He also wondered how far the PM's jaw could drop before reaching its limit.

"He showed me humanity and compassion."

"At any stage, he could have called 999, and got you the help you so obviously needed."

"He didn't want to be implicated in my disappearance."

"He could have asked you to leave and turn yourself in. Would have saved the country hundreds of millions of pounds."

"He showed me friendship. We walked his dogs!"

"Canafanta asked his group of fellow dickheads what they would do if they had you. He wanted ideas. Wasn't sure what to do. Played for time while he decided. Then he disappeared off the site. Scrubbed all his history. Are those the actions of someone who genuinely wants to do right by you?"

"Oh, come on Martin. We played golf together! No threats. Didn't shoot me…"

The gulp after he said it told Barnwell all he needed to know.

"Pope has a gun?"

The PM waved his arms in front of him, as if fighting through cobwebs.

"I found it at the back of a wardrobe in a box full of various items. He probably doesn't even remember it's there."

But Barnwell was no longer listening - focused instead on his phone and getting through to his assistant or her driver. Neither answered.

"That's the problem with that area. Dodgy phone signal. Try texting," said the PM helpfully, but not looking or feeling very helpful. Barnwell's look confirmed the suggestion's value. The PM watched the man he regarded as a good friend, as well as the ultimate consigliere.

"How long have we known each other, Mart? Must be about ten years."

"Eight years, ten months," replied Barnwell, his eyes not shifting from the text he was preparing to send.

"About ten years," mused the prime minister. "We really must work on our communication."

85

Dave Westlake walked into the police station locker room to change into his work attire and found a note wedged in his locker door.

Whitwell ASAP.

He changed quickly and hurried to Whitwell's office.

The superintendent was watching a short video compilation on her computer, created overnight by some bright spark in IT.

"From the golf club CCTV," she said, stepping aside so Westlake could get a better view. "It corroborates Pope's statement and that of Mister David Davies. He's the big lad squeezing out of the car."

Westlake watched as the prime minister walked into view carrying his golf bag, approached Davies and engaged him in conversation. He saw both men walk towards the putting green and interact with Pope, who was already practicing, before all three proceeded to the first tee. Almost two hours later, according to the video timer, Davies walked past police vehicles and officers on his way to the practice range.

"He left the game after nine holes to practice a new swing," said Whitwell, "The other two cut their game short a while later, as you can see."

Both men walked into shot and headed across an almost-deserted car park to Pope's car, before saying their goodbyes. The PM headed off towards the course entrance while Pope went into the changing rooms. Eight minutes later, according to the video timer, Pope emerged from the clubhouse, got into his car and drove off, just as Davies came back from the range.

"We were there, and he walked right past us," mused Whitwell.

"Easily done, believe me," said Westlake, "I gave him a lift. And I'm supposed to be a recognition expert."

"Your report says you recognised him just before offering the lift. Unsure of the circumstances or his mental condition, you extracted him safely from the house and took him where he wanted to go. You left him when you recognised Amanda Abbott waiting for him in the lay-by. Stick with that. The report delay was an administrative oversight."

Westlake left the office, promising to report the meeting as soon as it was over. He picked up his holdall, signed out his equipment, and headed out to the patrol car.

86

Barnwell's text message finally made its way through to Mindy's phone just as she and Curtis were five minutes away from Pope's house.

"We're early anyway," said the driver. "Want to stop?"

"No. We only want to hear his story. We're no threat. The police searched his house just last night. Jenny Barrett's been there this morning. Besides, I want a few minutes with him before Dave Westlake arrives."

"The spare's in the glove compartment."

"No."

"Do it."

Being told what to do was Amanda Abbott's pet peeve. But she knew Curtis was right, despite him losing bedroom privileges as a result, at least for the next week. She took the box out of the glove compartment, removed the handgun and one of the extra magazines and stowed them in her handbag. If all went well, Pope need never know they were there.

"I'll search him and the downstairs," said Curtis. "If he decides that he's going upstairs, you prepare for his return."

Mindy nodded. Two minutes later, Curtis turned into Pope's lane and parked outside the last house on the right. The front door opened just as they arrived.

"Mister Pope?" asked Curtis.

"Yes?"

"I'm Curtis, sir, from the prime minister's office. I'm afraid I have to search you, sir, and have a quick look around your house before Ms. Abbott can enter."

"Then Ms. Abbott can stay out there," said Pope. "I'm fed up with people searching my house. You'd be the third in the last fourteen hours and…"

"Quite right, Mister Pope," interrupted Mindy, smiling at their host as she pushed past her current - possibly former - lover, "Mind if I come in?"

Pope shook her offered hand, then stood to the side as she sailed past and walked into the kitchen, pausing only to greet the two dogs on their eternal quest for treats.

"It's been quite a journey, Mister Pope. How can a girl get a drink here?"

"Ask."

"Then how about something cold and fruity? Maybe a cana… orangeade?"

The mind's ability to process new data quickly had always fascinated Simon Pope. Unfortunately, that still left time for his eyes to widen before he shook his head.

"I used to be a big fan, but it was very gassy. Made me full of wind so I gave up on it. I have tea, coffee, water or beer."

Message received and understood, as was the response, thought Mindy.

"A beer sounds splendid."

Curtis shook his head when Pope gave him an enquiring look.

He wandered into the hallway, then the lounge, while Mindy sat at the kitchen table and Pope headed for the fridge.

"Sounds like you've had a busy couple of days… it's Simon, isn't it?"

"It is. And I have."

"First, thank you very much for showing your guest such kindness and consideration. I had a good talk with the prime minister. I wanted to share what he told me." She produced a stapled document.

"After you've read this, I'd like to discuss both your and Constable Westlake's recollections to ensure I have the complete story."

"I don't want any publicity…"

"Neither do we, but that'll be a tough ask. It's a big story, but we can minimise it if we all collaborate."

Pope handed over an open bottle of Monk's Perm and sat down, pulling the document towards him.

Mindy sat quietly and watched his facial expression as he read, noticing the faint scars on his cheek and the more vivid one on his neck for the first time as she did so.

From her position at the table, she saw Curtis walk quietly out of the lounge and towards the stairs.

"Just using your bathroom. Hope you don't mind," he said.

Pope threw Mindy a knowing look.

"Help yourself," he said, then returned to the PM's account.

Mindy stood up and wandered over to fuss Fred and Ginger, who had retired, disappointed, to their beds. She loved dogs, particularly the unconditional love they gave if you treated them right. That kind of made their love conditional, but she was happy to overlook this. There was nothing unconditional in her life. Hadn't been for a long time. There was always a deal to make. Maybe it was time that changed.

"Treats in the pot by the toaster," said Pope, pen in hand, eyes on the document. Mindy made a great fuss of removing the treats - partly to attract the dogs, partly to hide the footsteps on the floor above.

"What's he looking for?" asked Pope, still reading.

"A handgun."

"He's wasting his time."

"Do you have one?"

"I had one given to me several years ago, for my protection."

"I've read the reports." If Pope was minimising the event, so would she. "Do you still have it?"

Pope hid his surprise that the reports were so easily accessible, but the one doing the accessing was the prime minister, so maybe it wasn't such a big deal.

"Not at the moment," he said. "I'd be happy if I never saw it again, but... you never know."

You never do, she thought. Ensuring his story remained secret was probably one of the biggest challenges she faced. Pope's life could change if the story became public knowledge, possibly for the better, but as he said, you never know. Maybe he would need protection at some stage.

"Ignore this if you like," she said, her curiosity getting the better of her. "How is your faith? After all that happened... I just wondered."

Pope read the last page silently before returning the document to her.

"There are some questionable parts in there," he said, "But overall I'm comfortable with it."

87

Westlake turned into the lane and pulled up behind the car parked outside the end house. He grabbed the folder on the front passenger seat, then heaved himself out onto the small pavement.

Cigarette smoke curled up from behind the hedgerow that masked the boundary fence. The smoker stood up to identify the new arrival. It surprised neither man that they recognised the other.

"Small world," smiled Curtis, taking a break after his fruitless search for a weapon.

"Getting smaller by the day," replied Westlake, shaking Curtis's hand slightly longer than the norm.

"My name's Curtis. I brought Amanda Abbott here to meet with Mr. Pope and your good self."

"Then you know my name already."

"Is it Dave or Constable Westlake? I'm not sure if you're on actual duty."

"I am, but Dave's fine."

Curtis decided not to mention the handgun at the police officer's side. If he'd requested its removal and safe storage in the police car, he was pretty sure what kind of response he'd get.

Besides, as he had a gun concealed beneath his jacket, with another weapon hidden in Mindy's bag, such a suggestion would have been hypocritical.

"Sorry about the other night."

"Not a problem. Strange times. Just pleased everything turned out okay."

Curtis nodded and stubbed out his cigarette.

"Come on in."

Pope and Mindy were side by side on the sofa when Westlake and Curtis entered. Mindy stood up and introduced herself to the constable, leaving the framed photograph she'd been looking at on the arm of the sofa. She noticed him glance down at it.

"That was some day, wasn't it?" she said, with outrageous understatement. "I read the War Diaries yesterday."

Westlake remembered submitting his own account of the action. He hadn't given it a moment's thought since doing so, believing someone would bury the entire event forever. The existence of his report among others was surprising, but not worth dwelling on.

Pope hadn't moved off the sofa and looked troubled. He felt out of control in his own home. Too many people, talking about things he didn't want to discuss. His brief chat with Mindy over the picture had filled the awkward silence whilst waiting for Westlake's arrival but had been a reluctant one. Her reading had left her with a more detailed understanding of the day than he wanted or could recall.

Sensing the consternation, Westlake surmised it related to the previous day's police action. He sat down next to the man he considered a friend, even though the feeling wasn't mutual.

"I'm sorry about yesterday Simmo," he began.

"What?"

"Yesterday. You understand why I had to…"

"You were just doing your job. The moment I saw Paul's photo on the news and recognised him, I knew it would happen."

Mindy gave Westlake the copy of the prime minister's statement. In return, Westlake issued copies of the police statements from Pope and himself, together with the statement of Coldfront Davies.

"I also have a video compilation from the golf club's CCTV records. This corroborates the statements of both Simon and Mr. Davies," he announced, producing a USB stick.

Mindy plugged the stick into her laptop, and everyone crowded round to view the footage.

Pope felt a sense of relief as third-party visual evidence of the statement he had given to the police played out before him.

Thank God the club's system had been working properly for once. It was perfect.

The timely arrival of Coldfront and the occasional appearance of police officers also showed how difficult it was to recognise the PM in real life.

Pope smirked occasionally while reading Westlake's account, especially when reading the superintendent's additions.

Ten minutes later, Mindy completed the few amendments needed for the prime minister's account of events to corroborate the others.

"It's watertight," she told Barnwell in a brief call from the back garden. "I've added their electronic signatures and am sending it over to you now. Get the PM to sign it and we're done."

"He's not happy that you're back up there. This should calm him down."

"We're just finishing. I'll come straight to yours and we'll sort out his speech for tomorrow."

Mindy rang off, threw the remaining treats onto the grass for the dogs, and walked in to help Pope make drinks.

She observed the former pastor lining up mugs and cups. Clearly, he wasn't used to entertaining. He stepped back and surveyed the crockery, massaging his neck as he tried to remember what each guest wanted.

"The scar on your neck?" she asked. He nodded, but kept his eyes focused on the kitchen top.

He wasn't happy, she observed, although that could be down to her topic of conversation. Still, now that she was there…

"The war diaries reckon you barely wasted any ammunition," she said.

"The fog of war does strange things to people's memories. I remember clawing at the earth, crying like a baby, desperate for shelter. One of my protection detail died beside me. I picked up his gun and started firing. Random shots at shapes behind the flashes in the smoke and the dust. I doubt any of that made the records."

Mindy knew it hadn't. "You know," she said, "What you do. How you act. They're vital to who you are; what you become. But they're not the full story, because it's how others perceive those actions that will dictate how you're viewed and remembered. How you choose to deal with that. How it affects your self-regard, your self-belief. That's what defines you. Your weekend guest is a prime example."

Pope considered her words and nodded. Mindy tried again.

"Where did you learn to shoot?"

"I spent ten weeks with the regiment before being posted," he replied. "I wanted to know the lads, so I joined them everywhere, on manoeuvres, even at the ranges."

"And that was your only experience?"

Pope placed a tea bag in each cup and coffee in the mugs.

"I had an air rifle as a kid. I had a good eye."

"What did you shoot?"

Pope smiled at the memory. "Cans off walls mostly. Corks out of wine bottles. Acorns out of oak trees."

Mindy nodded appreciatively. Not too different from her childhood then.

"Takes some doing, but in the heat of a battle… wounded… scared?"

Pope held the sugar bowl in mid-air as he turned to look at her. Finally.

"I was very lucky," he said.

She held his gaze.

"Perhaps you were," she said. "And perhaps you weren't."

She smiled and walked to the fridge, then handed him the milk.

"Maybe you weren't on your own in that hell," she murmured, gently touching his arm before walking past him to join the others in the lounge.

88

Police sergeant Angus Grace had spent most of the night sorting out what he hated with a passion, a domestic incident.

As per the norm, it had started with a 999 call from the spouse. Unusually, the husband was the caller. Returning early from a night out, his wife had attacked him for disturbing her television viewing.

The issue had simmered for a couple of hours before the call. The original officer attending had successfully reunited the couple. They both turned on him. Wonderful for the marriage. Not so good for the officer, who was in hospital with a suspected broken arm after being hit by a walking frame.

The husband and wife, both in their seventies and in supported living, were now in custody.

On his way back to the station, Grace dealt with a road traffic accident assigned by control. It took two and a half hours to resolve.

Tired, hungry and rather bad tempered, he found himself stuck in a queue of vehicles at temporary traffic lights.

As the line of traffic crawled forward, the lights ahead changed to red and the vehicles ahead of him came to a halt.

At least, most of them did.

A top-of-the-range SUV and a van pulled out and raced through the red light to join the line already travelling through the roadworks.

Wankers, thought Sergeant Grace, as he switched on his blue lights, turned on the siren, left the queue and followed them through.

Once in the roadworks, he signalled to the drivers ahead to pull over.

To his disappointment, they both complied and pulled over between the bollards onto some hard ground.

Grace parked to the right of both vehicles, between them and the road, and radioed in their registration numbers.

He got out of the car and walked towards the SUV driver's window. As he did so, a tall, thin man in a grey suit emerged from the rear door, fumbling for ID.

"Apologies officer," said the grey suit. "We need to get to Sidwell. ASAP. It's a national emergency." He finally found his photo identity card in his wallet and handed it over.

Grace took a quick look with tired eyes and took nothing in.

"Back in your vehicle, please, sir. I need a chat with your driver."

He walked past the grey suit towards the car, when he felt a hand pull on his shoulder, spinning him around. Instinctively, his right hand slipped towards the Taser holster.

Taking two steps backwards, he pulled the gun clear and pointed it at the man with the rapidly reddening face. As he did so, the doors on the driver's side of the van opened, revealing an assault rifle and a handgun pointed at him.

"Drop your weapon!" shouted someone in the minivan.

Sergeant Grace had not survived twelve years in the police without learning some extremely important life skills. He dropped the Taser and stepped back with his hands in the air.

Murdoch held out his hand for his identity card.

"Very sorry about that," he said. "They're MI5 in case you want to put in a complaint. We're from the Met and none of my men assaulted or threatened you."

"You assaulted a police officer."

"Let's just say your shoulder hit my hand. How long will it take us to get to Sidwell?"

"Why do you want to go there?"

"How long?"

"Twenty minutes."

The deputy director retrieved his ID card, then flashed a big smile at the sergeant.

"We have blue lights," he said. "Let's go for fifteen."

Sixty seconds later, the sergeant was back in his car with Murdoch beside him and the SUV and the van immediately behind. The police radio squawked into life and Murdoch nodded to signify he could answer.

"Tell them you've had your car commandeered by the security services and we're going to Sidwell," he instructed.

By the end of the brief conversation, Angus Grace knew the people in his convoy were legit.

Superintendent Whitwell knew what was happening, and how long she had to protect her force.

And Menzies 'Ming' Murdoch had done his best to protect the life of an innocent man and to bring a semblance of sanity to the day's proceedings.

89

Dave Westlake left the house when the radio call came through from the station. Reception was much better in the front garden. It wasn't long before he was back.

"Someone has hijacked a police sergeant at gunpoint. He's being forced to escort two vehicles here," he said, his reddening face betraying the calmness in his voice. "The vehicles contain armed men from the Met, MI5 and special forces. Help is on its way, but we're on our own for a while. My orders are to deny them access to Simmo."

While the three men worked on the group's options, Mindy updated Barnwell on events. He was as calm as she had ever heard him, but as blazingly angry as she had ever known him, both at the same time.

"I have to make a call," he said. "The PM added his signature to the paperwork you sent through. I'll send a completed copy back to you in case it might help. On absolutely no account, put yourself at risk."

He wanted to say more, but time was of the essence.

Avoiding the concerned stare of the prime minister sat across from him, Barnwell called Crockett to bring him up to speed with events in the Midlands and to urge him to cancel the mission.

Crockett's lack of shock told Barnwell everything.

It firmed up his plans for his own future and reinforced his determination to take down whoever needed taking down on the way, including this idiot if necessary.

"This is the only way to protect the Met, regain some credibility for RaSP and to bring things to a satisfactory conclusion." Crockett sounded as if he was reasoning patiently with a small child, even if the discussion was about the potential death of an innocent man.

Listening in to the planned demise of his new friend, the prime minister couldn't help himself.

"This is an outrage," he thundered. "You'll be the prime minister, not God. Call this off now, Damien. Otherwise I'll withdraw my resignation. You'll be a busted flush before you've even started."

"Oh, have a word with yourself," snapped Crockett. "Will anybody listen to you? You've lost all credibility in the party and in the country already. You're an embarrassment. A grubby footnote in the more unsavoury pages of our nation's history."

The prime minister looked like an angry, gently deflating balloon.

"Enough," said Barnwell, then fell silent. So did the others. They had crossed several lines in just a few seconds. Eventually, he spoke again.

"Damien, we've talked over the last couple of days about what you could do in this role. Do you really want your first act in office to be sanctioning the execution of an innocent British citizen?"

"Not just innocent," interjected the prime minister. "A man who helped to save my life. A war hero."

"Remember, we have signed affidavits from witnesses and CCTV evidence that account for Simon Pope's involvement. None of them suggest any illegal action on his part."

Crockett gave himself a few seconds, so it looked as if he was listening respectfully to the points being made.

"Look at the bigger picture. If I am to stand on a platform of law and order, the public need to have respect for the offices responsible for underpinning that platform. This issue could severely damage the credibility of those offices and hole my plans even before I can float them."

The prime minister was about to interject, but Barnwell raised his hand.

"Damien," he said. "This will get out. There are too many people involved already. It will be a massive scandal. Bring down the government. You'll end up behind bars. You're building a legacy on foundations of straw. The whole thing will come crashing down. Your reputation will be in tatters and irrecoverable."

"Marty. This is my chance. Might be my first and last opportunity." Crockett caught his breath and reflected on a ruined reputation and the chances of a former police commissioner surviving prison.

The PM couldn't help himself.

"Then don't start with the blood of an innocent man on your hands. God knows, there'll be plenty of that before you've finished. And don't throw your big opportunity away just because I walked out of a warehouse."

The words gave Crockett even more pause for thought.

"Look," he said, "I don't want last weekend to destroy anybody or anything. Give me a workable solution that protects the services and I'll call them off. Now, I have to go."

Barnwell ended the call as quickly as Crockett and updated Mindy.

90

Mindy hung up after listening to Barnwell and stared at her reflection in the window of the kitchen door.

How had she ended up here, in the back garden of a terrace house, in the middle of a bad dream that was developing rapidly into a nightmare?

The air felt thick with uncertainty, and the sound of rustling leaves added to her growing unease. Had it all been worth it?

For the first time in ages, she felt sorry for herself, then shook off the self-pity. It wasn't her life at risk, after all. Whatever she faced was nowhere near as challenging as the problems facing Simon Pope.

She ran through the house, into the lounge and stared at three faces showing varying levels of concern.

She pointed at Westlake but addressed the group.

"What he said, but with secret top level backing. And the outcome looks bad for Simon."

Westlake broke the stunned silence.

"Options. We can get away in the two cars," he said. "I could arrest Simon for suspected kidnapping and take him to the station."

"We could take him back down to London," offered Curtis.

"News conference with the prime minister, explaining his involvement. They couldn't touch him after that, surely?"

They all looked at Pope, who shook his head.

"Running away makes it look as if I've done something illegal, but I've done nothing wrong," he said. "Whatever escape option we choose just prolongs the endgame. Also, it increases the number of people who know about me. I don't want that. They could still have a crack at me further down the line. And the publicity means someone else might. Plus, I have the dogs to think about."

"Then our only option is to stay here and keep them out until help arrives," said Westlake. "That won't be too long."

"I won't have anybody putting themselves at risk for me." There was a vehemence in Pope's voice as he struggled with his emotions. "I have enough deaths on my conscience already. I don't want more."

The comment about risk was laudable, but it sparked like a Roman candle in Mindy's head.

"I need to make a call," she said. "Work out how we play for time."

Struggling to come to terms with a situation out of his own control, Pope simply picked up the cups and mugs and washed them in the kitchen sink.

Westlake and Curtis agreed a plan and disappeared out of the front door, having determined to block the top of the lane with their vehicles.

Pope finished washing up and turned to find both dogs looking at him expectantly.

"You've not had your walk, have you?" he asked, already knowing the answer even if they didn't provide it. Finally, he had a decision to make. God knows he needed the break and removing himself from the scene may buy some time and keep the others out of harm's way if he wasn't there to protect.

He checked Mindy was on the phone in the garden, then put the leads on both dogs and left through the open front door.

By the time Curtis and Westlake returned, weighed down with weapons and body armour, Pope and the dogs were nowhere to be seen.

Mindy was still on the phone to Barnwell, talking slowly. His arthritis hindered his already weak note-taking abilities.

"So," he said after a silence whose length severely tested Mindy's patience, "The statements and video negate the need for a public inquiry. We've established the facts - why it happened; how it happened; who was accountable. We're not sure what lessons we can learn to prevent a reoccurrence, unless we test the sanity of the sitting prime minister every day. There's no civil or criminal liability to be established. Therefore, the inquiry doesn't need to be public and expensive. The security services and the relevant government departments can run an internal inquiry, with a final report published in due course."

"Yep. We'll curtail media coverage by issuing defence advisory notices. These will reference special forces operations and personnel working in sensitive positions. They're usually respected by the media. Editors will want to curry favour with a new prime minister, anyway. We could also apply for a court injunction on the grounds of national security and endangering life. We don't want to put innocent people at unnecessary risk. The last bit was Pope's idea."

"Leave it with me."

Barnwell called Crockett. The future PM had been mulling over their previous discussion and recognising the wisdom in Barnwell's viewpoint.

"I can buy that," he said, wishing he could keep this man and conscious that every time they talked, he pushed him even further away.

"It was all Mindy's idea," replied Barnwell, to whom the thought of retirement, or at least a change of career, grew more attractive by the minute.

Crockett called Sir Michael Stanfield with instructions to call off the operation. The Met head passed those orders on to his deputy director of RaSP. Or rather, he would have done, were it not for the lack of signal. Instead, he left a voicemail, then asked his secretary to keep calling to ensure Ming received the message.

To cover his bases, Sir Michael called his opposite number at MI5, but found out he was attending a team bonding event in the New Forest. Since nobody else had needed to know about the operation, nobody else knew anything about it.

The Ministry of Defence denied all knowledge of any UK operation involving members of E Squadron because that's what they do, whoever is on the line.

A last throw of the dice resulted in a call to West Cumberton police station. The receptionist explained that the superintendent wasn't available. She had just rushed out of the building with some heavily armed officers.

Sir Michael put the phone down. He felt as if he were on top of a mountain, watching the boulder he had pushed, gathering destructive momentum despite his desperate efforts to stop it.

91

Pope stepped over the sturdy wooden stile, the rough texture grazing his palm, and followed his two dogs into the field.

He couldn't help but feel a twinge of melancholy. It could be his last opportunity to enjoy this simple pleasure, at least for a while.

As he absorbed the scenery, his eyes darted around, trying to capture every minute detail, every fleeting moment.

The dogs ran wild for a minute, then, remembering their noble greyhound lineage, slowed down gracefully, gliding across the grass, noses gently sniffing the scents of the world.

He wandered to the edge of the woods and easily located the trees where he'd buried the phone and the gun. He briefly considered digging them up, in case they might be useful at home. Instead, he elected to sit down with his back against another tree, take several deep breaths and contemplate the current situation.

Mindy's words echoed in his head. Maybe God was with him that day. He had saved lives by being willing to give his.

A bit like Jesus.

He experienced sheer terror, then horror, when the smoke and dust settled and the noise of war abated, leaving images that were carved into his memory.

There had been no elation. Not even relief. Just numbness.

Then the aftermath. The nightmares. The fights in the pub. The depression and the effect on his relationships.

His actions had created potentially massive issues for others as well as himself. He knew that.

There was no way he could have stayed.

He could understand - and now maybe he could accept - the church's decision to release him, but that had been the decision of men and women, not God.

The weight on his shoulders lifted slightly at the thought.

He'd felt abandoned, lost, spiritually alone, and hadn't had the courage to lift his head and look around him.

It was simpler just to look downwards; easier to lose some of his faith rather than fight to retain all of it.

And if he'd looked up at the Father, prepared to argue his case, maybe he'd have seen a nod of understanding. "I know, son. Life can be a bitch. Just ask my lad."

Lifting his head, he felt more alive to the sights and sounds around him. Even the dogs had wandered back and had settled on the grass beside him. White clouds scudded over the distant woods. Wind rustled through the leaves of the trees nearby.

He thought of his life. Of Pippa. All the good things he had never really appreciated, blinded by drink, guilt and his resentment.

Now, he recognised them; weighed their genuine value. But now may be too late. Usually, that thought would bring Pope down, but not today.

Today, he felt a fresh resolve, eager to make amends, take on new challenges and leave the past behind. He wanted to hold onto this feeling, this new life.

However, to achieve that, he had to confront the current realities, as he had seven years ago, but peacefully this time. No weapons.

He reached over and hugged Ginger and Fred, then set off down the field.

Both hounds immediately followed him, one on each side.

He'd looked the devil in the eyes, the RSM had told him.

Now, he was staring God in the face and was not afraid of what he saw.

It was time for his second day of reckoning.

92

In the house and at the end of the road, two groups experienced similar consternation, but for different reasons. Angus Grace recognised the police vehicle helping to block the entrance to the lane. Dave Westlake must have been nearby to arrive so fast. The other vehicle he didn't recognise, but Murdoch recognised the plates as a government car.

"What's down the lane?" Murdoch asked.

"Field behind left side hedgerow. Twelve houses on the right. After the houses, the lane runs between farmland and woods to another small settlement, then joins a larger B road that links to a small town."

"Define a larger B road?"

"One with no grass growing down the middle."

Murdoch shook his head, struggling to comprehend, then stepped out of the car to strategise with the MI5 lead. Once alone, Grace reduced the volume on his radio and then called the station to report his location and current status.

"Dave Westlake is in the end house, Angus. He's being interviewed by a member of the government about the recovery of the prime minister. Delay the people with you if possible. We're on our way. Whitwell's bringing the heavy mob. ETA twelve minutes."

With so many guns around, it was tempting to drive off, thought Grace. But that wouldn't be of much use to Dave Westlake.

It would also deny himself the opportunity of smacking the snobby twat in the suit. He wrapped his front teeth in his handkerchief and put the bundle in his pocket.

Now he was ready for whatever came his way.

Back in the house, a swift search for Pope and the dogs revealed nothing. Westlake and Curtis assumed they were in the back garden with Mindy, while she had imagined they were all in the house.

"He wasn't happy, was he? And this kind of takes the pressure off a bit, doesn't it?" said Curtis. "Now we have nobody to protect, so there's less chance of one of us taking a bullet meant for him. All we do is delay until the cavalry arrives."

"Let's hope it's that simple," said Westlake, just as a text message appeared on his mobile. "The bad guys have arrived. Eight of them. Armed. Angus Grace is with them, under duress. He'll be so angry."

"We stick with the plan then?"

"We stick with the plan."

With his handgun in its holster, Westlake made his way across the low side walls, marking the boundaries of three neighbouring front gardens.

He reached a large privet hedge that gave him a view almost all the way up the lane whilst remaining under perfect cover. Angus Grace led a group of three men in suits slowly down the middle of the lane. Five others, wearing body armour and carrying light weapons, hugged each side of the lane, utilising any cover available.

Westlake waited until they were forty yards from their starting point, then used his key fob to unlock the doors of his vehicle.

He saw the lights flash and the group's reaction but couldn't hear the clunk. Most of the group stopped, turned, and looked around, confused about what had happened and its implications.

Three others stayed in cover and remained focused on their front, wary of any ambush or escape launched by the distraction.

Now we know who and where the members of E-Squadron are, thought Westlake.

The man at the rear of the group walked back to the vehicles, covered by two others, and gingerly opened the driver's door on Westlake's car.

He couldn't move the vehicle out of park and was just getting out when Westlake pressed the fob again.

The car emitted a loud alarm noise because of the open door. The surprised agent stood up quickly, banged his head on the top of the doorframe and discharged his handgun, blowing out the front passenger window.

One suit spoke to another, who trotted back up the lane to help. Westlake amused himself by continuing to press the key fob and creating additional confusion.

Eventually, the group restored order and reassembled. Westlake waited until they tentatively reached the first of the terraced houses and then made his way back to Pope's house.

He sat down on a bistro chair next to a small wrought-iron table on the front lawn, just in front of the closed front door.

Adrenaline pumping, he checked his gun by his side, then took a couple of sips of water from his mug.

93

Pope heard the car alarm at the top of the road, but it was the gunshot that caused him to stop and take shelter with the two dogs in the woods alongside the lane. The sharp crack sent a tremor through his body, causing him to lose focus for a moment, but the lack of any follow up gunfire calmed him down. Taking a deep breath, he stepped out and peered cautiously to check on the situation.

Everything appeared still, devoid of signs of life or death. Correctly thinking that everybody's focus was on events further up the lane, he walked down the side of the house to his garage. Using his remote control, he opened the garage door and ushered his dogs inside.

Once the main door locked again, he took out his mobile phone and, from memory, called the number the prime minister had texted to him. He was actually relieved when the call went straight to voicemail, and he heard the personalised message. He didn't have time to talk.

"Hi. Hope you're doing okay. There's a lot happening near the house at the moment. The weekend was… memorable. Whatever happens now is not your fault. I've realised that about my time in Afghan. Don't take as long as I have to come to the same conclusion. Look after yourself."

Then he sent a text message to Pippa.

Can't talk. Pls take care of dogs if I don't contact you in next three hours. ILY. X

Taking deep breaths, he crept out of the garage and into the garden, where he left the dogs with the rest of the treats. Entering the empty kitchen, he closed the doors at each end before, as quietly as humanly possible, putting on the kettle.

94

Sat behind the small iron table, Westlake glimpsed three men positioning themselves across the road, away from the front hedge. Seconds later, Angus Grace walked through the front gate, followed by the three suits.

The two MI5 men didn't follow, but stopped just outside the gate as if they were unwilling interlopers, fervently wishing they were somewhere else.

"That's far enough, Angus. What's going on?"

Angus Grace stopped and said nothing, but smiled, revealing an enormous gap in his teeth. It was his trademark move before somebody, often more than one, was about to be hurt.

Westlake's face gave nothing away as he turned his attention to the tall man on Grace's right.

"Officer. My name is Menzies Murdoch. I'm the deputy director of the Royalty and Special Protection unit in the Met. These are two of my associates. The gentlemen accompanying us are from the counter-terrorism unit, supported by members of the special forces. I'm here to talk to Mr. Pope."

"Mr. Pope is talking to Amanda Abbott from Number 10 about his role in the safe return of our prime minister, sir. Ms. Abbott has instructed that nobody disturbs them."

"I'm afraid that won't be possible, constable."

"Both Ms. Abbott and I believe it will be, sir."

For a person of his status in RaSP with all the backup currently at his disposal, Murdoch looked decidedly uncomfortable. Unhappy, even.

Raising his voice slightly to ensure everyone at the scene could hear, Westlake decided it was time to play what he hoped would be his trump card.

"I need to tell you, Mr. Murdoch, that Mr. Pope is not who you think he is."

Murdoch's eyes narrowed and his head titled slightly backwards.

"Go on," he said.

"The special forces know him well. Anyone who served over the last several years will know his story."

Murdoch didn't say a word. He wasn't the target audience and he knew it.

"In a previous life, Simon Pope's name was Stephen Popp," continued Westlake. "Changing it protected his safety once he returned to the UK seven years ago, when the army discharged him following an incident in Afghanistan."

Westlake remained determinedly silent, waiting for a response. Eventually, it came from a disembodied voice beyond the hedge.

"The padre?"

"The padre."

"Prove it."

Westlake picked up the framed photograph resting against his chair. He offered the photograph to Grace, who took it and returned to the gate to hand it to someone from E Squadron.

"They took this that morning. You may recognise some lads on it. On the right side of the picture, the padre is looking at the group."

The soldier and another who joined him examined the print. He pointed at two smiling faces from all those years ago.

"Where did you get this?" the other man asked.

"It's mine."

The soldier holding the print looked hard at Westlake as the police officer removed his cap. He studied the photograph and pointed at the tall man crouching uncomfortably in the front row.

Concealed behind the net curtain over the bedroom window, Mindy Abbott held her breath as the group at the gate talked quietly between themselves.

"Mister Murdoch sir," Westlake said quietly to the deputy director, "Mobile signal is shocking in these parts, but it's not too bad out the front here. You should check your voicemail."

Mindy watched as Murdoch listened to Sir Michael's frantic message, his eyes never leaving Westlake's face.

He hung up, nodded at Westlake, and walked to the gate with his two men. Mindy took this as her cue to get down there, leaving Curtis with Westlake's submachine gun in Pope's bedroom to provide cover if needed. As she reached the bottom of the stairs, she heard noises in the kitchen. She crept down the hallway, removing the handgun from her bag as she moved, then quietly opened the kitchen door. Pope was placing a couple of beers amongst several hot drinks on a couple of trays.

"What the hell are you doing here?" she whispered.

"I've run out of cups," he explained, pointing at the beers.

"Just… just wait here."

She walked back down the hallway, opened the front door, took a deep breath and stepped outside.

A brief discussion between the group at the gate was just concluding and Murdoch walked back towards Westlake, accompanied by Grace.

Murdoch spotted Mindy over Westlake's shoulder and gave her a curt nod of the head.

"We'll be off," he said, "But you'll understand I can't leave without checking that all is as it seems and you're not under any duress. Also, some of the group are very keen to meet Mister Pope, and I assume the interrogation by Number 10 has ended…"

Westlake turned and looked at Mindy. So close to the end, but not quite there. Damn. To his surprise, she was smiling.

"Nobody is under duress. My interview with Mister Pope is done and I'm sure he'd be happy to meet anybody who wants to say hello. No guns, though, please. He's had enough of guns."

The two MI5 agents plus Murdoch's men set off to their vehicles at the top of the lane, weighed down by several weapons.

As they headed back, Pope's front door opened wide and two dogs raced out, followed by Pope and Curtis, each carrying a tray of drinks.

"Sorry for the delay," said Pope with a broad smile on his face. "Have I missed anything?"

He put his tray down on the table, then turned and shook Murdoch's hand.

"Simon Pope," he said, "Pleased to meet you."

"Menzies Murdoch, Mister Pope," replied the director. "Sorry about all this. I guess you're becoming used to the occasional unusual occurrence."

Pope nodded. He turned to see three men approaching from the gate, dealing with the excited dogs.

"Gentlemen," he said, then walked forward with his hand outstretched. "A pleasure to meet you."

"Padre," came the response. Each man stepped forward to shake his hand. None had been unlucky enough to be there that day, but each felt like they had been.

Each noticed the scars on his head and neck. The tears pricking his eyes matched those of their own. All three also shook hands with Westlake. Like the padre, one of their own.

Murdoch, Abbott and Curtis watched it all play out in front of them and knew what should happen going forward. Nothing. Or, at least, as little as possible.

Murdoch walked back up the lane and set off with his team back to London, but only after apologising once more to Sergeant Grace and avoiding a headbutt by doing so.

Curtis and Grace walked up with him and removed the vehicles blocking the top of the lane. Grace radioed a stand down message to a relieved Superintendent Whitwell. The cavalry was just entering the village and simply sped through as if off to an incident elsewhere.

Mindy left the boys to chat. She didn't want to re-live the war diaries again. She called the dogs, walked through the house to the back garden, and scattered treats on the grass. Then she took out her phone and called Barnwell.

95

As two members of E Squadron swapped war stories with Dave Westlake and Curtis listened in, the third member helped Pope gather the empties and take them into the kitchen.

He looked around carefully, then locked onto Mindy, pacing the lawn while she talked on her mobile to her mentor.

"That weapon you mentioned Padre, you're still keen to keep hold of it?"

"For the moment, yes. Gives me a certain amount of reassurance. You never know what's around the corner. The last few days prove that."

The soldier handed over the mugs to be put in to soak.

"If it's of help, I'd be happy to give it a quick once over for you. Three years is a long time for a weapon to lie unused. You won't want it misfiring when you need it. It won't take me long."

Pope stopped washing the crockery, grabbed a tea towel and dried his hands.

"That's not a bad idea," he said. "It's only a couple of minutes away. We'll go through the garage so I can grab my trowel."

Before either could move, the back door opened.

"Don't let me stop you boys," grinned Mindy, glancing at the washing up as she marched through, "A woman's work is never done."

The men walked through the garden, Fred and Ginger joining them on the way.

A couple of minutes later and all four were heading over the field alongside a line of trees leading to the copse protecting the gun. Pope stopped, fell to his knees at the base of a tree and started to dig.

"Do you remember the guys who were with you that day, Padre?" The tone of the soldier's voice had changed; the warmth of the earlier conversation now cooled slightly.

Pope stopped digging for a moment and half turned to face the man silhouetted by the morning sun.

"I didn't know all of them. It was a bit of a mishmash. A few special forces were involved, plus a couple of advance intel officers from the Americans who were on their way."

"But you knew Lance Corporal Jamie Jameson, right?"

"Jam Jam? I did. He was part of my protection detail. A really great lad." Pope turned back and continued digging, not because he wanted to retrieve the gun, but to conceal the pain in his face and the worry in his eyes. "Was he a friend of yours?"

There was a moment's silence behind him, but Pope watched the shadows move out of the corner of his eye and knew without knowing that this situation was going downhill fast.

"He was my brother. And my best mate."

Pope stopped digging and stared for a moment at the base of the tree in front of him.

"Then you must be John. He talked a lot about you, you know. Was very proud of you."

Still on his knees, he turned around to face the soldier once again.

Despite the silhouette, he could make out the form of the handgun being pointed at him.

"Are you going to kill me John?"

"What happened to him?"

"You must've been told."

"I want it from you."

Pope gathered his thoughts, trying to resolve his current predicament through a fog of memories he would prefer to bury alongside the gun.

"We visited the local Shura to say our farewells and to introduce our replacements. I was on good terms with the local imam. We stayed about an hour. Much too long, but there was a lot to get through. On the way back we ran into an ambush. It wasn't even meant for us. An IED hit the side of our vehicle. The blast threw three of us out."

Pope hesitated, partly to chase the demons out of his mind, partly to work out how to phrase the next part of the account. "I don't know how long I was out. Probably only a minute. When I came to... Jam Jam was dead. He took most of the impact. Likely saved my life. He can't have known anything about it, John. The blast... I'm sorry. Very sorry."

"Did you do anything for him? Pray for him? Give him the last rites?"

"Not then. Later. When it was over."

The handgun fell, but only slightly. John Jameson was shaking, but Pope didn't know why. *Upset? Angry?*

"That was after you'd been hit."

"Jam Jam was a friend. A good friend. We'd worked together for several months. Been in some scrapes. He did his job for me. I needed to do mine for him."

"But if you hadn't been there..."

"He would still have been on that mission."

"But you were there. He had to think of you as well as himself."

The soldier fell silent but raised his weapon once more, the metal glinting in the sunlight.

"I've dreamt about this day between the nightmares," he said, almost in disbelief. "My shrink talks about closure. Now I have it handed to me on a plate. If you hadn't been there, he might still be alive. Now, take your gun out of the hole."

Pope shook his head but did as he was told.

He'd just been in the wrong place at the wrong time and was now in a whole load of trouble, none of which was of his making. The weight of the situation was suffocating. He'd never felt more like a health secretary or, indeed, a prime minister in his life.

"This will be murder, John. You're destroying the rest of your life. Killing me isn't going to make you feel any better."

"I'll take that risk, Padre. Besides, you're a potential terrorist. You turned on me with your gun and I shot you to protect myself. Now, get up and face me."

Pope stood up, his legs feeling weak beneath him, and turned around slowly, noticing a slight, unnatural movement along the tree line closer to the stile as he did so. He unwrapped the gun, removing it by holding the cold barrel between thumb and forefinger.

Thinking it may be time for a treat or two, Fred and Ginger stirred in the grass. Still holding the gun, Pope put both hands in the air.

"Nice try Padre," sneered Jameson, "But I'll make sure your prints are all over it before raising the alarm."

Pope grimaced, then flicked the gun away to his right, hearing it thud as it hit the ground. He clenched his fists. As Jameson's eyes swivelled towards the fallen gun, both dogs leapt to their feet, hackles raised, their fierce barks piercing the stillness of the scene.

The soldier took two steps backwards, hesitating again as both dogs fell silent and lay down once more, then swung his gun back towards Pope, who simply stared at him with a disconcerting smile on his face.

Two shots rang out, the sharp cracks of gunfire slicing through the air, across the field and reaching the men in Pope's front garden a split second after being created. Westlake reached for his handgun, then sprinted for the gate, closely followed by one of the two members of E Squadron. Curtis ran back inside the house. Moments later, he emerged with his own weapon and handed Westlake's submachine gun to the remaining solider. Both took off in hot pursuit of the others.

By the time they reached the field, the action was all but over. Pope and Mindy, escorted by Fred and Ginger, were helping a pale and injured Jameson towards the stile.

"We had a slight issue with my old handgun," explained Pope. "I'd left a round in the chamber three years ago and it just blew up in John's hand. Fortunately, the wounds are only superficial."

"But we heard two shots."

"Really? Must have been an echo."

Jameson's skeptical comrades took over supporting the injured soldier. Westlake and Curtis ran ahead to retrieve and prepare the trauma kit from the police car.

Pope and Mindy caught their breath, leaning against the stile while the two dogs mooched around.

"Are you okay?" asked Mindy.

"I'm fine. Adrenaline's pumping," Pope said. "What made you follow us?"

"I was just going out of your front door when I heard somebody say Jameson had lost his brother that day. You'd disappeared when I came back to the kitchen, but the garage door was open. I just had a feeling."

"I didn't know you could shoot."

"We all have our secrets. You know that better than most."

"Fair point."

"You're not pressing charges?"

Pope shook his head. "He needs help. Just make sure he gets it."

96

Sometimes in life, you don't realise the magnitude of a situation until you're almost done with it, thought Mavis Barnwell.

Nursing a mug of coffee fortified with a nip of whisky, she watched her husband take one call, then make another from the comfort of his chair in the lounge. Eventually he rang off, then just sat there, slumped forward with his elbows on his knees and his forehead resting on slightly trembling hands. She walked to him, sat on the arm of the chair, and gently stroked his head.

"Are we there yet?" she asked softly.

"Almost. Mindy's on her way back. Crockett is telling the Minister for the Cabinet Office there's no point in a public inquiry. Stanfield's happy."

"So nobody got shot."

"One superficial injury. And somebody mortally wounded a police car window. The Met and MI5 might have hurt pride, but we all move forward. And so does our democratic institution."

"All of you move forward?"

Barnwell looked up and smiled.

"Mavis Barnwell, you are probably the smartest person I know," he said, "But you are so easy to wind up."

Before Mavis could reply or hit him with a cruise brochure, the guest room door opened. The prime minister emerged, flustered yet relieved, with his phone in hand.

"We know," said Mavis, before he could speak.

The prime minister grinned, then retreated to his room to put on some trousers.

* * *

Stuart Morris was in the kitchen making a cup of tea when Westlake walked in through the front door, carrying the framed photograph.

"I thought you were on shift," he said.

"We're all entitled to a break. You, more than anybody else in the entire universe, should know that."

Morris nodded sagely and pulled another mug from the cupboard.

"How did it go?"

"Interview was fine. Then it got interesting. The Met, MI5 and E Squadron turned up. My car got shot. A gun exploded. Angus Grace took his teeth out. Nobody got badly hurt."

Morris held the tea bag over the second mug, struggling to make sense of what he'd just heard and requiring urgent clarification.

"Nobody?"

"Nobody."

"But he took his teeth out…"

"He did."

"Bloody hell."

Westlake gently took the tea bag from his friend's hand and made his own tea, while Morris leaned against the worktop.

"One day retired," mused Morris, "And the entire world has turned upside down."

97

Having called in sick first thing Tuesday morning, Pope took the dogs for a walk, then gave the house a quick clean. After recent events, it felt empty and unusually quiet.

Mindy had departed after hugging him and making sure he had her number on speed dial in case anything - absolutely anything - happened and he needed help.

The special forces lads had insisted he put another number on speed dial in case anything - absolutely anything - happened and he needed help. It was a number he had kept in his head for the last seven years - The Garden Club number - but he took it anyway.

A while later, Superintendent Whitwell had called to check he was okay. She made sure he had her number just in case anything happened - especially anything involving the Metropolitan Police.

So much had happened so quickly he completely forgot about his message to Pippa until the key rattled in his front door. It hadn't mattered. She had been so happy and relieved to see him.

They sat down together on the sofa. He told her everything that had happened, first describing his brief walk with the dogs and then detailing the subsequent events at the house.

He ended with an apology.

"I shouldn't have cut you off, Pip. I did that even before you left, and I'm sorry. I thought it was right for both of us, but I was wrong. Very wrong."

"How daft are we?" she smiled, feeling tears well in her eyes. "I never pushed. I didn't want you facing things you were trying to forget. I was protecting you. You were protecting me. We just never told each other."

"Just two lost soles lying in a shoe shop."

"Yeah. Something like that."

The key in the door told him she was back. This time, he was expecting her. She walked in carrying a bag of goodies and a pack of Monk's beer bottles. He took them off her, gave her a long hug, then stepped back and looked her in the eyes.

"Are you sure about this?"

She broke into a wide smile.

"I am absolutely certain."

Pope grabbed a bottle opener and led her into the lounge, followed by the dogs, who focused on the carrier bag. Pippa sat on the sofa next to him as he stretched for the remote control and switched on the television.

Show time.

98

Mindy sat on Barnwell's desk in his Downing Street office watching the television, while Martin cleared his desk. It didn't take very long because there was barely anything on it. He had filed or shredded his paperwork. He had assiduously removed anything private on a weekly basis and had stored it securely. He decided early in his career at Number 10 to never leave looking surprised. The picture the press and TV cameras would never get. He'd be gone before they even had a sniff. And today was that day.

Mindy understood and respected his decision. The desk in her office displayed her usual detritus, without a packing box to be seen. It would stay that way until Martin left.

Outside, the prime minister's removal van had just departed, and Crockett's bits and pieces were pulling up in a similar vehicle. Staff had roughly ninety minutes to get everything out of it and into place. The world's attention would then focus again on the famous black door and the podium in the middle of the street.

Currently, that attention focused on the cars at the front of Barnwell's apartment building. The world eagerly awaited the first public appearance of a man who had vanished just four days previously.

99

"There was a time when I found this kind of attention quite exciting." Mavis peered down at the road two storeys below her, careful to keep behind the net curtain. She wanted to avoid being on her own television screen, especially with a gin in her hand at this time of day.

The prime minister finished tying his shoes and walked over to join her, standing further back and peering over her head. The road was empty apart from three police motorbikes, one police van, two police cars and a government limousine. A large gaggle of cameras set up on the opposite pavement faced a phalanx of police officers.

That'll please the commuters, he thought. *Another thousand votes down the pan.* Then he caught himself. *Not that I care.*

His mood brightened by yet another load off his shoulders, he walked to the dining table and picked up the whisky on the rocks Mavis had prepared for him. He turned around, his glass tumbler raised in salute.

"To you, Mavis. The veritable force behind my good friend and a marvellous hostess."

She turned and lifted her own glass.

"A momentous day, prime minister. Welcome back to your real life."

"And you to yours!"

They looked at each other after taking a sip, unsure what to say next.

"You have your speech with you?"

The prime minister patted his pocket.

"Mindy's finest work," he said.

"And you plan to use it? This being your moment in history?"

"I do plan to use it," he smiled.

"But will you?"

The smile grew wider, then the door buzzed.

"I must go," he said. "Thank you, once again."

He put down his glass and gave her a hug, inadvertently knocking her glass and spilling gin on the floor.

"Oh get out, you fool," she laughed, "And break a leg."

He opened the door and exchanged pleasantries with RaSP officer Freddie Jackson, who he had specifically requested for this event. It was time to leave his safe place and face the world again. He walked out and closed the apartment door behind him.

"But don't really break a leg, you accident-prone idiot," Mavis murmured, walking to the kitchen to grab some paper towel before the gin soaked in.

100

Westlake and Morris sat in Westlake's lounge, watching the prime minister walk out of the building and onto the road.

He thanked the media for coming and the police for keeping the media from him, before apologising to anybody inconvenienced by the closure of the road. All the time he was talking, the media took their pictures and video.

When he reckoned they had enough, the prime minister waved and climbed into the limousine, with Freddie Jackson getting in the front passenger seat. Before the entourage had made it onto the main road, the news channel had photographs comparing the prime minister today with a week previously.

"I can see why you didn't clock him straightaway," said Morris sympathetically. "He looks thinner and smarter now."

"Cheers Stu."

"Much more like a prime minister," Morris smirked.

Westlake didn't bite. He remembered the video he'd taken of his snoring, dribbling friend on Saturday evening.

Any more comments like that and the video's audience would grow significantly.

101

Sat in the back of the car, the prime minister listened again to the voicemail from Pope on his mobile.

"Whatever happens now is not your fault. I've realised that myself about my time in Afghan. I don't want you to take as long to come to the same conclusion."

He pondered the headlines of his last fourteen years in politics, like a drowning man's last moments. There were successes and failures, both at home and abroad.

He had often pointed the finger at individuals or events for the failures. Being honest with himself, he knew similar catalysts were behind most of the achievements as well. It was just that his signature was on the final document. He had stood on the shoulders of giants, but the same had trampled him.

Being a prime minister was such a fake role. It was like captaining a rudderless ship, with a crew permanently on the edge of mutiny. Responsible for a manifest of passengers who, to various degrees, believed in and relied on his control of the vessel to guide them safely from port to port. Dependent on the vagaries of the weather and the mood of the sea. Reliant on the support of vessels of all sizes, each of which was busy plotting their own course.

Like Napoleon's generals, the best prime ministers were those who had been lucky.

Maybe there had been a wealth of talented people inside and outside of government, or an upturn in the economy. Possibly a settled time of peace, or when war had galvanised the nation.

He led the team, made speeches, and set agendas, but external sources had an enormous influence on these actions.

External sources, or his burning desire to secure his own future.

Media popularity had been key to the latter, and had been an area in which he had truly excelled.

But even there, his influence had grown stale as time had worn on and editors realised bad news about him sold more papers and gained more clicks.

He observed the empty pavements from his tinted window.

"Have the police cleared the route?" he asked.

"No sir," said the driver.

For a moment, the PM bristled. A historic day for the country and nobody gave a toss. No supporters. No protestors. Not even general curiosity. Just shoppers, commuters, homeless people and drug dealers, all going about their usual business.

He caught sight of his frowning reflection and laughed at himself.

If he couldn't attract any attention in a cavalcade of cars and motorbikes, he was going to have no problem doing his weekly shopping at the supermarket.

"The Palace and outside Downing Street will be busy though," added the driver helpfully, conscious he may have hurt his passenger's feelings.

The prime minister smiled and nodded. His phone vibrated in his hand, and he checked his messages.

Miss you too. That was not what he had expected to see from Mindy. Talk about taking your time.

Good luck. Catch up later. He barely had time to process the message when another appeared.

And stick to the bloody script for once in your life. X.

He smiled again.

Time would tell.

102

Mindy put her phone down, already regretting the message and second guessing the response. It had been a sod-it throw of the dice, but the last couple of days had made her reflect and review what she wanted from life. Politics and the ability to make a positive impact? Sure, but did it have to cost her happiness?

Certainly, she knew when she'd been happiest, when life and her future felt exciting.

She'd seen how traumatic events had affected Pope's life. Now he was finally looking to get it back on track after going off the rails for a while.

She'd had front row seats as her erstwhile lover achieved the position he wanted before being worn down by the role. Finally, he'd either had the guts or the mental breakdown required to walk away and find himself once more.

Maybe she needed to do the same.

She glanced at her boss, absorbed in the television images that would define his departure from Downing Street. He had changed in the last week. Older. More haggard, if that could be possible. As if he'd realised the events and their consequences had been beyond even his unparalleled ability to absorb, reflect and react.

Both were at the end of this road. Each would now take a different direction.

The car on the screen transported the man who had decided enough was enough.

By doing so, he had inadvertently motivated others to do the same and make their own decisions. Life-changing decisions. Possibly nation-changing decisions in Crockett's case.

And all because of a sausage.

"What are your plans for tomorrow, Mart?"

Her craggy boss frowned slightly, then his face brightened, smoothing out some of the many wrinkles on his forehead.

"I'm going to switch off my phone," he smiled.

103

"Do you think you'll see him again? Hear from him?"

Pope reached for his mobile and handed it over to Pippa, then took another slug of beer.

"Who's Paul Morgan?" she asked, scrolling through recent calls and text messages. "Ah. PM. Duh."

She read through the messages. On the television, the author sailed past groups of supporters or protestors with banners carrying a variety of messages.

Next time, take me with you!

Why did you bother coming back?

Piss off, then when you've pissed off, piss off some more.

The cameras caught the prime minister smiling and waving at the crowd and laughing and pointing at the ruder signs. Opinions differed amongst commentators and their guests. Was the PM enjoying his last moments in the sun or displaying signs he had truly lost his marbles?

"He's having a ball," observed Pope from the sofa, "But I have inside information."

Pippa had to agree. The PM's texts over the last couple of days reminded her of a child, waiting impatiently for Christmas. As she handed the phone back, yet another message appeared.

"Not long now!" reported Pope, replying with a thumbs up emoji.

"You should keep all these texts. For posterity or something."

Pope briefly considered, then shook his head.

"They're private messages," he said. "They'll stay private."

"Simon Pope!" Pippa laughed. "An opportunity like that and you're not taking it? You've changed, mister."

Pope grinned.

104

Just a couple of minutes later, an aerial camera showed the prime minister's car and escort driving along the Mall.

It slowed as it passed significantly larger crowds outside Buckingham Palace, then turned through the central gates. The limousine pulled up in the courtyard, where an equerry opened the car door for the PM, then led him to the King's Private Secretary, Sir Timothy Pontefract.

"To what do we owe this unexpected pleasure?" asked Sir Timothy as both men walked up the steps and into the Palace.

"Oh, you know me, Tim. Bit of a loose end today, so thought I'd pop over."

"Try not to overstay your welcome. He wants a bite to eat before his next appointment."

"No problem."

105

The PM disappeared from view and the studios switched back to talking heads or reporters in the crowd.

Mindy reached for her laptop and pulled up the formal statement that she, Barnwell and the PM had written the day before.

"How many, do you reckon?" she asked.

Barnwell walked to the window and observed the media across the road.

"Thirty is plenty," he said. "It'll go online at the same time it's distributed."

"They're going to be pissed off."

"Oh, I hope so."

If one thing had annoyed Barnwell more than anything during his time in politics, it was the media's smug, insufferable arrogance; their assumption of entitlement and the vindictive petulance that could follow if they weren't treated like the spoilt little shits they actually were.

Similar, in fact, to politicians themselves, who were number two on his shit list for exactly the same reasons.

Mindy waited for the thirty copies to appear, collated, from the printer on the far table and then stapled the two separate sheets together.

"Shame it's not raining out there," mused her boss, albeit only for the next five minutes. "I like it when they get soaked, just so they can shout some banal question at a government minister with absolutely no expectation of a response. Journalism at its finest."

Mindy smiled but made no comment.

Martin rarely opened up, making his soliloquies intriguing.

"At its finest," he repeated, shaking his head before stopping abruptly, as if something important had occurred to him. "But that's not all journalists. Oh no. Some are genuinely brilliant. Diligent. Thoughtful. Thorough. Fair. They're like a dog with a bone when they believe they've found a major story."

Barnwell took a sip of his coffee and watched the three-minute compilation of the PM's years in office being broadcast on one of the satellite channels. Three minutes. As if someone could fairly distil years of power into a three-minute summary. As he suspected, it ended with a photo of a sausage that resembled a human turd. This then faded out as an image of the prime minister stood outside Barnwell's apartment building less than an hour earlier faded in. Vindictive petulance indeed. Now, where was he?

"Our role is to suppress some stories as much as we promote others," he mused to himself. "The best approach is to identify and address issues before they become prominent."

Mindy sensed where this might go but stayed quiet. Barnwell watched the split screen, showing four different channels. Each displayed the same pooled photograph of His Majesty greeting the PM. A second image followed, showing the PM handing over his letter of resignation.

"That book, *Inside The Number 10 Den*, is making the author a lot of money at the moment," he continued, still looking at the screen.

"The author is being very cute. The publishers have to use a very random email address. They make payments into an anonymised Swiss bank account. Now, I have the account number. A journalist discovered it."

Mindy barely dared to breathe. She focused on tidying the sheaf of statements on the desk. Television coverage shifted to the Palace. The now former prime minister, Andrew 'Andy' Blackwell, walked down the steps to his car, waved to the crowd and slipped in.

"Even with the account details, it's a major challenge to identify the author. Unless, of course, they continue their account of life here, which will show they are still walking these corridors," said Barnwell. "If all goes quiet, it's likely a departed advisor is the author. Their lack of access will kill any future editions and the issue disappears off your to-do list."

Mindy nodded, then used the office phone to call in an assistant to collect the statement copies. Once the assistant had gone, they watched the limousine, now with just one motorcycle outrider, turn right at a junction where it should have turned left.

To his great satisfaction, Barnwell noted that the panic in the television studios was being mirrored outside his window. The reporters mobbed the poor assistant for the statement, then started to-camera pieces with no clue how they were going to finish.

"My work here is done," he smiled, then walked over to Mindy and gave her an enormous hug. "This isn't the end," he said, noting the tears in her eyes. "Just the beginning. Enjoy it, even the tough days. I'll be around if you need me, but I doubt you will."

He kissed her cheek and left the office without looking back. The lobby was full of people wondering what the hell was going on.

They didn't notice the now-retired chief-of-staff amble past them and into the passageway to the Treasury building.

A car waited with hazard lights flashing outside the front of the building in Whitehall. The driver leaned against the bodywork, chatting with two uniformed police officers.

"Good day at the office, boss?" asked Curtis, opening the rear door.

"A very good day," smiled Barnwell, patting him on the shoulder. "Now, take me home."

106

"He's going the wrong way," laughed Pippa, leaning forward as if being closer to the screen would improve her comprehension of what was happening.

People in the television studio were even closer to the action.

Judging by the looks on their faces and the garbled chat that had replaced the erudite comment, it was doing nothing for their understanding of events.

"He's going home."

"How do you know? Did he tell you?"

Pope shook his head. After recent events, it surprised him that this man's unexpected act would shock anyone. The programme switched to Downing Street, where a flustered reporter tried to read out the statement she had grabbed in the melee.

The cacophony engulfing her meant she struggled to make herself heard.

"For God's sake, shut the fuck up!" she yelled in frustration, thus ending her career on one channel, but ensuring offers of employment from elsewhere. A hush fell, but only for a moment, akin to clapping one's hands under trees full of nesting birds. Then the clamour started again.

Back in the studio, the presenter apologised for 'technical issues' and read out the statement, which was now available online, from his mobile phone.

The former prime minister started with an apology for the inconvenience caused by his disappearance, followed by a brief account of events.

Pope was relieved Mindy had omitted the identity of anybody - genuine or fictitious - who had helped over the weekend. The statement explained what prompted the PM's decision.

It credited the media with maintaining public interest in politics but mildly admonished them for misinterpreting events in order to do so. He highlighted the sausage saga as a prime example and expressed sympathy for the worker who had died in the van blaze, holding onto the offending item.

He discussed how being prime minister affected his mental health. He urged the state to consider this when seeking lessons from the experience.

"I am resigning in order to address my issues, and I respectfully ask for time and privacy in order to do so. Some may view today as historic. Certainly, it's a chance for growth, both personally and nationally. Considering this, I have decided not to address you from the front of Number 10. That platform should be for our next prime minister, and I am happy to play my part in ensuring that is the case."

"The focus should be on getting our great nation back on track," it continued. "I failed in this regard, and I am deeply sorry for my failings. My successor, with the support of his party and the British public, will make the changes needed to get us where we belong. I wish him and you the very best of luck. Thank you."

The presenter read the statement as helicopter shots of the limousine leaving the centre of London played on the screen. In the silence that followed, the picture switched.

Damien Crockett left his party's headquarters, hugged his family and headed to his own appointment at the Palace.

"That's that then," said Pippa, before taking a silent but deep breath. "Fancy taking the dogs to the pub?"

"Sounds good," said Pope, trying not to punch the air. "Let's just hang on until he gets home."

Ten minutes later, yet another convoy heading to the Palace started to bore people inside and outside the studio. In desperation, the producer switched to a view of a leafy suburb and the former prime minister arriving at his private home. There were no family or friends to greet him. Even the neighbours didn't bother to secure an easy few seconds of national fame by wandering out to welcome the prodigal.

Andrew Blackwell emerged from the car, carrying a bag of groceries from a supermarket he had detoured to during the journey - an episode completely missed by the media.

The complete absence of recognition and respect in the store and the car park had simultaneously bruised his ego and boosted his hopes for the future.

He shook hands with his much-maligned RaSP officer, then turned towards his front door, only to find a camera and a microphone in his face.

"Welcome home, sir," said a young man in an ill-fitting suit, borrowed from his brother. As had been the case over the last few weeks, he had spent the day shadowing the camera crew. Now, he found himself substituting for the reporter who was currently riding pillion on a motorbike heading to Downing Street to replace the overwrought swear monster. A unique moment in the national spotlight that could put rocket fuel into his burgeoning media career or destroy it before it had barely started.

"Thank you. It's good to be back."

"Yeah. Just wondered if you had any last words before descending into obscurity, ultimately followed by oblivion."

Blackwell stopped short, an expression of bemusement on his face.

"Have you been in this job long?" he asked.

The interviewer hesitated.

"Two minutes. I'm on work experience for a year."

"And was this your first choice?"

The reporter shifted uncomfortably, his earpiece telling him to focus on asking the questions he'd been given.

"It's okay if it wasn't," Blackwell smiled. "This wasn't mine."

"What was yours?"

"To save the world and everything on it."

"I wanted to be a lawyer, but I didn't get into university. Poor results. Ended up at college doing journalism."

"You've still got plenty of time."

"And you?"

Blackwell laughed.

"Not as much."

"But you can still give it a go though, right? Otherwise, what's the point?"

Blackwell regarded him for a moment, then nodded.

"I can still give it a go," he said, "But first things first."

"And they are?"

The entire production team, studio, and millions at home held their breath.

"To get my life sorted, play some golf and drink a bottle or two of Monk's Perm." Blackwell smiled and patted his interrogator on the shoulder.

"Thanks for the chat," he said, as he put his key in the door and stepped inside, "And good luck with whatever you end up pursuing."

Nonplussed, the reporter turned to face the camera, pulled a face and whispered, "Monk sperm?"

A shriek of laughter from Pippa broke the stunned silence.

Pope grimaced and shook his head.

"He simply cannot help himself!" he said. "The man's a walking disaster zone."

"He'll be okay, though, right?"

"I think so. Once he's sorted a few things."

"So, he's just like the rest of us?"

Out of the corner of his eye, Pope caught sight of the framed photograph of a couple walking by the canal.

A record of happier times. Proof they had existed. Promise that they could again. Maybe.

"Just like the rest of us," he smiled. "Let's get the dogs."

107

Try as he might, the Regimental Sergeant Major always felt uncomfortable in civilian gear. He hated wasting time and brainpower on an unnecessary distraction. The army's instructions on what to wear and when were perfectly acceptable. Unfortunately, for civilian life, the army merely shrugged its shoulders, which accounted for his outfit as he knocked on Pope's door.

A brown tweed suit, sporting a black leather elbow patch on each jacket sleeve, covered a red and white striped shirt, set off by a thin black tie. A pair of worn but highly polished black formal shoes completed the ensemble.

Not wishing to attract attention, the RSM had opted for his civilian funeral attire. The strategy worked, although that was due more to the quiet location of Pope's house and the fact that his neighbours were out working or shopping on a Wednesday morning.

Six months on from the dramatic events in the front garden, Spring was in the air. Yellow daffodils and tinges of green on the branches of the surrounding trees and hedgerows signified its arrival. The smell of recently applied gloss paint on the wooden frames of the home's front door and windows simply reinforced the sense of new beginnings.

The door opened, revealing a familiar face. This time, the person had sparkling eyes and a wide, welcoming smile, a stark contrast to the incandescent fury he remembered in Afghanistan.

"Hello stranger," said Pippa, walking forward and shaking the RSM's hand, "Long time no see."

"It's good to see you, Pippa. How's life? I believe congratulations are in order."

Pippa grinned. She pulled a small, thin presentation box out of her paint-stained overall pocket and handed it over. The RSM opened it and looked admiringly at the contents.

"I've never seen an OBE before," he lied, being the owner of one himself. "You must be very proud."

"It was a lovely day," she admitted, "And it's helped boost our work with the kids."

"That's good to hear. Is he in?"

"Just cleaning up. He'll be down in a minute. Come on in."

Three minutes later, they both sat on the sofa in the lounge, each holding a cup of tea. The two dogs lying at their feet stared hard at the biscuits on the table, willing them to fall to the floor.

Footsteps on the stairs interrupted the small talk. Pope walked in, wearing jeans and a khaki T-shirt, the smell of soap failing to hide the occasional whiff of the paint cleaner he'd been using.

The RSM stood up and shook his hand, barely flinching when Pope followed up with a quick embrace.

"Hello RSM. Or is it Pete, as you're in mufti?"

"Pete's fine, Simmo. Thanks for agreeing to meet."

The RSM settled back on the sofa and Pope sat in his favourite armchair, uncertain what was to come next. If it involved returning the gun, he'd have to recover it from its resting place on the edge of the nearby wood.

Small talk focused on Andrew Blackwell and his earnest but futile efforts to avoid the spotlight.

Following a couple of months of rest and recuperation, which had done him the world of good, the former prime minister had finally answered the hundreds of invitations he had received for interviews, media appearances and speeches around the world. He had declined them all, but that had simply increased public interest and his market value.

"He's been talking with Amanda Abbott about writing a book," reported Pope. "It'll show how he reached breaking point and will explain something he's calling his *path finder* philosophy."

"Sounds fascinating," said the RSM, without sounding particularly fascinated. He cleared his throat.

"I want to talk to you about The Garden Club," he said, referring to the clandestine support system operated by a section of the military for club members in need.

"I'd like to know why you didn't call our number six months ago, firstly when you had the then prime minister as your guest and then when the government was trying to kill you."

"Never occurred to me," Pope frowned.

The RSM nodded and sipped his tea, resolving to work on his own communication skills when introducing the concept of the club in the future.

"We could have taken the prime minister off your hands and returned him or kept him safe elsewhere, with no record of your involvement. We have links with E Squadron and MI5 and could have called them off. Finally, we could have guided you to a secure location while we resolved the issue."

"I thought you'd only be interested if I was in immediate danger."

"That's not the case, although you actually were in imminent danger."

Pippa leaned forward. "So. What exactly is The Garden Club?"

"Retired soldiers who had fought with the Duke of Wellington at Waterloo founded it around 1830," explained the RSM.

"During the two decades before the Duke died, he split his time between Apsley House in London and Walmer Castle in Kent. The retired men maintained the Apsley grounds during the Duke's time in Kent. If more help was required, their contacts in the military would use the resources at their disposal to provide it. Someone called it The Duke's Garden Club. Been shortened since then, of course."

The RSM fell silent a moment, allowing the prestige of the club's origins to sink in. Tired of waiting for a biscuit, Fred got up, shook himself, and left the room. Ginger continued her hopeful vigil.

"By the time Wellington died in 1852, the club had grown in size to help others who had served their country with distinction. The range of support had grown as well, from gardening to home improvements, legal counsel and financial help."

"Impressive."

The RSM eyed Pope and Pippa carefully, before deciding on his next words.

"It's meant to be, but it's bullshit," he said. "Completely fabricated. The historical documents are brilliant fakes. It's a much younger organisation. The legend provides us with legitimacy." He took a sip of tea and glanced at their confused expressions before continuing.

"It started after the army's deployment in Northern Ireland in 1969. After leaving the service, men and women faced ongoing terrorist threats. Successive governments didn't want to know; the police weren't prepared, and the top brass were too busy."

"The Garden Club provides support and physical protection. Sometimes we take preventative action. Strong preventative action. We step in whenever the institutions fail us. Those instances have increased significantly over the last decade or so." He nodded at Pope. "You're a prime example."

He took another sip of his tea.

"But you still do gardening, though?" asked Pope, more in hope than expectation.

"Rarely."

"So, who funds this?" asked Pippa.

"The Ministry of Defence unknowingly provides resources. If anybody raises questions, the Wellington legend persuades them to look the other way. Former service members who have done well for themselves - either legally or otherwise - make substantial donations. Some charities get involved as well. And we rely a lot on carefully selected volunteers who want to make a difference and help on a mission-by-mission basis."

"And where do you get your carefully selected volunteers?" Pope asked, wondering who would want to join an unofficial team carrying out missions ranging from weeding and social care to illegal assassinations at home and abroad.

The RSM took another sip from his mug before placing it on the table.

"I'm glad you asked," he smiled.

108

AUTHOR'S NOTE

Thank you for the time you've spent with Paths Not Yet Taken. I hope you enjoyed the book much more than I did writing it - and I had a blast, eventually.

Paths Not Yet Taken was what you might describe as a slow burner.

Covid caused many things including - way down the list - yours truly deciding to write a novel.

You've spent your entire career writing for other people, I told myself. *Now's the time to write for yourself.*

The question was, what?

It was during the first lockdown and my fourth weekly tidy up of the garage (anything to get out of the house). I opened the side door and stepped into the already immaculate space and thought, *What if I'd opened the door and somebody was already in here?*

A few moments into sweeping the already pristine floor: *What if it was the prime minister?* Then, two minutes later: *What if it was the prime minister having a nervous breakdown?* I grabbed my laptop, and started writing.

A couple of years, two or three vaccinations and just eighteen thousand words later, I gave up. There was no point. Real life superseded anything I downloaded from my imagination onto the electronic page.

My book wasn't sharp, hopefully humorous fiction; it became a contemporary chronicle of the top-down madness enveloping society and suffocating humanity, toned down to avoid upsetting readers of a sensitive disposition.

I didn't want to write a book offering a glimpse into a gloom-filled void with little sense or promise of a positive outcome. I played golf or walked the dogs instead.

I gave myself time, and that gave me hope. Generally, politicians don't set off with a dream of destroying the economy, tearing the fabric of the nation or jeopardising lives and futures.

At all levels of society, life gets in the way of what we hope to do and where we plan to be. Circumstances can be way beyond our control. Seemingly innocuous decisions we make sometimes come with big unforeseen consequences.

Some may well be content with the hand dealt to them. Others less so. Whatever the case, we each have a choice - to accept our norm or to change it; to stay on the current path or to choose another. Whichever path you choose, I wish you well.

Please consider leaving a rating and review on your preferred book retailer website.

If you'd like to stay in touch, then please visit **www.philrennett.com** where you'll find my blog, plus a free subscription to the bi-monthly Path Finders newsletter.

This will keep you up to date with my writing and a host of other bits and pieces, including prologues for the characters you've already met.

I look forward to seeing you there!

Printed in Great Britain
by Amazon

48961459R00199